NDIMA NDIMA

A Novel in Stories

BY
Tsitsi Mapepa

CATALYST PRESS
ANTHONY, TEXAS

For further information, write Catalyst Press at
info@catalystpress.org

In North America, this book is distributed by
Consortium Book Sales & Distribution, a division of Ingram.
Phone: 612/746-2600
cbsdinfo@ingramcontent.com
www.cbsd.com

In South Africa, Namibia, and Botswana,
this book is distributed by Protea Distribution.
For information, email orders@proteadistribution.co.za.

FIRST EDITION
10 9 8 7 6 5 4 3 2 1

Library of Congress Control Number: 2023932123

Cover design by Karen Vermeulen, Cape Town, South Africa

To my whole family, but mostly,
my lovely mother and father
who raised me to be who I am today:
my guardians of yesterday, of today,
and of tomorrow.

When a moon meets the sun,
they create the ring of fire
to bear a star...

Table of Contents

SUNSET STREET

Autumn 1990
ZUVA

The morning sunlight flared through the green leaves of the water berry tree. Zuva stood underneath the broad branches with Nyeredzi, her youngest daughter. Zuva was holding a sickle in her right hand, studying the tall brown prairie grass swaying from side to side in front of them. The grass, bowing to the winds in their backyard, fenced their cottage like a wild creature gnawing at their home, as though they were living in the forest.

But this was not a forest, nor the countryside; they had moved to Zimbabwe's capital city, Harare, located in the northwest of the country. So many high–density suburbs were being developed at the start of this new decade, and Southgate 1 was one of them. The suburb was in the city's southwest, where Zuva's husband, Mwedzi, had bought the last stand on Sunset Street to build his family a new house.

It was April, and in this new raw land, the birds chirped in the scattered trees, bees buzzed, and hares, and rock dassies ran to hide from the eagles and snakes. If it was very quiet, Zuva could hear the snakes hissing from afar, slithering within the grass from their holes.

They'd moved here from Marondera, which was two hours away from Harare, a small city in Mashonaland, to the east. Zuva only had a few weeks to sort themselves before her daughters started school again. This meant starting by clearing the field that was before her.

Mwedzi had already dug the foundation of their main house. Big heaps of red soil piled to the sides of the foundation. A small four-walled toilet sat further away from the three-roomed cottage he had built for them as a temporary home. The house next door was plastered, with red-brick pillars on the veranda. The burnt umber floor reflected on the glass of its French doors. Behind them was a black tarred road sandwiched by their new neighbors' houses, which stood in long rows. They were all finished and freshly painted, some fenced by Durawall or hedge.

Zuva couldn't help but notice that people kept looking at them from their yards. In Marondera, Zuva and her family lived in a low-density suburb. Here it was different: there were too many houses, too close to each other. She didn't mind that. It was what it was. All she ever wanted was to live in a house built by her husband, and this was where they ended up: the capital city that was going to bring fortune to her family. But were all these hopes she had going to make her regret her decision?

Earlier, Zuva had left three of her daughters to unpack the boxes inside their cottage. She'd squeezed her own bed into the smallest room, the wardrobe overloaded and bursting, large bags filled with extra blankets and clothes tied to the beams of the roof. The other room was her daughters' bedroom, which all four were going to share. They were to use the third room as the lounge/dining/kitchen.

Zuva disappeared into the bush, clearing it with a

sickle. She'd told Nyeredzi not to follow her, so the little girl didn't move from her spot. When Zuva got back, she found Nyeredzi still standing under the tree.

"Oh, you are still here?"

"Yes, I'm still here," Nyeredzi responded. "Are you going back in there, Mama?"

Zuva nodded, pulling off her red gumboots to shake out the dry grass and soil.

"Can I come with you this time, Mama?"

"Not yet," Zuva said, walking back into the bush. Nyeredzi was left alone under the tree again, her arms folded in front, scratching the beads of sweat forming on her forehead.

Once Zuva had cleared a specific area, she began to pile the grass onto the cleared section. The ground was covered with holes scattered everywhere. Nyeredzi's squeal told her she'd spotted the snakes' heads peeking out, as if they were playing peek–a–boo.

"Ruth, Hannah, and Abigail, come and see the snakes," Nyeredzi shouted at her sisters inside the cottage. Zuva saw them looking at Nyeredzi through the window as though she were insane or making up things.

"Mama, I saw snakes peeking out," Nyeredzi called to her mother.

"I know, just stay there." Zuva wiped the sweat off her thick brows. "This is why you can't come with me."

She asked Ruth, her oldest daughter, to bring two galvanized buckets from inside so she could fill them with water from the tap outside. Next, she started a fire, burning the grass she had piled before. She placed the pails on rocks to boil water, then poured hot water into each hole. The flames and smoke disappeared into the air, forming a thick gray blanket.

Her other daughters had come out to see what she was doing. They all began to laugh when they saw the snakes breakdancing on the ground. Zuva used a stick to toss the snakes into the ring of fire, where death waited for them. Each one of her daughters watched them burn, flesh shrunk into a thin thread before they vanished into ashes. Three of her daughters couldn't take it and soon she was left with only Nyeredzi to inhale it all. It was not the first time Zuva had encountered the stinking burning flesh smell in her life. She'd smelled worse things than snakes.

During the course of the day, Zuva could see people watching her from their houses while she cleared the bush, and some came to introduce themselves to her.

"Sorry to bother you," one of the ladies said. "I am Mrs. Dutu, and the blue house you see over there is mine."

She pointed at her house that was about two hundred meters away.

"I am Mrs. Taha, and this is my youngest daughter, Nyeredzi," Zuva said, touching Nyeredzi's shoulder.

"How did you clear the dead grass and snakes in your area?" Mrs. Gwenga from next door asked. "We are so afraid to go in there."

Zuva placed her sickle on the ground and scratched on the white patch between the lines of her braided hair.

"I can teach you if you're interested," she said. Bravery was a feature she'd inherited from her father, Togara.

"Absolutely, we would love to," Mrs. Dutu said, stepping closer. She seemed anxious but willing to learn. Zuva was pleased her neighbors would come to help. This was a big job that she couldn't do by herself.

Day by day during the April school holiday, women, boys, and girls showed up at Zuva's cottage carrying

sickles and buckets to fetch water, all dressed up to protect themselves in worn–out sweaters and jeans, Tommy
shoes, and gumboots. Mrs. Dutu had her own style: she
wore palazzo pants over layers of laddered pantyhose that
looked like bandages, and because of that, people started calling her Lazarus. Sometimes men would come on
weekends when they were not working, but these were
the days Mwedzi built their main house, brick by brick.

After clearing a few hectares of the land, the place
looked better. It kept snakes far from the houses and people started to feel safe. Those who were once petrified now
relaxed like jelly in bowls.

For young children in the neighborhood, the cleared
section became their playground. Zuva never took her
eyes off Nyeredzi and other children kicking bright plastic balls across the red clay. The balls were burnt on the
outside layer to make them look rustic and to protect them
from tearing. They drove cars made of wires and tucked
themselves in the old tractor wheel Mrs. Dutu had brought
from her farm, and the big boys would spin it from a steep
ground. All they got from it was laughter and dizziness
and bruises that lasted days after the wheel tipped sideways, banging their heads on the side.

Everyone in the street could now see there were hectares and hectares of dense red and black soil holding the
roots of plants firm in the ground. The fresh breeze that
was once blocked by the tall grass now brushed their skin.
Trees were scattered here and there, nesting birds and
other animals, and granite and igneous rocks spotted the
landscape.

The land was neither too steep nor too flat, and there,
in the river that flowed through the middle, peoples' sins
were washed away, especially those who had just killed

someone. Sometimes Zuva and other women saw ragged clothes with bloodstains chucked on the ground. If they went to the river in the morning, while the sun was still rising, blood trails were still fresh and visible along the bank.

Far across the bush, there was a hill surrounded by buildings and laced with pine trees and dense shrubs, but bald at the tip of its skull. The red bald top beamed in the daylight even from afar. In the afternoon, Zuva could see people walking on top of the hill, and they looked so small from a distance. To the left were houses that stood in rows, painted in different colors.

If she stood close to the river, Zuva could hear the sound of the grinding mill and loud music from a bar called Monstrous Joy in front of the hill. An Agric company and a bridge that went over the train tracks lay on the right side of the hill. Duva dam was close by the bridge; it belonged to the Agric company. Zuva knew about—but could not see—the train track that divided the bush and this suburb called Majuba, a couple hundred meters away from the hill.

In the evenings, after dinner, if the moon and stars were bright, Zuva and her family sat outside circling the burning fire. No electricity in their cottage forced them to entertain themselves a lot. Nyeredzi pretended to be a journalist and often danced, and Abigail sang Michael Jackson's songs while she slid her sandals backwards moon walking. Ruth had her own elegance: she just shook her tummy up and down, and that was it. Hannah preferred to sit back and make jokes. Zuva laughed at their girls.

Sometimes Mwedzi told them stories from his old life, other times about how he got the scar on his forehead.

In the late 1960s, war was still ravaging the nation,

blood still sinking into the soil. New rules said that no civilians were allowed to be seen out after 6:00 p.m. If they were seen by soldiers, trouble awaited them. One day, Mwedzi was traveling from Chimanimani to Harare, and it got dark before he arrived at his destination. He came across a group of armed comrades in Chakohwa. When they started harassing him, Mwedzi threw a punch at one of the comrades. The rest of them joined in, and it was suddenly one man against six.

When they could see that Mwedzi was not backing down, one of them hit Mwedzi on his forehead with a gun. Blood gushed out from the torn skin. They surrounded him and harassed him, angry that Mwedzi had challenged them. A rifle was pointed at his face, but Mwedzi did not bother to wipe or press on the wound to stop the bleeding. Instead, in the middle of being tormented, he opened his trousers' zip and began to pee on the comrades.

"Are you crazy?" one of the comrades shouted. Mwedzi didn't respond. He just continued to splash urine on them.

"He's crazy, really crazy," the other one said, pulling the rest of his fellows away from Mwedzi. They all walked away, leaving him standing there in the dark, but still alive.

Mwedzi wanted to mention that it was Zuva who had saved him that evening, but he stopped talking when the train going to Bulawayo was passing. From the fire outside their cottage, they all watched it zip by so fast and race far across the bush. The silhouettes of people sitting and standing under the bright lights inside the passenger train made Zuva ask herself if those people had seen what she was thinking about at that time—the girls Mrs. Dutu told her about.

Young, beautiful girls with bright futures ahead of them, but lost with nowhere to find help. The impregnated girls were neglected by their boyfriends, frightened to tarnish their families' image; they were left with only one option. The girls knew the time the train came, and this was where they took their lives. They would lie on the train track before 9:00 p.m. and leave a message on a piece of paper with their last words placed under a rock.

Parents would later come with police to collect a bag with the minced dead body. All they saw was their daughter's bloodstains on the granite stones along the tracks, some of it already sunk into the red clay. The unknown boyfriends hid, with secrets that haunted them to death. For those with their names revealed by the letters, they had nowhere to hide.

Later, in bed, Zuva lay awake next to Mwedzi, still thinking about those girls. When a girl lay on the train track, did she open or close her eyes? Did any of them cry before the train crushed them? Had they told their friends what they were planning to do?

Zuva stared deep into the dim room lit with a paraffin lamp. Unanswered questions kept roaming through her head. She was learning a lot about this bush. She'd been raising her daughters in a bubble, in a simple, small city, but now they were going to be exposed to all this. Would the snakes come back? Would the boys who impregnated other girls come for her own?

It seemed whenever she was settling in, that was when new things popped up. Even if she wanted to, she was never going to be able to just sit back and relax. Although Zuva was strong and would do all she could to protect them, the danger this bush brought might prove too much.

PALMS OF LIFE

Winter 1990
NYEREDZI

There was something about the smell of the earth to Nyeredzi that made her feel alive. When the weather was dry, a fine dust of clay coated her clothes and found its way under her fingernails and into the fine hairs in her nostrils. When she was a little girl, she loved to play in the dirt. At their old house in Marondera and at their neighbors' farms, she ran through fields of maize, the red soil damp beneath her feet, hiding in the sweet potato beds when her mother called to her to come home.

They moved to Harare when Nyeredzi was six, though she turned seven just two months later. There were many more houses and people here, and instead of fields, a vast expanse of dense bush. But she could still find happiness burying her toes in the red soil.

The energy she got whenever she stepped into the bush was something special—the connection between her and this land was magnetic. She was drawn to the tiny hills that frothed termites—large and small balanced rocks—trees that danced to the whistles of the ancestors—animals that spoke in different languages while they bathed in the warm sun. It was as if the land was communicating with her, signaling what it had sucked, what it had devoured, and what it had birthed.

The richness of the red dirt contrasted with the beige grass, the naked trees, and some lush green plants that refused to be undressed by the gusty winter winds. Nyeredzi craved the taste and texture of iron–rich dirt on her tongue and was eager to lick it, but she was shy about being judged by her new friends. She never told them that back in Marondera, she used to lick her muddy fingers while she played with Cleo and Tariro. Or that she ate soil from the termite hill at the edge of Mr. Davidson's farm.

Nyeredzi had seen pregnant ladies picking dirt from the trees that were clothed in soil by termites. When these women spoke, their reddened tongues were visible, but they didn't seem shy or worried about being judged. Still, Nyeredzi was afraid of being teased that she was pregnant. That's why she only tasted the red soil when she was by herself.

Sometimes she stepped on large thorns without realizing they were not just dead grass on the sides of the pathways worn down by other people. Other times she tripped on her feet and the skin peeled off, leaving her with dangling flesh and bleeding toes. Whatever pain, she endured; it made her strong. Stronger than she was in Marondera. Her soft feet were long gone, they had hardened, but she didn't mind.

Other days Nyeredzi wrote the list of the most important things in her life on the soil. Little did she know who was watching from above and reading from underneath. Even though she was still young, it seemed as if she was now sure of who she wanted to be.

For Nyeredzi, the dirt was freedom. Her friends were terrified that they would get into trouble if they went home covered in dirt. Nyeredzi didn't mind the days she skipped bathing and went straight to bed with dusty legs, not to mention smears of oil from the chicken soup she'd had for lunch. Zuva never told her off because she liked the outdoors as well.

They moved from the small three–room cottage into the four–room house with a bathroom built by her father. He planned to add another three bedrooms, an open liv-ing–dining room, and an extra bathroom when they had enough money. Her parents rented the cottage to two young men from Bulawayo, Edward and Dingani. They spoke Ndebele and had moved to Harare to look for jobs.

But even in this new house, the sleeping arrangements weren't that much different for the girls. Ruth was the lucky one who had her own bedroom, because she was the oldest, and because there was only space for one bed. The rest of the room Zuva had stacked with furniture—a sofa, dining chairs, a mattress—as well as their suitcases and a wardrobe at the foot of Ruth's bed.

The other three girls shared a room with two double beds, and a laundry basket woven from reeds that Zuva bought from a street vendor. Under each bed were their shoes, picks, and hoes for digging in the garden, and nests of galvanized tubs used to carry dirty clothes outside for washing. The hand–painted artwork of a curved road was hung on a nail above Nyeredzi and Abigail's bed. Nyeredzi and Abigail shared a brown wardrobe with a mirror and drawers.

One side of it was cluttered with hooks carrying school satchels and sun hats. Hannah's freshly-ironed clothes sat neatly on the wooden hangers hung on a thick gray nail above her pillows. The view from the window was of pawpaw trees, and sugarcane along the boundary. On the other side was the neighbor's veranda with its red–brick pillars.

Nyeredzi shared one of the beds with Abigail, who didn't like dirt at all.

"Your whole body is stinking of sweat, and you're dirty," Abigail shouted at her. She kicked Nyeredzi off the bed they shared and threw her pillow onto the floor.

"Why do you care so much?" Nyeredzi pushed her pillow back onto the bed. "It's not your body—it's mine and mine only."

"Well, you need to know I'm older, and you have to listen when I tell you what to do."

"You don't have to order me around," shouted Nyeredzi. Abigail was only three years older. "Mama never complains about me being dirty. She likes me the way I am. You are jealous that she allows me to go to the bush."

"Ha! Who cares about the bush?" Abigail said. "I don't care about the bush or this place. I just want to go back to Marondera."

Tears trickled down Nyeredzi's cheeks. She tried asking Hannah if she would sleep with her, but it was always a big, stretched *No*. If it wasn't for the snakes, she would go outside to sleep on a smooth, wide branch of the gum tree in the bush. Besides, Zuva and Mwedzi would never allow her. Instead, she screamed her lungs out, her voice echoing off the gray unplastered blocks of the new room.

Abigail kept pushing Nyeredzi off the bed as if she was dirty, marking her territory. She would move her pillow into the middle, followed by her body. And Hannah never bothered to side with Nyeredzi.

"You guys, you don't like me," Nyeredzi would complain before she lay down on a thin blanket on the cold floor. "I'll punish you one day."

Hannah and Abigail didn't take her seriously, but one afternoon Nyeredzi surprised them. Nyeredzi and her neighboring friends Hope and Marvellous were in the middle of the bush, standing under the jujube tree with broad branches hanging on the sides. They were looking for ripe fruit, but being careful of the spiky thorns all over the tree. When Nyeredzi reached out to grab one, she saw a chameleon crawling on the same branch. She grabbed a long stick from the ground and picked the chameleon from the tree. It changed its colors several times as Nyeredzi walked to the front of their yard where her sisters sat in deckchairs in the tree shade.

Abigail was busy painting her nails with lilac nail polish, Hannah inserting golden beads on her braids. Her sisters cringed, thinking Nyeredzi was going to throw the chameleon at them, but she didn't.

"If you two make me sleep on the floor again, I will put this in your blankets."

"Go away, lizard girl," Hannah said.

"Oh, she frightened me," Abigail whispered to Hannah.

For the next few days, Nyeredzi was able to slide into the bed next to Abigail even if she had dirty legs, without any quarrels. She had won the battle without having to fight. She was happy, because the chill of winter still lingered in the morning breeze, and she didn't want to sleep on the floor. But this feeling didn't last long.

Jossey, their cousin, arrived from Rusape in the east of Zimbabwe. She brought her two small children, all under the age of three, along with much of her furniture, because she had run away from her husband. She was done with the beatings, Nyeredzi heard her tell Zuva.

Nyeredzi had never met Jossey before, and Zuva had to explain how they were related. With extra people in the house, Nyeredzi and Abigail had to sleep on the floor. They had to give Jossey their bed since she was older and had little children. Nyeredzi didn't like it. Nor that these relatives she didn't even know only showed up when they were in trouble and wanted something from her mother. It seemed as though adults were always put first before young children, and because of that, Nyeredzi knew it would take a lot of years before someone listened to her— before she got to do what she wanted.

At first, when Jossey was having a conversation with Zuva, she seemed too talkative, but when she removed her scarf to reveal the scars on her head, swollen bruises on her chest and neck, Nyeredzi stepped closer to calm her crying children. Some mornings when they woke up, Jossey appeared to be upset and so lost, sitting at the edge of the bed with her children in her arms. Nyeredzi wondered if this was what happened when you got married. Being beaten. Being sad all your life.

Jossey had promised to stay for a few days, but weeks passed. Nyeredzi and Abigail were still sleeping on the floor. To make things worse, Abigail made Nyeredzi sleep on the side of the door, which meant everyone stepped on her if they got up in the night to go to the toilet. The breeze that constantly blew through the gaps made her body cold as the ocean. If she tried to wriggle close to her sister, Abigail would fart to keep her away. Nyeredzi decided that she never wanted to sleep with Abigail or anyone else ever again.

After three long weeks of Nyeredzi having to deal with Abigail and her farts, Jossey finally left with her children and all her furniture. What the girls didn't know was that Jossey's blankets were infested with lice. And all the time she stayed, the eggs spread in the mattress and the unplastered walls. Back in their bed, Nyeredzi and Abigail were bitten by lice. Even Hannah who slept on her own was bitten. The lice had taken over the whole room.

Nyeredzi asked if her father would allow her to sleep in his Peugeot pickup truck, but he said it was not safe. Zuva had to move the girls into Ruth's room. In there, Ruth wanted Nyeredzi to sleep in her bed. Hannah and Abigail were stuck together, sleeping on the floor next to the furniture that was piled on one side. Nyeredzi felt loved when Ruth chose her, she liked talking with her before they fell asleep. Sometimes it was jokes. Other times, it was folktales, but Nyeredzi preferred those about animals that spoke. Some days Nyeredzi would ask Ruth to repeat the same story.

"The hare was not willing to share food with his uncle baboon, so he sends him to go and wash his hands by the river, but on his way back, he dirtied them because he touched the ground again, so the hare sent him back again while he ate all the food."

"So, if I call out to a hare in the bush, will it speak to me, Sis?" Nyeredzi asked.

"Perhaps we should try if we see a hare in the bush another day—what do you think?"

"Ha! That'll be fun if the hare talks back to me."

Nyeredzi yearned for the night not to end. She just wanted to continue listening to Ruth's soft voice sing all night telling her folktales. She loved it in Ruth's bed. There were neither fights nor farts. Because of that, Nyeredzi made an effort to have a shower before she went to bed.

Once, in the middle of the night, they heard baby rats squeaking. Abigail and Hannah didn't wake up, but Ruth and Nyeredzi did. They looked under the bed but couldn't see anything; then they realized the squeaking came from under their covers. Ruth threw back the top blanket, and there were six or seven pink newborn rats crowded together at the foot of the bed. The sight of their twisting bodies made Nyeredzi feel sick. Ruth got a dustpan, collected the rats, and dumped them outside the front door.

They went back to sleep, but soon they were awake again: the baby rats were back on their bed. This time Ruth didn't take them outside. She flushed them down the toilet. Nyeredzi watched them swirl in circles before disappearing into the curved part of the pipe. They waited to see if the rats were really gone. Nyeredzi's impatience made her press the button of the tank several times, though she could see there wasn't any water coming out.

Later on, when Ruth and Nyeredzi were back in their bed, the rat mother came back for her babies. The rat crossed the bed several times, squeaking, looking for a loose part to get inside the blankets, but Ruth had tucked all the corners tight and covered their heads, so the rat wouldn't bite them. Nyeredzi felt each step of the rat as it ran from side to side. She fell back asleep to the sound of the rat squeaking, mourning for its babies. The following morning, Ruth and Nyeredzi didn't tell anyone. They kept quiet as if nothing had happened.

After Zuva had sprayed their bedroom with pesticide and washed everything in hot water to get rid of the lice, Nyeredzi, Abigail, and Hannah were able to return. She wondered, though, why she couldn't sleep with Ruth every night. The bed was big enough for two people. It felt like everything that brought her happiness was always taken away, swooped from under her feet. The nights loomed faster and seemed to stay longer. There was nothing fun about bedtime anymore, Nyeredzi missed sleeping with Ruth—their long talks, the adventure of killing the baby rats in the middle of the night.

But in the mornings, she couldn't wait to get out of the blankets and chase the sunlight drying the mist on the beige grass and tree leaves. When she followed Zuva to the field, her footsteps were the first of a young child on the red clay. The energy she got whenever she stepped on this land was miraculous, as if she was offering herself in the palms of life.

THE KISS OF DEATH

Spring 1990
ZUVA AND NYEREDZI

Zuva had promised to teach her daughter a lot of things. So, Nyeredzi followed the steps of her mother the same way their neighbors did. Since Zuva was the one who'd started clearing the bush and everyone else was scared to death to do so, it was as if this land belonged to her—as though she'd known all along what she was going to do with it—as though her ancestors buried under the red clay were guiding her to her own destination.

Zuva would dig holes with a hoe to mark her territory, and that way the neighbors would know the place was taken. She rubbed a handful of clay soil in her palms to see how dense it was and rich in color, to determine if it was worth growing something in that area. This was new territory for Nyeredzi. Sometimes she learned by asking her mother a lot of questions.

"What do you think, Mama, is it good soil?" she asked, rubbing soil in her palms too.

"It's all right, the land is fertile, but it still needs a boost with fertilizer." Zuva paused, sniffing the soil. "When it comes to maize crops, it's a little bit weak."

"I love the soil. It's red! So red, Mama."

"Yes, it looks beautiful, but we are going to use the soil for what it's meant to be used for. We are going to grow maize here."

"More like a garden?"

"No, more like a farm."

"Whoa, a farm, in this bush?"

"Yes, in this bush," Zuva answered.

Nyeredzi had seen farms before. Behind their suburb in Marondera, the farmlands were so huge, she had to squint to see where the boundary was. Plus, they didn't have rocks nor thick grass that was difficult to get rid of or tree roots that had taken over beneath the land.

On their old street in Marondera, they had neighbors who owned farms. Mr. Davidson grew tobacco. Mr. Crockett planted maize and groundnuts, and Mrs. Dhana specialized in potatoes and mushrooms. All these farmers had employees who helped them, but her mother was about to start on her own. Even though Nyeredzi and her sisters were there, they were inexperienced. Nyeredzi had seen Zuva gardening behind their old house, but she never thought her mother could cultivate a large piece of land like that.

After Zuva decided what this land could do for them, they started digging the area that was close to the main road. There were no problems because Zuva had burnt most of the snakes that lived in the holes closer to the houses. At first, it was fun for Nyeredzi, slicing the ground and then flipping the soil with a sharp hoe so the dust swirled in the air, coating her perspiring legs, nostrils, and turning her black braided hair ginger. She laughed at her sisters after seeing the same thing happening to them.

Mid–spring, Zuva and her daughters had finished digging most of the fields she'd chosen but were left with the termite hill field, the one that had black soil. Zuva told Nyeredzi and Abigail to put on some old shoes and follow her. She carried her old basket containing a large bottle of water, broken wristwatch, towel, matches, and sandwiches wrapped in plastic. The girls dragged their worn–out shoes on the dry grass. When they arrived, Nyeredzi and Abigail pushed the stalks of grass to the edge of the field with their hoes.

Nyeredzi had always wanted to know what it was like to be so close to a snake. On the day Zuva was clearing the bush, she wanted to go with her mother, but Zuva wouldn't let Nyeredzi go with her. Nyeredzi couldn't understand why. She was ready to face what was coming on to her. She wasn't scared of snakes. There was this part of her that wanted to know what would happen if she held one in her palm, felt its coldness in her warm skin. Would it slip off her hand like butter? Perhaps today her wish was going to be fulfilled.

Soon, Nyeredzi started digging the black soil, but the tiny holes she thought belonged to ants were the homes to baby snakes. She looked at other people who were close by in their fields to see if they were also experiencing the same thing, but she noticed they all wore gumboots, and the girls didn't.

Zuva had warned them it was a matter of life and death, but she didn't really tell the girls what to do; the instinct just kicked into their bloodstream. Abigail jumped here and there, screaming while Nyeredzi had her fierce face on, as if she were possessed by something—a spirit. The bloodline of her ancestors who hunted wild animals rushed in her veins from her tiptoes to her skull.

The tiny, slim reptiles were encapsulated in their little holes under the ground and with each dig Nyeredzi took, they came out fast—twisting their bodies before her. At that time, she wasn't thinking about grasping one in her palm. Nyeredzi sliced them into pieces and tossed them by the termite hill with her hoe, where ants crawled on the bloodied, threaded bodies. The heat from the sky shrunk their skin and the thickened blood turned brown. Nyeredzi kept her hoe in the air, wide–eyed, scanning for the snakes on the black soil, which was difficult because the snakes were grayish in color and blended in.

Soon the girls were exhausted and burning under the hot sun. To entertain themselves, they gathered dried grass and began to stuff it in the wide hole. Zuva was on the other side of the bush when Nyeredzi took a box of matches from her mother's old basket.

"Do you want me to show you what Mama did when you were at school playing netball the other day?" Nyeredzi asked.

"What? Just show me," Abigail said. "I don't have time to muck around. I don't want to be here—I want to go home, you know."

"Yeah, I know." Nyeredzi nodded but she wasn't concerned about her sister. She had other things on her mind.

Nyeredzi scratched a match on the brown side of the box. Flames were born, and she threw the stick on the stuffed grass inside the hole. The girls bent their bodies with hands resting on their knees and waited, staring at the hole. It wasn't the second–hand ticking on Zuva's wristwatch in her old basket which told them how long the girls waited but each bead of sweat flowing from their foreheads until it dropped on the soil. Perhaps it was the smell of blood from the baby snakes they had just killed or smoke that lured out what was inside the hole. The top burnt grass had turned into black ashes but still it produced waves of smoke that disappeared into the atmosphere. Nyeredzi could still hear the sparks popping underneath the quiet, dark hole.

Just when the girls were starting to lose their patience and their curiosity about what was going to happen, something knocked the burning grass into the air and landed a few feet from them. They leapt back in fear, unsure what had come out of the hole.

Long and thick, its tummy, neck, and head were gray, the rest of the body was blackish with a shiny herring-bone pattern of scales. It was a black mamba, only a few meters away from them. Its head was raised, mouth open, ready to attack. Nyeredzi had never seen a snake that big and angry, and she could feel Abigail shiver next to her as fear took over. The adrenaline of bravery had worn off. Nyeredzi couldn't blink—she was frozen.

"What do we do?" Abigail asked, sounding as though she wanted to run away.

"Nothing," Nyeredzi said. "Mama, Mama!"

Zuva turned around. "Don't move," she shouted.

She grabbed some stalks of half–dead grass and walked fast toward Nyeredzi and Abigail. The box of matches that Nyeredzi had used before by the termite hill lay on the ground. Zuva used them to set the stalks alight. They created a dense, dark smoke. Then, cautious of the black mamba, she moved closer to the girls and placed the burning stalks around them. Nyeredzi and Abigail stood, crying and trembling, but their mother remained calm.

The black mamba's head was now swaying sideways, neck stretched in the air, trying to bite the girls with its glistening fangs. They'd been told by Zuva to stay away from this termite hill, but Nyeredzi was curious. She'd wanted to know what was in there. What Nyeredzi thought she could handle wasn't what she had imagined all along. She thought it would be small snakes coming out of the hole—the ones she was chopping off with a hoe or stomping with the heel of her shoe when they were half–dead.

When Nyeredzi discovered that there were many snakes in the bush, she wished that one day if she came across a snake, and if it looked into her eyes, maybe it would understand her. But now, standing there in front of a venomous snake with seconds to live if it attacked them, there was nothing to be understood. It was clear that both creatures were enemies—prey versus predator! If it were to come closer like Nyeredzi had wished, she would only have the kiss of death.

Although the black mamba was furious, the stalks of grass that Zuva had placed around them released heavy smoke, which clouded the snake. This subdued its anger, making it drowsy. The black mamba uncoiled itself, its shiny herringbone pattern of scales gleaming under the sun. It slithered away slowly, defeated, toward the dense bush. That's when they realized it was between one and two meters long. They did not wait for it to return.

"All right, I think it's time we go home," Zuva said, picking up the basket and their hoes.

"I don't want to come back here anymore," Abigail shouted, facing Zuva, her body still trembling.

"Go and tell those people we have a black mamba in the bush," Zuva said, looking at Nyeredzi.

"I think we should set a trap for this snake, Mama, that was really long," Nyeredzi said.

She ran toward their neighbors who were digging in their field. Her fear had turned into excitement. Once again, Nyeredzi was curious to know what would happen if they captured the black mamba mother. They had already killed some of her children, and she wondered if this snake was going to take revenge at some point, and death would fall upon them.

Zuva called the Snake Park from the call box down the street and asked the authorities to come and capture the black mamba. Nyeredzi saw the men with their equipment, small cages, long sticks that had hooks at the end, and the large snake bags to tie the snakes inside. Although the men found some snakes in the bush, which they took to the Snake Park, Zuva's family weren't sure if the black mamba was captured too. The men told Zuva to put the bush on fire to chase the rest of the snakes away, but she was against it. It would have affected other animals and Nyeredzi wouldn't have heard the beautiful sound of the pigeons cooing in the wild berry trees or run after the hares again.

Nyeredzi lay in bed, the only one awake. Her sisters were fast sleepers, and if she woke up, she lay still, staring at the gray asbestos roof. Two days had passed since the incident with the black mamba. Her mother had decided to leave the termite hill field alone for a little while.

The nights were getting warmer, so Nyeredzi had pushed off the thin blanket she shared with her sister. Nyeredzi felt Abigail stir next to her, then scratched Nyeredzi's hand.

"Nyeredzi," Abigail whispered. "Don't move. A snake has coiled around my leg."

Nyeredzi wasn't sure if Abigail was dreaming, but she didn't dare move.

"How big?" she whispered back.

"Maybe the length of my forearm."

"Then don't do anything stupid," Nyeredzi said.

She looked into Abigail's eyes: all they were saying was, "I'm dead, goodbye my sister, I love you." Nyeredzi turned her head to look at the top of their blanket, a big bump was there by Abigail's legs. As Abigail stayed still, Nyeredzi didn't want to alert the snake, but its head was moving. She slowly moved out of the bed as silently as she could, tiptoed to Zuva and Mwedzi's bedroom through the dark passage, and knocked on the door.

"Mama, wake up, a snake has coiled Abigail's leg."

"What?" asked Zuva, shuffling Mwedzi's shoulder.

"I said a snake has coiled Abigail's leg. Hurry! It's going to swallow her."

"Oh, my Lord, save my daughter," Zuva said.

No one knew how deadly the snake was. Mwedzi, in his shorts, ran outside in the dark to grab the gabhu–gabhu sticks from the chicken coop, where Zuva kept them. The sticks released a thick, intense scented smoke that snakes didn't like, and Zuva had only kept them to chase snakes from her chicken coop. Within a few seconds, he was back in the girls' bedroom, holding the sticks next to Abigail's head. Mwedzi lit the gabhu–gabhu sticks from the burning paraffin lamp, now adjusted to light up the room for them to see. Mwedzi held the sticks, pointing them underneath the blanket and the smoke circled the room.

Zuva had put a wet towel on Abigail's face for her to breathe easy. While Nyeredzi was on the other bed within the room, watching, her eldest sisters were waiting in the corridor. Zuva was holding a thick log by the door. Though Mwedzi told Nyeredzi to leave the room, she didn't move. Instead, she held her hands together and prayed silently, asking for the snake to let go of her sister's leg, for it not to get angry and attack Abigail, who was still lying on the bed, frozen. She'd forgotten how much they fought.

Wide–eyed, they watched the snake slowly uncoil it-self from Abigail's leg underneath the blanket. Nyeredzi, Zuva, and Mwedzi tried not to cough. The smoke was not only making the snake drowsy; it also turned their eyes red and teary. The brown snake poked its head from the edge of the bed. First, the head touched the floor, and once its whole body was on the floor, Zuva swung really hard, aiming at its head with a log, but missed the first time. The snake twisted its shape on the floor, trying to escape, heading to the wardrobe doors that were open.

Mwedzi was now holding a hoe he'd grabbed from un-derneath the bed, waiting to chop the snake in half, but Zuva hit the snake several times with the log.

When everyone in the room was sure that the snake was dead, Abigail was still in bed, still frozen. Nyeredzi brought the paraffin lamp closer to study the creature. It was long, slim, and brown. She then remembered she'd seen a brown snake a few days ago. She had stared at it while it slithered into their neighbor's yard on the grass. When it disappeared into the dead leaves, she had called for her mother. Zuva decided not to look for it since it was dangerous for her too.

While Mwedzi took the dead snake outside to burn it, Ruth and Hannah were busy checking if there were any snakes left inside, under the bed, the drawers, and inside the blankets. It turned out Abigail was okay except she had wet herself so Zuva kept rubbing Abigail's leg with a towel to clean her.

While everyone seemed unsettled, Nyeredzi knew it could have been her leg coiled with the snake if she had covered herself in the blanket too, but she got lucky. She wondered if the snake had come for her. Perhaps it was her wish. Supposedly the snake had seen Nyeredzi before while she watched it slithering on the grass. Maybe it was just revenge from the snake family. They had killed lots of snakes, after all.

GOLIATH

Autumn 1991
NYEREDZI

Mr. Jombo used to come over when the sun was tilted low, heading west under the blue dome. The Taha family welcomed him because he was a caretaker at their church even though Mr. Jombo often ran away from the jobs he was asked to do like cleaning the gutters, fixing the broken lamps, mowing the lawn, and so many other tasks.

But when Nyeredzi's father went away to Zvishavane City, where he had to build a client's second house, Mr. Jombo said he would look after the Taha family while Mwedzi was away. He thought Zuva and her daughters needed a man to check on them, so he popped in almost every day. And when he came, he would make sure the girls made him a cup of tea.

Usually he wore khaki trousers, a light blue shirt, and a gray blazer, which matched his hair. He limped from the corner of the street, the outer layer of his black shoes peeling like a lizard's dead skin. Nyeredzi wondered if it was due to being exposed to water, or just negligence. The holes at the front tip of his shoes grabbed her attention more. Each step he took, they collected red clay from the bare ground. When he reached the front yard, their green lawn circled with flowers, he kicked at Zuva's plants with that *I don't care* attitude.

On the days when Zuva went to the local church where she led late afternoon prayers with the parishioners, her daughters stayed home to prepare dinner. They took turns cooking as well as going to Thorville Shopping Center to buy essentials. Nyeredzi mostly gambolled outside with Hope as if she was guarding their territory. Whenever Nyeredzi saw Mr. Jombo striding toward their house, she ran to warn her sisters that he was coming and then carried on with her business.

Mr. Jombo would call out to Nyeredzi when he was getting closer. She'd run toward him with Hope, giggling, tiptoeing along the edge of the lawn. She would pass him in zigzags while he spread out his arms hoping for Nyeredzi to jump in, but Hope would jump in instead. He would throw Hope in the air with a disappointed face.

Zuva had warned Nyeredzi not to jump in any man's arms that were not her father's. She watched Hope leap, screaming with excitement and fear. Nyeredzi liked to fly, even if her heart went up to her throat. Even if the wind blew her skirts away from her thighs, she still loved to fly.

Mr. Jombo would put Hope down, walk around the house, and stand under the branches of Zuva's fruit trees. Sometimes he slapped the maturing trunks with his broad palms. Other times he whistled while staring at the bush like Hope's father did when he got back from work or when he had a shower in his bathroom. Nyeredzi would get moody from her missed opportunity to fly and run to the back to make mud houses with wet clay instead.

But one day she followed Mr. Jombo's trail inside the house. The dusty shoe prints on the shined floors of the passage led her to the room that served as kitchen, dining room, and lounge. In here, two tall brown kitchen units stood on either side of the window, sandwiching the wooden workbench with a two–plate paraffin stove on top. Underneath the bench were woven baskets filled with vegetables and three containers of water. The sunlight flared through the lace curtain, covering the floor and the long coffee table with its legs that looked like lion paws.

Two long carved giraffes guarded the Taha's ancestors in wooden frames, who randomly floated on the nails plugged into the gray wall. The main furniture was a dining table and chairs, and an old maroon sofa and two armchairs of the same color. The cabinet for their black–and–white TV and radio was decorated with carved lions, elephants, tiny little drums, a man stretching a bow and arrow at an angle, and a woman holding a child.

Nyeredzi peeped through the gap of the wooden door and the frame. Mr. Jombo was already sitting on one of the armchairs, talking to Hannah who was putting the kettle on the stove. He gawked at Hannah's back while she bent to get the utensils from the cupboard. Hannah was the prettiest of her sisters, and her body had only started curving into that of a woman's, and Nyeredzi didn't like the way he looked at her. She marched in and slapped Mr. Jombo on his knee.

"Get off Papa's armchair."

"Well, it's my chair too. I'm your guest."

"No, it's Papa's only." She pointed to the other one. "And that one, it's Mama's."

"All right, Miss Taha, I hear you."

He got up, looking irritated, and moved to the three–seater sofa. Hannah went outside to get water. Nyeredzi sat in the armchair across from Mr. Jombo, still watching him. He opened the sugar basin on the coffee table and scooped sugar into his palm with a teaspoon, spilling some on the clean floor and sofa as he licked the crystals with his tongue. Nyeredzi cringed, the hair on her arms standing on end. The urge to slap him was huge.

"That's bad manners," Nyeredzi said, looking at him. She rested her chin in her palm. "Mama doesn't like it at all."

He stared back. "Bad manners are only noticed in young children like you. I'm an adult."

"Then why don't you do that when Mama is here?"

"Because I respect her so much," he said, and yawned.

"Well, too bad. I am going to tell her."

When Mwedzi was preparing to go to Zvishavane, he had mentioned to Mr. Jombo he would be away for a few weeks. Nyeredzi had overheard their conversation. She thought Mr. Jombo would stop coming, but he was always there, waiting for her siblings to make him a cup of tea. She'd also overheard Mwedzi asking him to become his laborer a few times because Mr. Jombo complained a lot about his job.

"Hmm, I'll think about it," he would say. "I don't know much about building, you know." Then he would start whining about how his leg got hurt when he was hit by a car.

Mr. Jombo was married and had two children, a girl, and a boy, but his family had left him. Each time his wife spoke up, he would punch or slap her and the children, so they packed their belongings and took off. The church members had warned him several times about how unacceptable his behavior was, how one day he would look back and regret it.

Now that the Taha family had moved here to Harare, and Zuva was a church leader, their home had become a world for Mr. Jombo to escape to, and it seemed as though he wanted to move in and take over.

Hannah walked in again. She picked a teabag from a jar and threw it in the boiling water before pouring in a little bit of white liquid from a 500 ml Chimombe milk packet. She folded the corner, pinched it with a wooden peg, and then placed it in a bowl half–filled with water so it stayed fresh. Mr. Jombo's gaze was back on Hannah's waist, watching her every move while she made sandwiches and spread butter. Nyeredzi frowned and folded her arms but he just grinned down at her. Mr. Jombo slid his hand inside the front pocket of his faded gray blazer, pulled out a coin, and put it on the table.

Nyeredzi admired the coin. It was shiny, gold and still newish, unlike Mr. Jombo's clothes. She took two steps closer to it, still staring.

"It has a bird on one side," he said.

"What bird?"

"Come and see for yourself. This is a foreign bird."

Nyeredzi picked up the coin, and placed it in her hand. "Have you ever been to South Africa, Mr. Jombo?"

He glanced at Hannah, who was humming a church song and carrying the tea things over to the coffee table. "Tell you what—you take the coin. Go and keep it somewhere safe."

Before Nyeredzi walked out with the coin, Hannah shouted, "Nyeredzi!"

"It's fine," Mr. Jombo said. "It's only one coin. Let her take it, she's just a child."

"Exactly, Mr. Jombo. She is just a child who you should not encourage to love money," Hannah said, pouring tea into a mug. She was standing close to Mr. Jombo.

He smiled at Hannah. "Hmm, well said. You are all

grown up now. It's only today I am giving her the money. Let her take it, honestly."

Nyeredzi looked at Hannah, searching for approval in her eyes, then walked into the passageway, thinking of where to keep the coin. When she turned around to ask Mr. Jombo a question, she saw him put his hand on Hannah's buttocks. Hannah jumped aside, startled. Mr. Jombo smiled at Hannah, raising his hands in the air, gesturing as if nothing was wrong.

Nyeredzi shouted, "Mr. Jombo, you touched my sister's butt! I'm going to tell Mama!"

"Why did you touch me?" Hannah interrupted.

She was walking around the table to get out of the room, but he got up quickly, grabbing Hannah's wrist before she reached the door. Nyeredzi rushed to break his grip, but it was strong. She tried to push Mr. Jombo's body away from Hannah, who screamed, attempting to break free. The coin fell on the floor. Nyeredzi thought of going to call for Hope's parents, but she didn't want to leave Hannah alone with Mr. Jombo.

"Let go of my sister!" Nyeredzi shouted, trying to pull Hannah away.

Mr. Jombo pushed Nyeredzi off with his free hand and she fell onto the armchair, hitting her head on the wooden arm. She felt as though she was hallucinating. The room was spinning as pain pounded in her skull. She was confused. Why would an adult man do that to a girl? Why did he behave so wildly?

Nyeredzi got up again to pull Hannah away from Mr. Jombo, tears falling. He pushed her back again, but she instinctively grabbed the mug of tea from the table and flung it at Mr. Jombo's face. He screamed, letting go of Hannah's arm to rub his face. Then he was growling, his anger echoing off the walls. Before the girls could leave, Mr. Jombo reached out to get hold of Hannah again.

At that very moment, Zuva stepped into the room, holding her Bible. She had left the church service early that day. The girls dashed toward their mother, both in tears and shivering. Mr. Jombo stood fidgeting, adjusting his blazer.

"What's going on here?" Zuva looked concerned.

"He is trying to hurt Hannah, and he pushed me on the sofa," Nyeredzi reported.

"Come on," he said with a grimace. "Why would I hurt Hannah? She's like a daughter to me. I just popped in to see how you all were."

"Well, we are in fine fettle, as you can see," Zuva said.

"No, he's lying, Mama." Hannah was sobbing. "He really wanted to hurt me."

"I splashed tea on his face when he wouldn't let go of Hannah," Nyeredzi told her.

Zuva glared at Mr. Jombo and gestured for her daughters to move away.

"How dare you?" Zuva stepped closer to the coffee table. "How dare you come into my house and lay your filthy hands on my daughters?" She placed the Bible upside down on the coffee table.

Mr. Jombo touched his scalded face with his fingers. "Who do you think you are?" he asked. "You are a woman, and you should know by now where you belong."

"Hannah, go and call the police," Zuva commanded, and Hannah ran off to the call box that was located at the end of their street. Nyeredzi didn't move.

Mr. Jombo stepped closer to Zuva. He was twice her size. He ran his hand down Zuva's face and brushed her braided hair behind her ear quickly.

"Aren't you ashamed of yourself?" Zuva shoved him backwards. "Get out of my house, you pervert."

Nyeredzi was shivering, tears trickling down her cheeks. She clung to the door frame with her fingers. She'd hoped that Mr. Jombo would leave once her mother returned, but he didn't. He didn't even care the police were coming.

"I like that in a woman—that kind of energy," he said, smiling now. "I like how you lead everyone in the church, they listen to you. Your voice is so strong and soft at the same time."

Zuva shook her head. Nyeredzi could see she was furious.

"I hear them talk about you," he continued, "so I'm here too, letting you know you are such a beautiful woman with beautiful daughters."

He adjusted his blazer again, and for a moment Nyeredzi thought he was leaving, but instead he leapt at Zuva. In one movement, he tore her blouse open. Nyeredzi stood frozen, but Zuva was pummelling him, fighting with all her strength. Mr. Jombo jammed one hand under Zuva's chin, strangling her. She gasped for air, her eyes red and watery as she tried to break free.

Nyeredzi stood trembling with fear like a twig in the wind. Mr. Jombo was fast, and he was strong. He was used to hurting women—Nyeredzi had heard this from the lady gossipers at church. She didn't know what it meant, but now she could see it happening before her. Zuva's left hand groped for the cutlery drawer behind her until she got hold of a knife. She swung it at Mr. Jombo, but he was too quick for her: he grabbed the knife and threw it onto the floor. He was still throttling Zuva while his other hand unzipped his trousers, pulling at the belt. When Nyeredzi saw his erect flesh part popping out between his thighs, she screamed.

Her mother was cornered by the kitchen unit. Mr. Jombo pulled her long skirt up, his bottom silhouetted in the dimming light. Although Nyeredzi was shaking, she picked up the knife and lunged at Mr. Jombo's thigh. She didn't know where the strength came from. For a moment, he stopped moving, and all Nyeredzi could hear was her mother's heavy breathing. Mr. Jombo inhaled with pain and let out a mighty bellow. He staggered backwards, almost knocking Nyeredzi over, the knife sticking out from his thigh.

In a flash, his right hand was on her throat, choking her against the wall. His pants were now down to his knees. He didn't bother pulling them up. Nyeredzi feared two things: dying and seeing Mr. Jombo's bottom. Zuva was coughing and choking, but she staggered a few steps and pulled the knife from his thigh. He yowled, turning around to face Zuva to strike her, but she stabbed him, piercing deep into the femur. Mr. Jombo collapsed like a pillar struck by an earthquake, his body still half–naked, blood everywhere.

Zuva pulled Nyeredzi into her arms, turning her away from the sight of Mr. Jombo's private parts. He just slumped there, unable to move as blood kept oozing out, so they stepped outside the house, locking him inside.

Hannah arrived with the police in their Santana Land Rover. She was lucky, she told Nyeredzi later. They'd picked her up on the roadside on her way home. They pulled over in front of the house and Hannah hopped out of the vehicle, followed by three officers, two males and one female, their brown boots shining against their navy–blue pants, shoulder badges dictating their status. Their blue caps gave them enough shade from the sun setting. Guns were buttoned in their cases and buckled to either side of their hips.

"I have locked the man inside," Zuva said, handing a key to the police officers.

Two of the officers unlocked the door to collect Mr. Jombo. Inside the room their furniture was displaced, armchairs and coffee table tipped on their sides. A large pool of blood surrounded the smashed mug and teapot on the floor. When he emerged, Mr. Jombo's pants were now pulled up to his waist. He was limping, and in handcuffs, led away by the male officers.

The female officer scribbled in her notebook while she questioned Zuva and Hannah. Some of their neighbors skulked along the street, glancing inside the vehicle and at them. Nyeredzi didn't like it.

"Clean the blood," Zuva demanded. "I don't want it on my hands, nor my daughters. And please, try to make it look tidier inside?"

"We can clean the blood, Mrs. Taha, but we will need you to make a statement at the station."

"I can't leave my daughters alone," she said with a stiff face. "I'll have to come tomorrow morning."

Mr. Jombo sat at the back of the vehicle; its windows barred with wire net, his head lowered. The image of what had happened still played in Nyeredzi's head.

She looked up to her mother and asked, "Mama! Is Mr. Jombo going to come back here again? I don't want to see him ever again."

"No, he is going away for a long time." Zuva stared down into Nyeredzi's eyes. "I will never let anything happen to you, my daughter."

THUGS

Winter 1991
ZUVA

Everyone was already deep in dreams when Zuva heard someone banging on their back door. She shook Mwedzi to wake him up.

"My love, what is it?" Mwedzi said, his voice groggy with sleep.

"Someone is trying to break in," Zuva said, getting dressed in the dark. The banging continued. Mwedzi lit the paraffin lamp and she bent down to grab a crowbar from underneath the bed.

"Auntie Zuva, it's me, Lameck!" a quivering voice called. "Tell Uncle to come out first. Uncle, please bring a cloth to cover my body?"

Zuva assumed Lameck was naked, but the question was why? Zuva put the crowbar back and pulled out a bath towel from a washing basket. This, she handed to Mwedzi who walked out to their nephew. Zuva stood just inside, holding the paraffin lamp, and glimpsed Lameck lying on the ground, holding a log in his hand.

"Oh, son, what happened?" Mwedzi asked while he covered Lameck's shivering body.

"There were so many of them," Lameck answered, his

voice thick.

"You can come out, my love," Mwedzi shouted to Zuva.

"Oh, my Lord what happened to you, son?" she asked, holding the light up to Lameck. His face was swollen, his half naked body covered in blood and mud.

"Auntie." He paused, trying to regain some strength. "The thugs took everything."

Zuva recalled one of their neighbors saying there were thugs who stayed in the bush at night. They hid in the trenches dug by the city council for sewer pipes and were after people's valuables. She linked her arms under Lameck's upper body and Mwedzi held his legs as they carried him into the kitchen and laid him on a mat. Zuva lit the paraffin stove to boil some water. When it was ready, she poured the water in the galvanized tub and Mwedzi began cleaning Lameck. Their nephew was wincing in pain.

After Lameck was bandaged and clothed in Mwedzi's extra pair of pajamas, Zuva fed him some warm soup and Mwedzi drove to the pharmacy to buy some medicine. He also went to report the incident at Southgate 1 Police Station. Zuva was keen to know what had happened to Lameck, but she decided not to question him until the police arrived because he couldn't speak properly.

Mwedzi returned with betadine and paracetamol. Two police officers had followed him home in their Santana Land Rover. They sat on the sofa and Zuva offered the officers some tea because the questioning was going to take a long time. Lameck explained everything that had happened bit by bit, struggling to speak properly due to pain. When he mumbled, Zuva had to speak for him if she could understand what he was trying to say.

Lameck had been traveling from Chinhoyi City, where

Zuva's cousin lived. Zuva wasn't aware her nephew was planning to come to their place and if she'd known, she would've warned him. Alone, under the dark sky, Lameck walked across the bush by himself, carrying a bag full of Seiko watches, which he was planning to sell. Thugs accosted him and demanded it, then battered him with barbed wire when he refused to give the bag. Though the thugs didn't stab Lameck, they took what belonged to him, including the clothes he was wearing. And when they were done with him, he dragged himself across the cold dirt, shivering in pain until he got to the Taha's place after midnight.

The police took Lameck to hospital, where Zuva visited him. It wasn't pleasant to see someone close to her with wounds that still reeked despite being dressed daily with fresh bandages. It reminded her of how deadly the bush was. It took Lameck a month to get out of his hospital bed.

Edward and Dingani, who rented their cottage, were kind enough to let him use one of their rooms after he was discharged from the hospital. The betadine scent lingered, and each time Zuva entered Lameck's room to give him food, she left with her own clothes carrying the heavy scent of the medicine.

Zuva understood it was dangerous for the police to patrol the bush in the evening by foot as there were poisonous snakes, but this meant the family's lives were in danger since their house was on the edge of the bush. She was horrified at the thought of them trying to live peacefully in this suburb, when every night the bush awakened, reverberating with wild animals and humans. People were being murdered right in their backyard. It forced her family to be on guard all the time.

It all started because of the famous Monstrous Joy bar,

in front of the hill across the bush. Thugs knew a lot of men went there and it was easy to get money and valuables from drunken men. The bar was lit up each day from late afternoon until the early morning hours as men traveled from their workplaces, even those who lived far away. They would loiter for hours in the bar, drinking from bottles of lager—Castle, Zambezi, and Lion—or Black Label alcohol. Some preferred masese or hwahwa.

Men drank one bottle after another, buying rounds for strangers whom they had befriended while sitting on stools circling small round metal tables. If their conversations went well without arguing, they got up and danced to Stella Chiweshe, Aleck Macheso, Oliver Mtukudzi, and Thomas Mapfumo, singing along with the loud music that brought them joy.

Some mornings, when the sun was beaming from the eastern side, Zuva woke up to see drunken men crossing the bush from the bar. One day it was three men staggering on the pathway, coming from Monstrous Joy. The short one from the back shouted as if they were a hundred meters away from each other, his words unclear. He bent down, and the vomit poured out of his mouth. The one in the middle threw himself onto the ground and fell asleep. Their friend who was leading walked back to take a look at the one on the dirt and started to cry.

"Oh, my friend Trevor, don't die on me now—who will buy me a beer?"

His friend shouted back from the dirt, "Let's go back! I shall buy my friend more beer." He managed to get up, and they all began walking toward the bar again.

Zuva was watching the group from afar. She was trying to understand why they would stay out so late before she remembered the girls in bikinis who showed up at the top level of the bar. These men didn't want to miss out on seeing them pole dancing. It wasn't as though they had never seen naked women before, but it seemed new and exciting to them. They would get drunk until they couldn't stand on their own anymore, throwing money at the girls.

It satisfied their eyes and perhaps even their souls. If only the men were that lucky when they crossed the bush. If only they died peacefully without growling in pain after being tortured by the thugs. The bush was a shortcut that saved them hours from using the main road. But what happened to Lameck was horrifying. People must have heard that the bush wasn't safe to cross at night, so why would they risk losing their lives?

One night, two drunken men crossed the bush together and both of them were attacked. The first place they thought to come and ask for help was the Tahas'. The family had finished eating dinner and were sitting in their main room. The moon was bright outside that evening. They saw shadows of two figures passing by their window, and everyone stopped talking, listening for footsteps.

Zuva looked at her daughters and the next minute she was up, pulling a crowbar and a hammer from under the kitchen unit. Perhaps the thugs had come round their house to do wild things to them. Mwedzi took the crowbar and gestured for his daughters to stay inside, but they weren't willing to do that. Zuva took the hammer herself and hid it behind her in case it was only Edward and Dingani outside. All of the Tahas marched out in a single file to the front of their house.

The two men staggered, falling onto the concrete slab of rooms that were still being built. It was hard to tell if they really needed help because they were so drunk. But when Zuva stepped closer to them, she realized the men were injured. One man had a ravaged face; the skin of his left side was dangling. Blood mixed with saliva and tears oozed out of him. He tried to take off his blue jacket but couldn't.

It wasn't the first time Zuva had seen a person whose body parts were torn as though a bomb had exploded inside them. She realized the two men were harmless and placed the hammer by the pile of bricks. The man growled in agony, struggling to stand on his feet. The other one was bruised and had bloodied clothes, but he looked better and seemed to have no broken bones. He had managed to escape, leaving his friend in the hands of thugs holding knives, machetes, and chains.

"What happened?" Zuva asked.

"I'm sorry for coming here. We could only see your place from the bush." The man paused, as if trying to think what to say next that would make sense. Clearly, he was very drunk. "I'm Nathan, and we were attacked by thugs in the bush before we crossed the river. We thought if we left early, it would be safe for us to cross."

"How many were there?" Mwedzi asked, placing his crowbar by the bricks.

"There were many of them, but we couldn't really see. Probably more than ten. I heard some laughing from the trenches, while the others tried to beat us to death."

Zuva asked the girls to bring a towel and water for the men. Nathan drank and poured some water on his bloodied hands. She remembered how her nephew Lameck looked, and now, the blood oozing out on this man's torn skin made Zuva realize that the thugs were not the kind of people you could negotiate with.

"Tell us your friend's name so we can help him," Zuva said.

"I don't know his name. We just met outside the bar and figured if we crossed the bush together, no thugs would touch us."

The man who was severely hurt could not speak. His ravaged jaw was unable to form words while his swollen hands pressed a towel to his face to stop the bleeding. After Zuva gave him a pen and paper, he wrote down his name: he was Stephen Dhuba and he lived in Brown Stone, a suburb further away.

Mwedzi knocked on the cottage door to get Edward and Dingani, who were already in bed. They came out, looking surprised by the sight of the bloodied men standing by the slab.

"Boys, can you take these two men to the police?" asked Zuva.

"Yebo, Gogo, we can do that," Edward said in Ndebele. He was still learning Shona. Everyone who met Zuva called her Gogo, though she wasn't even that old. Perhaps it was because of the white patch of hair at the top of her head.

They went back inside the cottage to grab their jackets, then the four of them set off to the police. Mwedzi could not leave his family alone after this happened. That night the girls were scared. Whenever Nyeredzi shut her eyes, all she saw was the man with the ravaged face. Abigail would wake up whispering, "The thugs are here, Mama." Nightmares had possessed their brains. They both lay crying and shivering in fear until Zuva let them sleep on the floor of the main bedroom. Days passed, but the girls still had bad dreams. Only when Zuva let them get into her bed did they finally start sleeping peacefully.

The taking of people's lives never ended.

One afternoon, Zuva decided to take a shortcut

through the bush to pay school fees at Majuba 1 High. She was walking with Ruth and Nyeredzi, and they had only walked three or four kilometers. Zuva was mostly talking to Ruth while Nyeredzi walked behind them on the narrow path, hunting for lost treasure by scraping the dead grass areas with her black canvas shoes.

"Mama! Ruth! Someone is sleeping over there." Nyeredzi pointed to something she'd seen in the dense bush.

"What?" Ruth turned around in fear.

Zuva wasn't surprised to hear that, or to see a man's head and the side of one shoulder lying in the shrubs. They all walked back toward the man, and Ruth called out to him, to see if he was drunk or asleep. The man didn't respond. Ruth grabbed Nyeredzi's hand as though to protect her—if the man woke abruptly.

Zuva knew he was dead, but Ruth was in denial. It looked as though he'd been there for a couple of days because no one slept lying like that, with their mouth and eyes wide open, body naked and unmoving. They peeked from behind the shrub again, realizing he was half–covered with grass. His body was pale as though he'd been in the mortuary for a long time.

Zuva shook her head and said, "He's dead."

Nyeredzi bent down, stretching her hand out to touch the dead man's leg.

"Stop it!" Ruth shouted and pulled her sister backwards.

Now Ruth was trembling so much she couldn't walk steadily without heaving. While they walked back home to call the police, Zuva wondered what had happened to the man. Was he poisoned? Did the thugs strangle him or break his neck? Why did they have to take his clothes too?

First, Lameck was stripped of his clothes and now it

was this stranger lying dead on the ground. When Zuva looked at him one last time before they left, he was old enough to be a father, a husband to someone else. She wondered if those people existed in that man's life. If he had children, it meant they were already fatherless, and if he had a wife at home waiting, she was already a widow.

In that moment, she felt blessed to have a husband who didn't drink alcohol. Otherwise, he would be tempted to cross the bush too.

When they arrived home, it was Hannah and Abigail who went to call the police. Ruth was now in the state Abigail and Nyeredzi had been after they saw Stephen, the man with a ravaged face.

Later, the policemen showed up and walked through the bush with Zuva. It would be up to them to find out who the man was, to call his family members and tell them their son, brother, or father was dead. And if he did not have any relatives, after lying on the cold concrete of a mortuary for so many days without anyone showing up, they would bury him.

It was her daughters Zuva worried about. Was this the life they were going to live everyday—showing the police where the dead bodies were, helping attacked people who knocked on their door? This was not what she ever hoped for in her lifetime. She wondered though, if sooner or later she would have to face the thugs too when they surrounded her house? If Mwedzi was away and that happened, how could Zuva save all four of her daughters at once?

THE HOLLOWED SCAR

Late Winter 1991
NYEREDZI

Nyeredzi was eleven years younger than Ruth, but she still worried about her, especially the scar on her sister's foot. All day Ruth wore her canvas shoes while others wore flip–flops inside or outside the house. Even that time they shared a bed—after their cousin Jossey left their room in-fected—Ruth wore socks.

It was hard to keep on asking questions about the same thing, wanting to know more about the past that Ruth was trying to hide. A deep hollowed scar was there on Ruth's right foot, where she was shot as a child in the Second Chimurenga War. The Rhodesian soldiers had been patrol-ling Marondera City. Zuva was out to buy the essentials, but there were screams, and soon, bullets started flying in the air. Zuva was carrying Ruth on her back and as she ran for safety, a bullet pierced through Ruth's little foot.

Nyeredzi wondered if the scar had healed, whether her sister felt pain when she carried her. She loved to ride on Ruth's shoulders, feeling the breeze brushing her face and seeing the earth from up high. It was satisfying enough without demanding Ruth buy ice cream for her. Nyeredzi just wanted to have that long walk again, to feel her sister's grasp when they held hands.

It was now late winter in August when the maize crops they harvested from the fields were fully dried. Zuva was sending Ruth and Nyeredzi with bags of maize to the mill across the bush. The maize was to be ground into mealie meal, and this was Zuva's first batch harvested from the cleared fields.

"Are you ready, Nyeredzi? I'm leaving right now," Ruth called. "It's already noon—can you hurry up? Mama is expecting us to be back early."

"Please wait for me, Sis?" Nyeredzi shouted from Zuva's bedroom, squeezing her feet inside her canvas shoes.

The back door slammed, and Nyeredzi could hear Ruth outside talking to Zuva. Their voices faded as though they were walking into the bush. Nyeredzi was trying to dress as quickly as she could. Her face crumbled; a dark cloud was building up inside her. Tears were flooding her eyes, falling on her cheeks. Nyeredzi didn't know how she ended up outside, but she let out a long sigh of relief when she saw Ruth standing by the sack bags filled with dried maize, under the water berry tree.

Zuva picked up the little sack and placed it on Nyeredzi's head.

"Aah, Mama, this is so heavy," Nyeredzi complained.

Her mother didn't respond to her, she placed a bigger sack on Ruth's head.

"Mama, why are you giving me a sack that is so heavy?" Nyeredzi demanded.

"You are the one who cried to go with Ruth." Zuva adjusted the sack on Ruth's head. "You are complaining but look at your sister's sack. It's five times yours."

Nyeredzi and Ruth set off into the bush, dead leaves

and bark crunching under their canvas shoes. Nyeredzi thought it was beautiful and scary at the same time. The Bill and Southern Tree Agamas chased each other on the ground, and girdled lizards lay still on large rocks, soaking in all the heat as much as they could.

After they walked for what felt like hours, they reached the Msasa tree and the river with its lush green reeds and algae-covered boulders. Nyeredzi was exhausted. Ruth crossed the river by stepping from one boulder to the next, and Nyeredzi followed, an eel swimming by in the clear water.

On the other side lay a narrow path. The maize was heavy, but Nyeredzi kept following Ruth, her hands grasping the bag on her head.

"You must be exhausted," Ruth called back. "Do you want us to rest a bit?"

"Yeah, I'm so tired." She could see that Ruth's sack bag was more cumbersome than hers. Even shaking her head sideways was impossible.

"Let's walk until we get to the next tree."

The sun had stopped warming the earth and was now burning it. Nyeredzi's lips were stuck together. Dry. She was thirsty. At first, she enjoyed stepping on little ants and other insects crawling on the ground, but it wasn't exciting anymore. She could barely lift her eyelids, and her feet were burning. The edge of the canvas shoes cut her skin as she walked. She wondered if Ruth was going through the same thing. When they reached the wide–branched jacaranda tree, they threw their sack bags by the trunk.

"Come and sit here under the shade," Ruth said, sweeping away the dead leaves and twigs.

They sat listening to the pigeons cooing from a branch.

Ruth pulled out a plastic full of water berries from her dress pocket. Surprised, Nyeredzi smiled, looking at her sister unfolding the plastic. They both began to gobble on the succulent fruit.

Later, when they finished eating the berries, Ruth took off her canvas shoes and shook the soil out. She rubbed her feet with her hands and rested them on her shoes. Nyeredzi did the same but was looking at her sister's feet. If she could get up from where she was sitting and touch her scar, perhaps that would satisfy her curiosity once and for all. Maybe she would stop thinking so much about her sister's past.

Nyeredzi imagined the soldiers who shot Ruth as the Pharisees with King Jesus. She had seen King Jesus revealing his scars on a large painting hung in her parents' bedroom, except his scars seemed reddish, still raw. Ruth's was big and brownish as if it had been repeatedly burnt by the sun. Too soon, Ruth put on the canvas shoes again.

"I know you still want to sit, but we have to go."

"Do you think we will have something to eat again when we get there?"

"I will see if I have spare change." Ruth coiled the top of the smaller sack bag and placed it on Nyeredzi's head. "Yours is lighter—you are so lucky." She smiled, lifting hers with both hands. She got it halfway to her chest, staggered, and threw it back on the ground.

Nyeredzi was worried Ruth would hurt her foot. "Are you okay, Sis?"

"I'm okay. It's just heavy."

Ruth lifted the sack bag again, leaning it against the tree. Slowly, she pulled it up to her chest and crouched down, ducking her head under the sack bag. It took time for Ruth to settle the sack on her head.

Halfway to the grinding mill, they reached the trenches dug by the city council. The rain had done them a favor by washing the soil back inside, but they still had to go up and down, which was time-consuming. Nyeredzi was now far behind her sister, struggling. Every part of her body was sore.

"How is it going there, Nyeredzi?"

Nyeredzi didn't respond; her lips got stuck together again. The boulders of red clay bruised her skin. Her canvas shoes were filled with soil again. Ruth stopped to pull the sack bag from Nyeredzi's head with her left hand.

"I can carry it. I just need to take the soil out of my shoes."

"You do that. When you finish, you can have it back."

Ruth was now carrying two heavy bags, going up and down the trenches as the sun headed west. Nyeredzi held her shoes, running after Ruth. She forgot to ask her sister for the sack bag until they reached the grinding mill. Sack bags and wheelbarrows sat in a long queue, deserted by people resting under shady trees. The grinding mill and the Monstrous Joy bar were quiet because there was no power. Ruth threw their bags in the queue.

They strolled to the shade where everyone else was and sat down. Nyeredzi laid on her sister's laps and fell asleep. By the time she was woken up by the grinding mill noise, the sun was setting, and the sky was an orange–peach color. Ruth and Nyeredzi crossed their arms, still waiting, while the stars came out. The bush was getting darker and darker until they couldn't see the houses in the distance. They were far from being served and were going to be there at the grinding mill for hours. A woman with three children came up to them.

"I thought I was the only one worried about crossing the bush," the woman said, looking at Ruth.

"Do you think we can cross safely?" Ruth asked.

"With kids?" the woman scoffed. "We will see."

She returned to her sack bag, and Ruth and Nyeredzi moved closer to everyone in the queue. Nyeredzi had goosebumps, cold flowing through her nerves. The dark was disturbing enough without looking at it. Hunger was gone, and fear had taken over. The bush was deadly not only with poisonous snakes but also with thugs that hid in the trenches. The bar was now packed with men drinking. Loud music banged in their ears.

A tiny light seemed to be getting nearer, and it was Edward who lived in their cottage with Dingani. Edward was riding the bicycle that belonged to Mr. Manjo, their neighbor. Zuva had sent him, he said, and began talking to Ruth in a quiet voice.

"Hey Nyeredzi," Ruth asked. "What do you think about going home now?"

"What about the mealie meal? Are we leaving everything here?"

"No, you go with Edward, and Papa will come and get me, okay?"

"But I want to be with you and look after you."

"I know you do, but I'd like it if you go home now."

Ruth lifted Nyeredzi onto the carrier. Nyeredzi held on tight to the bicycle bar, still confused why she had to leave her sister behind. Edward started pedaling the bicycle, moving away from the grinding mill toward the bridge that went over the train tracks.

Ruth waved. "I will see you at home, don't worry," she shouted, smiling at Nyeredzi.

Nyeredzi could hardly see her as Edward pedaled fast,

heading to the main road. She kept turning her head, looking at the hill, but soon it was just two buildings beaming with light, being sucked into the darkness.

When they arrived home, Edward lifted Nyeredzi off the bicycle. The bush was so dark that she couldn't even see the trees or rocks. Could it be her fault she cried to go with Ruth? Perhaps it was. If she hadn't delayed Ruth in the bush, complaining about being exhausted, maybe they both would have arrived earlier at the mill while there was still power. What if the thugs walked to the mill and did the worst to Ruth there?

Nyeredzi ran inside the house looking for her mother. Abigail and Hannah were sitting on the sofa looking nearly comatose with boredom. Mwedzi was talking to Mr. Manjo and Dingani. Her father slid a small axe and his black sjambok inside the coat. His curly hair somehow looked very long that night, like the mane on the male lion rug that was in her parents' bedroom.

Mwedzi, Mr. Manjo, Edward, and Dingani all headed off into the bush. It didn't take long for the darkness to swallow them. Nyeredzi stood next to Zuva at the back of their house, watching their figures disappear. She had not got the chance to say goodbye to Ruth earlier on at the mill, or to her father now, before he walked straight into the mouth of danger. She folded her arms and prayed for everyone to return safely.

Zuva had made the relish for dinner, but they were waiting for the mealie meal to make sadza. She built a fire at the back of their house and boiled some water for Nyeredzi to bathe. In the bathroom Nyeredzi forgot Zuva told her not to wet her braided hair in the evening, because it would take longer to dry. She couldn't stop thinking about her sister, father, and the other men walking with him. She imagined them coming face to face with thugs. Her father pulling out his sjambok to whip the bad men. And Mr. Manjo holding a long hunting knife he made himself, chopping off the thugs' body parts. She could see the boys, Edward and Dingani, lifting their legs in the air, kicking the thugs back.

The moment she imagined Ruth kneeling down, begging the thugs not to kill them, made Nyeredzi start crying. She lifted the whole bucket filled with warm water and poured it on herself because she wanted to get out as fast as she could. She was desperate to check the bush, to see if they were coming back.

She hurried to dress herself, and join her mother outside, watching the bush. All the procedures she usually did after having a bath weren't important. She didn't use lotion, and instead of changing into fresh, clean clothes, she wore the same clothes she wore on the long walk to the mill. Her hair was all wet and wrapped in a towel.

Zuva must have noticed this, but she didn't have the strength to scold Nyeredzi.

"Mama, maybe we can pray for Papa and Sis?"

"How about you do it there, where you are standing?"

"What about your Bible, Mama?"

"If you want to talk directly to God, you can still do that without a Bible. What matters is what you are saying from within," Zuva said, touching Nyeredzi's shoulder.

"But I always do that."

"Very well then," her mother said, folding her arms in front.

The evening breeze was battling with the warmth of the fire crackling behind them. Nyeredzi hoped her mother would start staying the words she usually said when praying for others, but Zuva stood still, staring at the bush.

After a while her mother turned around and walked back to the house. Nyeredzi followed her, watching her mother go to her bedroom; she stayed just outside the door, peeping in. The paraffin lamp was lit. Zuva knelt next to her bed, looking underneath the bed frame. She pulled out a locked safe, fiddled with the key in her hand but didn't use it. Instead, she pushed the safe back underneath the bed and stood up.

"Mama, what's in the box?"

"Nothing for you to worry about," Zuva said, and they walked outside again.

Nyeredzi stared into the dark bush, looking for any sign of figures walking toward them, but no one was coming back. Anxiety was crawling in her skin, raising the little hairs on it. She bit her lower lip until she could feel the pain. Was this pain the love she had for Ruth? Even her father?

They waited for two long hours, until two men with sack bags on their shoulders approached their house. Behind them was Ruth and the woman who'd talked to them earlier, holding the hands of her children. Mwedzi and Mr. Manjo were at the back, guarding the vulnerable.

"Sis! Sis!" Nyeredzi yelled and ran to hug Ruth.

"Oh, my feet are really sore," Ruth said.

"I can massage them in warm water if you want?"

The thought was kind and innocent, but later, when Nyeredzi sat on the floor next to a tub with warm water in the bedroom lit with two paraffin lamps, her gaze was drawn again to her sister's scar. All she ever wanted to do was touch it and know if it was hard or soft, but now she hesitated to do so.

Ruth moved some pillows behind her body to sit comfortably on her bed. Nyeredzi's back was against the piled–up furniture. She moved the tub close to the edge of the bed. Ruth sunk her feet into the tub and the scar bubbled as if it was breathing. Nyeredzi stared at it, as though she saw it through the magnifying glass, its size doubled underwater.

"What's wrong?" Ruth asked. "Do you still want to massage me?"

"Your feet need to be warm first," Nyeredzi told her. "That's what Mama said last time I was massaging her."

She doubted Ruth would believe her.

"Mmm, who knew?" Ruth said with her eyes shut.

Nyeredzi looked at the scar again.

Sooner or later, she had to do something with her hands—she'd promised Ruth after all. Nyeredzi sank her hands in the water and pretended to wash them, but when Ruth opened her eyes, she began to run her hands on her sister's feet, pressing onto the swollen muscles. She massaged everywhere but the scar area.

Somehow, distracted by the sound of water she was pouring with cupped hands onto Ruth's swollen feet, one finger dipped into the hollowed scar. Something splintered inside Nyeredzi. She could not explain it, but it was as if she felt the trauma Ruth endured when she was young. Now she understood why her sister always covered her feet. She continued massaging her sister, still circling the scar. And just like that, in one touch, Ruth's trauma passed to her.

THE CALL OF ANCESTORS

Spring 1992
NYEREDZI

At the age of nine, Nyeredzi was trying to work out who she was as a human being. After a couple years of beautiful harvests, drought arrived to devour people and animals. It was as if the sky's brightest star was angry at them. As though they had done something wrong and were being punished for it.

One day in November, she set off with her mother for the Duva dam. The bush that was once green was now just dirt littered with beige plants. Twigs and dead leaves crunched under Nyeredzi and Zuva's sandals with every step they took. After walking about four kilometers, they stopped to rest under the fig tree. The gully that criss-crossed the land was a reminder of what was once there— the riverbed was dry.

Nyeredzi ran around picking up round pebbles scattered on the riverbed and throwing them in the air. When she grew tired, she returned to stand in the shade of the fig tree with her mother. A pigeon fell from a branch like a rock onto the dry ground, a reminder that the drought took many lives. Its chest heaved, pulsating with its final breaths. It was as if the weak were being weeded out.

Nyeredzi bent down to touch it, but Zuva held her hand.

Within seconds, another bird dropped from the tree, and that's when Zuva said they should leave. If the birds that flew close to the heavens were falling upon them like that, then it was a bad omen.

They walked under the hot sun, following the path that people used by the banks of the river as though they were looking for something on the riverbed. The reeds had withered, and some had dried on the parched soil. Zuva and Nyeredzi were not sweating anymore but their bodies were sticky. When Nyeredzi touched her skin, it burnt her.

"Mama, aren't we roasting under the sun that promised to give us light?" Nyeredzi asked. "Why do we keep on digging the soil that soon buries us?"

Zuva turned to her daughter and looked in her eyes. "Because we are searching for our ancestors and when they hear the sound of a hoe digging, they know we are searching for them. In return, they bless us with what you and I eat."

"I thought that was God who does that," Nyeredzi said.

"Isn't God your ancestor? Weren't you created from his image?"

Zuva kept on walking. They passed the carcasses of small dead animals along the edges of the pathway, insects crawling over them. The stench reminded Nyeredzi of a rotten rat she had smelled once.

Under the burning sky, she imagined they were paddling on a vast red ocean with their feet. When she licked her lips, they were as salty as the sea and parched. It was not the first time she had felt like this. There were times when Nyeredzi played outside with her friends, Hope and Marvellous, and they would stop to rest their hands on their knees trying to catch their breath; dry, hot air had sucked away their strength.

At the Duva dam, there was nothing but a small muddy puddle at the center. All the fish were dead. Frogs blew bubbles and croaked underneath the shallow brown water. The sides of the dam looked iron–hard, cracked, like the landscape of a planet. An army of ants crawled through the gaps, marching toward the dead fish and back to the hole again to feed their queen.

Further away, the pine trees which surrounded the hill looked as though they were offering themselves before the sun. The buildings of Agric company were fenced with a gray Durawall. Its black corrugated roof rippled in the heat mirage. A few humming vehicles crossed over the bridge of Dargaville road, disappearing from the Durawall fence. To her right, the Olivine company's cyrindrical buildings stood tall, and then there was just the blue sky and the huge expanse of the bush with its rocks and dead trees.

Nyeredzi could see how concerned her mother was. It was as though their ancestors had forgotten about them and swallowed all of the saliva left above the Earth. There was no need to dig the land that year. No need to search for those who came before them, as Zuva had described. They would not be heard anyway.

Nyeredzi and Zuva had come to see if there was any water in the dam. Food grew scarce and expensive. Zuva sent Edward and Dingani, who rented their cottage to different places just looking for mealie meal. What they found was not white maize, but yellow mealie meal imported from other countries. Three meals became two meals. People learned to cope with that. Nyeredzi did too; Zuva had taught her to fast before. People were encouraged to stay indoors as the heat itself killed anything that breathed. They were encouraged to save water as much as they could but the Taha family were still forced to kill most of their chickens in a short time because they had started dying on their own.

Each day came slow and ended slow. In the evenings, the family had a little energy to walk around. Mr. and Mrs. Manjo came to their house one night to visit.

"Mr. and Mrs. Manjo, please come in," said Mwedzi. He got up to shake Mrs. Manjo's hand, and then gave Mr. Manjo a brief hug with a wide smile on his face.

Ruth, Abigail, and Hannah got up from the three–seater sofa and moved to the bench. Mr. and Mrs. Manjo sat down, looking surprised. Perhaps they were not expecting all of the girls to move seats. Nyeredzi hopped on to the sofa and sat next to Mr. Manjo, looking at his face that was now starting to wrinkle.

"We have come because death is knocking on our doors," he said.

"We do see that," Zuva said.

"What do you suggest?" Mwedzi asked.

"The Ndima Ndima dance," Mrs. Manjo responded. "We need the ancestors to hear us."

"All that bloodshed on the bush," Zuva said, shaking her head.

"We better do it now, I think," Mr. Manjo said, looking at Zuva and Mwedzi for their approval.

Nyeredzi was curious about what Zuva was going to do. In their community, if people had devoted their lives to being Christian, they should not be seen going back to their old traditional ways. Some people weren't bothered by being Christian and a traditional believer at the same time, but Zuva was a church leader.

"You know we can't get involved," Zuva told him.

"We thought we should come to you first," Mrs. Manjo said.

"We do appreciate that," Zuva said.

After Mr. and Mrs. Manjo left, Nyeredzi thought about what her mother had always told her. God was their ancestor; Nyeredzi was created from the image of God. But if everyone else was gathering for this dance, she wanted to be there, even if it was a clash between the religions. She wanted to know what lay beneath what other people believed, whether she had been praying to the right God.

It would be the first time in her life witnessing a dance that called upon their ancestors, begging them to hear them. She had seen some dances at school but not as serious and important as the one their neighbors were planning.

In the following days, Mr. and Mrs. Manjo went from house to house, telling people about the Ndima Ndima dance. From what Nyeredzi heard her parents say, a lot of them were on board, prepared to do anything that would save them from the drought—from death.

Mr. and Mrs. Manjo often returned to ask Zuva questions. Where was it suitable to perform the dance? How many people would be appropriate to participate? Was food needed too? Were the children allowed to come along? They seemed to seek Zuva's approval, and Nyeredzi wasn't sure why? Perhaps, she thought, it was because her mother was a church leader.

People had chosen to perform the dance on a weekend when everyone was not occupied with work or other activities. It was to start at noon. Next to the curve of the riverbed, the ground was cleared, and maponde were spread for people to sit under the Msasa tree. Its red leaves shimmered bright from afar. Some people said it was ancestors' blood rising from underneath, and that's why it was still alive. Others said that was where ancestors went when the land was dry. The tree was the communicator between the dead and living people, and it spat drops of water when people took shelter underneath it.

From their house, Nyeredzi saw people walking to the bush. Women had wrapped their heads in scarves, and around their waist they wore a large piece of fabric, zambia. Some were patterned; others bore the words, Madzitateguru edu tisunungurei. Set us free, our ancestors. Nyeredzi wondered if people always had those things in their wardrobes. Not knowing made her feel like she was an outsider among her own neighbors.

"Mama, everyone is going—should we go too?" Nyeredzi asked, expecting her mother to say no.

"We are all going," Zuva answered from her bedroom.

Nyeredzi was surprised because Zuva had told Mr. and Mrs. Manjo she couldn't get involved. Her sisters refused to join them, so Nyeredzi was the only one going with her parents. In her arms, Zuva held a bonde. Her father was holding a round clay pot filled with water. They walked toward the bush alongside other people, the streets quiet. No one was listening to the radio or watching TV that day. Nyeredzi noticed that, like her parents, people were carrying things related to their own cultures.

When they arrived at the prepared area, Mwedzi placed the clay pot he held in his hands under the Msasa tree. Zuva spread the bonde on the ground nearby, in front of the tree, and they all sat on it. Nyeredzi admired the drawings on the clay pots: small figures of women carrying pails on their heads from the river, men hunting in the forest. She wanted to get up to touch the crushed leaves that floated in the pots circling the tree. She wanted to step onto the dancing area covered with mealie meal and sand—feel the coldness of the animal horns set aside in a rutsero. She wanted to do everything and play the mbira, drums, and shakers placed next to the riverbed.

Many people were still arriving and Nyeredzi kept looking back until she saw her sisters approaching the dance place too.

"Mama, look—they are coming," Nyeredzi said, pulling Zuva's hand. Perhaps she would enjoy watching the dance with her sisters. Maybe they would start seeing things the way she did.

"Very well then," Zuva said. She didn't seem surprised.

"Why do we have to start the dance after midday?"

"Because we do not want to wake the ancestors in the morning, and if we do it in the evening, we don't want to disturb their sleep."

"Haven't they been sleeping all along?"

Zuva looked at her. "You may think they are sleeping because when you put someone in the box, they will be in a sleeping position, but the soul rises. It's not sleeping anymore."

"Like King Jesus did—he resurrected?"

"Exactly!"

Zuva folded her arms in front and looked out over the crowd. Mwedzi was talking to another man sitting next to him. Nyeredzi's sisters arrived and sat behind them on the bonde. They looked on with curiosity of the dance but pretended as though they weren't. Hundreds of people were waiting and Nyeredzi could see how anxious they were. Some ended up sitting on the dusty ground or on rocks because there weren't enough maponde. Others stood at the back.

One man wearing black shorts walked to the center of

the dance area. The crowd fell quiet. He had tribal drawings painted in white and red on his naked chest, arms,
and around his eyes. Zvuma dangled on his neck. He knelt
on the soil and raised his hands in the air.

"To our ancestors, your great–grandchildren are here
today. We are here. You sacrifice a lot for us, and still, we
break the rules. On behalf of my brothers who have killed
on this land, forgive us?"

He stood up and walked over to the men holding shakers. Within seconds, the mbira was on his lap, and his fingers moved swiftly. The rhythm drew everyone who was
sitting on the ground and rocks. A group of men appeared
from a dense bush, walking toward the drums, and picking them up. They began to tap on the drums, the sound
growing. Some of them grabbed the shakers and hummed
with deep low voices.

It raised hairs on Nyeredzi's skin. From that moment,
she knew she was not an outsider. The ancestors had arrived before they'd been summoned, before Nyeredzi had
devoted herself to them. They followed the line of the
blood, and she knew that she had it inside her veins.

Two lines of men appeared from behind the shrubs,
dancing slowly toward the dance area. Their upper bodies were bare, and they wore black shorts underneath the
animal skin patches of cheetah, leopard, zebra, impala
and more. Around their necks dangled zvuma made from
wooden beads; small arrows in the center of them matched
the bangles on their wrists.

Their long headpieces were made of the African fish
eagle feathers. Some of them had tattoos—their his-
tory dotted in darkened lines, and the images of animals
seemed as though that's where their strength came from.
Nyeredzi didn't know that some of her neighbors had

these emblems on them.

She wondered why they had come to Zuva asking for her approval to go ahead with the traditional dance. It was clear everyone in the neighborhood respected Zuva and Mwedzi, for who they were: Christians, down–to–earth people. Both of them had done a lot in the community and the Taha family prayed everyday for everyone to be saved. And for the Taha family to be present on this occasion must be important for their neighbors, although Nyeredzi still wasn't sure why.

The men held spears in their hands like the warriors Nyeredzi had heard about in folk tales. These were the warriors who were fighting evil spirits. The people who'd been killed on this land were moaning, haunting those who had taken their lives. Zuva had said it before to the girls: ghosts were haunting the murderers.

Before the men jumped up in the air in front of the drummers, they stomped on the ground and adjusted their headpieces so that they wouldn't fall. For the people sitting on the maponde, the land felt as though it was vibrating. It didn't take much time before the women who were wearing vivid colors of zvuma lifted clay pots onto their heads and joined the men. They swayed their hips in circles, the frills of their black skirts made from animal skin swooping up and down and sideways.

Their chests were covered in the manes of lions tied at the back. Bangles dangled on their wrists and zvuma on their necks. They all walked in a line and then knelt in front of the audience, placing the clay pots on the ground.

The women clapped their hands and began to ululate loudly, and other women in the crowd howled along with them. Nyeredzi wanted to do it too, but she was scared this was crossing the line. The women got up again, swaying their hips from side to side, fast, and jumped, throwing their hands in the air. They danced alongside the men, who sometimes moved to the front and threw their spears into the air. They looked serious, their bodies glistening with sweat. Dust swirled in the air. The Earth continued to vibrate, and their voices rang out, calling the ancestors.

Madzitateguru edu
matikanganwa here?
Dzokai muuye
kuzotisunungura vana
venyu vafa nenzara,
tinzwei woye?

Our ancestors, have
you forgotten about us?
Come back and set us free.
Your children are dying
from famine,
hear us?

Haa hiya hoye,
woye, woyeee,
madzitateguru edu
vana vofa.
Vakatadza vakadarika
vakawanda nedziro
ramakavaka.

Haa hiya hoye,
woye, woyeee,
our ancestors.
Children are dying.
Those who sinned
are hiding behind
the wall you've built.

Regererai,
vana vofa vasati
vakuzivai.

Forgive,
children are dying before
they know you.

Haa hiya hoye,
woye, woyeee,
madzitateguru edu
tinzwei…

Haa hiya hoye, woye,
woyeee,
our ancestors,
hear us…

Some people sang along with the dancers. Shouldn't Nyeredzi join in too, to beg the ancestors to hear them?

NDIMA NDIMA

She did, clapping her hands, while her sisters looked at her as though she was doing something wrong. Zuva and Mwedzi did not say anything. Nyeredzi ululated with the rest of the women. The women who were dancing looked deep into her eyes. At that moment, Nyeredzi knew the ancestors had heard them.

She had a vision of being transported to a place she'd never seen before. In this place old people sat on big rocks next to caves. Their bodies were covered in yellow fabric, like a rising sun. They held long brown walking sticks in their hands, earth in their palms, and red beads around their wrists and ankles, the blood of the ancestors. Gray–silver zvuma hung loose on their necks, like Mother Moon and the stars that shined upon them in the dark times. They stomped on the ground with their sticks, summoning their great fathers and mothers. The women ululated and sang while men hummed in deep voices, crouching on the ground.

One man with gray motsi that hung to his shoulders approached Nyeredzi and stretched his arm toward her. He opened his clenched fist and Nyeredzi saw a seed germinating in red soil. The old man gestured for Nyeredzi to take it. She hesitated then took the plant and dirt from his palm. Next, an old woman came with a clay pot filled with water. She dropped a seed into it and pushed the pot up to Nyeredzi's lips for her to drink. When Nyeredzi swallowed the seed, she felt full. Suddenly she found herself covered in a green fabric. The woman stared at Nyeredzi with a smile on her face.

"You, my daughter, you wear green. You are the wealth of this nation. What you bear in the future shall bring wealth in your palms. Your great grandfathers and mothers are there." She pointed to the men and women in yellow. "Gold, emerald, diamonds, whatever minerals you seek from them, they will give you."

She raised her hands in the air and water fell upon Nyeredzi, washing her whole body, as though she was being baptized or born again. Nyeredzi wiped water from her eyes and listened to the old lady's voice.

"I bathe you with holy water from our ancestors. Water shall pour on you whenever you call upon us, and if you ask, we will give you."

The old woman touched Nyeredzi's shoulders with both hands. Her grip was firm but gentle at the same time, as though she didn't want to let go of her. Fear rushed in Nyeredzi's veins. The old woman's voice was thick, and she was not the kind of person Nyeredzi had ever met before.

Her right hand moved from Nyeredzi's shoulder to her left rib and said, "This hand of mine on your chest is a red star of the aspiration I have seen in you. You have this endless burning flame in you no one can put out. You are like your mother who brings peace. She is the mother of this nation."

The old woman pressed her lips together, stepping away and pointing. Nyeredzi took two steps backwards, looking where the woman was pointing—the vast land sprinkled with green vegetation, the sun above beaming on the leaves and the red earth, birds gliding. A breeze brushed Nyeredzi's face, and it came from the old woman's mouth, as though she was waking her from sleep.

"My daughter, an African Fish eagle will fly you to places you've never been, but when you get there, don't ever forget where you belong like your mother has not forgotten the trail of her bloodline. You were blessed before you were birthed."

The old people were all looking at Nyeredzi, but because their eyes held a fierce intensity, she looked down as a sign of respect. When she raised her head again, they were gone. The caves were gone. Only the land was left. Nyeredzi had met the ancestors, and they had spoken to her. They had blessed and foretold her future.

At that moment, the dancing women had moved close to her and her family. Dust formed a thick blanket in the atmosphere. Zuva turned to look at Nyeredzi, and whatever she saw made her touch Mwedzi's hand and squeeze it. He turned to look at Nyeredzi, too. Both of them stared at her but didn't say a word. Her sisters were busy whispering, not paying attention to the dance.

"Fire is burning inside you like the Msasa leaves above us," one of the dancers said to her. Nyeredzi had never met this woman before and didn't recognize her from their neighborhood. "They are burning, and they will keep burning."

Most people were now singing along with the dancers. The women picked up the bowls of seeds and threw them in the air. They fell on people nearby, and one landed on Nyeredzi's head. She felt it at the core of her head and reached up, pinching it with her fingers. The women were still throwing seeds up into the air. Nyeredzi placed the seed on her tongue to swallow it.

When the Msasa tree began to spit on them, that's when the dancers stopped. Sweat dribbled from them, and their bare feet were coated in dust. The men picked up the horns which they blew, sending people home. No one talked after that, even on their way home. It was as though everyone had been electrified by the ancestors' spirit.

Days after the Ndima Ndima dance, the sky still burnt the

earth. Animals were still dying. More impatient people began to say terrible things, complaining that they had wasted time going to participate in the dance. Nyeredzi kept the secret to herself that she had met the ancestors. Who could she have told? Why would the ancestors come to her? She was a child after all. How could she talk to her mother about it when Zuva was a church leader and against the old ways?

One afternoon Mr. and Mrs. Manjo came back to the Tahas' house.

"Please, come in Mr. and Mrs. Manjo," Zuva said, gesturing for them to sit on the sofa. "Would you like a glass of orange juice?"

"Yes, please. Thank you, Gogo," Mrs. Manjo answered.

Zuva looked at Hannah, who got up and brought orange juice and glasses from the kitchen unit. Solid food was now rare to find, and it was only saved for the main meal like dinner. Mr. Manjo picked up the full glass and held it for a while, his expression deep in contemplation. He took a sip and looked at Zuva.

"Gogo, I want to thank you and your family for coming to the Ndima Ndima dance," he said. "It was an honor to have you all there."

Nyeredzi, sitting on the bonde, smiled when she heard this.

"We were supposed to be there," her mother told him. "We were not guests, Mr. Manjo."

"I am aware of that, but one of the spirit mediums where we went last time said there is something important about your family." He paused, glancing at his wife, who nodded at him. "It doesn't mean we've been looking into people's lives. It's just that the spirit medium said if you had not attended, the water would not fall on the ground and the ancestors would not hear us."

Zuva looked shocked. "Is that so?"

Mr. Manjo turned his gaze to Nyeredzi; instinctively, she hid behind the woven net of the armchair. She was scared that he might have seen the fire inside her eyes, just as the woman from the dance saw. She was also afraid that her sisters were going to see it and then they wouldn't want to sleep in the same room as her anymore.

"How soon do you think it will rain?" Mrs. Manjo asked Zuva.

"Be patient," Zuva said in a soft voice. Mr. and Mrs. Manjo gulped down all the orange juice and left.

Days came and passed, and soon the end of the year was approaching. The clouds formed in the sky, promising rain, but vanished as quickly as they had appeared. The sun burnt the clouds; it even burnt seeds under the ground. Nyeredzi kept her distance from Hope and Marvellous, her friends. She didn't want them to see the fire that was now in her. This meant she felt lonely. Each time she stepped on the bare ground, it was as though something was pulling her from underneath, talking to her. The Earth was trembling.

Quite often, she wandered off alone and hid behind the cottage under the water berry tree. She danced, thinking no one was there, until the day she realized that Zuva was standing right in front of her. Nyeredzi thought her mother was going to shout at her for performing the traditional dance.

Instead, Zuva looked deep into her eyes. "You have the fire. I saw the day we went to the Ndima Ndima dance under the Msasa tree," she told Nyeredzi. "Do not hide whatever you are feeling, my daughter. It's there to protect you."

Zuva walked away without another word, and Nyeredzi

resumed her dance. It was as if her mother had unlocked a gate, permitting Nyeredzi to follow her ancestors. The Earth vibrated as she stomped on the ground. At the end of her dance, Nyeredzi asked the ancestors to cleanse her. That way, she would know there were no clashes between the two worlds of Christianity and of their ancestors. Where she came from, and where she was headed: these worlds to her were blended into one.

The answer Nyeredzi was waiting for took longer. When the skies turned dark and dense one day when she was walking alone in the bush from school, she felt scared. She lifted her legs in the air and began to dance again. Her tongue mimicked the words that were sung at the Ndima Ndima dance, asking for forgiveness. She feared she might have had no right to ask the ancestors because her faith belonged somewhere.

Nyeredzi threw her satchel on the ground, unbuttoned the belt of her green uniform, and danced all the steps she saw being performed under the Msasa tree. Only later did she realize that this was what her ancestors had told her to do: ask, and we will give.

The clouds descended really low until the thunderheads swelled and blocked out the sun. The rain was finally here, and it was an enormous storm. At one point, Nyeredzi was frightened, thinking the ancestors had come to take her. The rain dampened the soil, penetrating the gaps of the cracked clay. It kept on coming down, hitting her body, the ground, the dead grass, and the thirsty trees that had wilted. Her green dress was now stuck to her body, as if she was born in it.

The fear that rushed in her veins somehow encouraged her to continue. This water that fell from the heavens revived her and gave her energy, she didn't know where it was coming from. She danced on alone in the bush, uncertain whether her great fathers and mothers had arrived to sing and dance along with her—to bless the land. Even with all the proof they had heard her, she didn't stop. Nyeredzi kept on calling upon them, not realizing in that moment that the ancestors had come to cleanse her, just as she had asked.

THE RETURN

Summer 1993
ZUVA

It was the last week of the school term. The morning was quiet, and Zuva embraced the warmth of the sun penetrating through the lace curtain. Mwedzi had already left for work, and all her daughters had gone to school. Alone, she could delve deeper into all that happened.

A year had passed since they had a drought. But had Zuva's attendance at the Ndima Ndima dance brought her spirit to a world she thought she'd escaped? When Mr. and Mrs. Manjo came to her house and said water would only fall if her family was present at the dance, had it reminded Zuva of who she was meant to be? Had she not felt her parents' presence in her bones when she sat down on the bonde with Mwedzi and Nyeredzi, and their spirits swirling in Nyeredzi's eyes even days after the dance happened?

All she saw in her own reflection in the mirror was a person her parents had anointed, their voices vibrating against the walls of the hut, because the rulers of Manicaland had spoken.

Zuva dropped her lilac morning gown onto the floor where the sunlight flared through the window. She looked at herself in the mirror. She was still in her undergarments, and her breasts lay full on her chest, emphasizing her tiny waist. The scar across her stomach was bigger than most of her other scars. They all told a story. Zuva caressed the stitches sewn into her skin. She counted them, one to eleven.

Her finger ran inside the dent on her shoulder, the bumpy skin made her shiver. She didn't usually touch it—the memories were too raw. Her fingers moved over the uneven surface. It made her think of a letter she had received from her brother, Garikai: the memory of bright blue words on white paper somehow made her probe the scar deeper, while the tears gathered. Garikai's letter. Why did he want her to revisit her past when she didn't want to remember it at all? After all these years, Garikai had summoned her home. Had her past not caused enough pain so much so that in the end she chose to leave?

> My dear sister, Zuva,
> It has been long. So long that I barely remember you anymore. Come. Mother and Father are not resting anymore. Come home. The spirit mediums said your absence has turned their bodies in their graves. You know you were the center of their hearts, why are you putting us into this misery? I beg you, make peace with us.
> Your only brother,
> Garikai

Zuva picked up the letter from the bed. *Your absence has turned their bodies in their graves.* That hurt. How could it be her fault? Had she not been set free by her mother, Nyikadzino? Both Togara and Nyikadzino were lying inside the curved rocks of the mountain, yet their souls were not at rest? How could he say such things?

She folded the letter and slid it under her pillow. She would only return for one reason: her beloved Togara and Nyikadzino.

The necklace she was wearing was the curved tooth of a lion, pulled from the last animal her father had killed, way back when he went hunting with his men. Zuva had brought him maheu to drink. She knelt to look at the tooth placed on the stool. It was fresh, stained with blood. Tiny pieces of gum flesh were still intact.

"My daughter," Togara said, "that tooth didn't come out of the lion's gum so easily."

She smiled. "I wish I had gone with you."

Afterwards Zuva sat cross–legged on a large mat of zebra skin in her father's big hut, where the light flared through the open door. Her father sat on a wooden arm-chair covered in lion's mane next to the face masks of old kings and queens hung on the wall. The walls were lined with shelves of clay pots, golden metal cups and round plates, carved utensils, and sculptures of animals. Anyone who entered the hut would think it was a kitchen, but the clay pots held mineral stones—gold, emeralds, diamonds of every color and other valuable things.

The breeze brushed Zuva's face and reawakened the fur of Togara's robes that hung next to his carved walking sticks decorated in gold. He took off his leather sandals that roared like a crocodile.

"Zuva, my daughter, fetch me some water before you leave?"

"Yes, Father."

Two pails filled with water were stored underneath the shelves. Zuva picked up a golden cup and pushed the timber block covering the pails aside to fetch water. She knelt before Togara, handing him the cup. He took the cup and placed the lion's tooth in her palm.

"My daughter, this is yours. Your mother and I chose to give you this, but take it to her, she will engrave it for you."

"Really? I thought you'd give it to Garikai."

"If Garikai wants a tooth of a lion, he should go hunting himself."

Zuva left with a wide smile on her face.

Two days later, she was summoned back by both Togara and Nyikadzino. Before them, she knelt with her head bowed. This was a special gift from her parents. Nyikadzino passed the tooth to Togara, then they both stretched their hands toward Zuva. She took the tooth. A hole was drilled into the end and a twine cord inserted. Wooden beads lay on either side of the tooth. Each bead was engraved with little stars underneath the letters that read Rugare.

There were other words, ones she wasn't expecting. The front of the tooth read ZM—Zuva Mutongi. The back read Mambokadzi. Zuva was shocked. She kept quiet for some time, struggling to swallow.

Finally, she said, "Father, Mother, you can't choose me, Garikai is here."

"Garikai," Togara said, and stopped, shaking his head.

Zuva placed the necklace back in her parents' hands. "But he is older than me."

"We do know that." Nyikadzino leaned forward and hung the necklace around Zuva's neck.

Now that it was on, Zuva was not supposed to take it off. She was not supposed to question her parents. She was to do what was now expected of her. Rule the land, and its people. She was an unmarried young woman.

How was Garikai going to take it? How were the people of Goho going to react? Their chief had chosen his daughter instead of his son. What about the chiefs under her father's rule who had expected a shot at the title? How was she going to do it all in a region dominated by men?

Her mother's dress remained stubbornly hidden in her wardrobe. Nyikadzino used to wear it on calm days when the sky shimmered during the day and sparkled at night. It was one of the few things Zuva was given when her mother died.

Usually Zuva only wore the dress on Nyikadzino's death anniversary, but today she needed comfort. She was desperate for a feeling of home.

She knew it was in there, somewhere, folded on the shelves. The fabric was printed with sunflowers. There it was, shining in a dark corner of the wardrobe. Zuva pulled it over her head. She tingled. Somehow, it still smelled of her mother's scent, earthy. The way it sat on her shoulders, hips, and hugged her stomach, made Zuva feel bold. Her mother's genes hid somewhere inside her body.

When her husband and daughters arrived home that day, they stared. After dinner, when the whole family was still sitting around the wooden table, Mwedzi asked her about Garikai's letter.

"We might have to go back where I come from," Zuva said.

The girls looked at her. "I thought we were never going to know where you come from, Mama," Abigail said.

"We will only go if your mother wants to." Mwedzi turned to his daughters and lowered his voice. "Maybe it's high time you see where your grandparents lie."

"Yes, it is important for you and me," Zuva murmured,

unsure of what she was saying, or of what she really wanted.

"Okay, when are we going then?" Nyeredzi demanded.

Zuva didn't respond. All of this upset her.

"If we need to go there, then we should all go," Ruth said, and all the girls agreed. "We are always here for you, Mama."

"What do you think about this December holiday?" Zuva asked, her voice faint, and it was done.

It had been more than two decades since Zuva last stepped on the beige sand of Goho Village. The village was approximately 105 km from Mutare City. Back in 1970, about 8,000 people lived there.

Round huts with thatched roofs were scattered all over the land on either side of the valley. She asked Mwedzi to drop her off by the well, where she used to fetch water when she was young. The girls went along with Mwedzi in their Peugeot pickup truck. Zuva took her canvas shoes off and left them by a green patch of grass, ready to sink her feet in the sand and breathe in her hometown. Hundreds of kilometers away from the well, the mountains of different heights, laced with bright and dark green vegetation, busy with baboons and monkeys, were the home of the Manicaland people.

The bells worn around the necks of cows and goats clinked from afar. Tall gangly boys herded the animals from steep ground. The boys shouted and whistled, running amidst the trees and grassy clearings, using sjamboks on the butts of the lazy animals. The cows mooed, and the goats bleated.

Zuva knelt by the well and looked at her reflection before she picked up a mukombe to fetch water. She held it up and drank. The water itself was cooling, but it reawakened the emotions of returning home. This was where she would fetch water with her mother and sister in the late afternoons.

Today, she was standing on the land where she'd sworn never to return. So great was her resolve, she had asked Mwedzi to lay her remains at their last stop. Her last stop: wherever she passed on, be it a strange land, an unknown place, she didn't mind. Mwedzi understood her perfectly. In some ways, she didn't understand herself—when she'd asked him, proud and determined, not to take her dead body home, a shadow had already darkened her soul.

This water she drank by the well was different from the water echoing in her ears, streaming down the valley. Down there was the last place her mother took her to bathe away the blood that had dried on her body. Her wounds had stayed open for days without anyone attending to them. Nyikadzino washed the blood off with water from the Yeredzo River, tears running down on her face. She'd tried to talk, but Zuva was silent. Her mother had already lost her. Zuva had already decided to leave.

Now it was time to pick up her shoes and walk along the dusty sand road. A group of women, young and old, arrived at the well with their pails. One of the most aged women seemed to recognize Zuva, walking up to her and touching her shoulder. When Zuva looked into her eyes, the woman threw herself on the ground.

"Ashe Zuva!" The woman peered up at her. "I remember you; you are back. What a grace."

"Please get up," Zuva said, picking up the woman from the ground.

"Welcome, Ashe, what a grace that you are back." The

old woman gave a curtsy. "So much has changed since you left."

Although Zuva recognized Mrs. Kaundi, she couldn't see what she meant. The soil was still the same to her. The mountains stood the same way she had left. Yeredzo River was still roaring down the valley.

"I hope all is well here," Zuva said, smiling. Though it was long ago, how could she not smile at the woman who once served them?

"It will be better now that you are back."

When Zuva turned to leave, the other women had finished fetching water and were standing around, waiting. They started arguing with Mrs. Kaundi, stamping their feet. Zuva's gaze met the older woman's eyes. She understood. The young ones before her seemed to disrespect the elderly woman.

Zuva walked slowly down the dusty road, breathing in the fresh air. Each step she took felt as though she was calling on her parents up in the mountain, telling them she was back, and that she was only back for them.

Closer to home, she saw that Mrs. Kaundi was telling the truth after all. When Zuva left, there was one large house painted white, surrounded by many huts. A shed down the road was where her father had meetings with his men. Fruit trees grew in the orchard. The flat land circling the dwellings was where they grew everything edible—maize, groundnuts, sugarcane, sweet potatoes, pumpkins, beans, etc. Even on that sandy land, the plants still grew.

Now everything was different. Their large house was gone, and so were the huts, except for Togara's chamber, still plastered but unpainted, as though it was kept as an unloved tribute. A black tarred road led to two large modern houses painted light green. Windows and balconies wrapped around the buildings. Green lush lawn sandwiched the driveway. Roses bloomed on bushes planted around the lawn.

Zuva wondered if her parents' things were still there. She slid her feet back into her canvas shoes. She couldn't bear stepping on that sticky black road going up the steep land in her bare feet. It looked as though Garikai and Maudie had raised the ground, so they had a better view than the other houses. The land was now fenced with electric wire to keep out the monkeys, baboons, and other animals, though Togara had allowed them to feed on the maize and fruit. The view of the entire valley was still spectacular, but Zuva felt disheartened.

She trudged up the steep driveway. Mwedzi had parked next to the bull–mango tree in front of a small house painted in white. He and the girls were waiting for her, sitting outside on outdoor furniture in the shade of a peach tree. They were drinking lemon juice and taking custard biscuits from a wide platter.

Zuva was about to ask them where they got these when a woman ran outside from one of the big houses toward her. She was tall, slender, and dark–skinned. Her short black permed hair glimmered under the sunlight. She hugged Zuva, who assumed this strange woman was Garikai's wife. The strong scent of chemicals on her hair lingered.

"My sister, welcome," she said and pointed to an armchair next to Mwedzi. "Come and sit—it's Garikai's spot, but you can sit while we wait for them to come back."

Mwedzi raised his eyebrows. Zuva sat down, irritated. Didn't this woman know what Garikai owned was hers, rightfully blessed in her palms by Togara and Nyikadzino?

"Mama, you didn't tell us you were from a rich family," Nyeredzi said.

"Oh, she didn't tell you?" the woman said. "Well, now you know."

Zuva turned to look at her, unsmiling. "Tell me about yourself," she asked, and the woman fidgeted and stuttered. Her name was Melinda. She chattered on.

"Whose house is that?" Zuva interrupted.

"Maudie and her family. It's for when they come for holidays."

Maudie was Zuva's little sister. The last time she saw her was in 1970.

"And this?" Zuva pointed to the other green house.

"This one is ours. Me and Garikai and our children."

"And this one?" She pointed to the smaller white house near Mwedzi's car, next to the bull–mango tree.

"Oh, that's a guest house," Melinda said. "I suppose that's where you will be sleeping."

Zuva shook her head. "When you look at me, do you see a guest?"

"Umm, not really. I'm sorry, sister."

Once Zuva had been the person who welcomed newcomers to the village. Now she realized that nothing belonged to her. Her siblings had cast her off because she'd left, and now all she was offered was the guest house.

Zuva walked toward her father's old chamber. The door was locked with a rusty padlock, and it seemed no one had opened it for a long time.

Melinda jumped up to look for the keys. "I hope I'll find them because no one goes in there," she said.

Zuva didn't bother responding. She lifted her leg and kicked the door. The padlock broke into two pieces, falling inside the dusty chamber. The creaky door swung back and forth until Zuva stopped it with her leg. Cobwebs woven years ago were hanging loose from the thatched roof, which had a huge hole on one side. The wall, rug, and floor had watermarks from the rain. It saddened Zuva that no one had bothered to fix the roof. If her parents were not at rest, this was the proof. They were even crying from above, but no one was watching.

It was dark inside the hut, and the dust made her cough. Dead bats lay on the floor. Skeletons of rats and dry feces lay on the zebra mat, chairs, and the shelves of clay pots. Everything was covered in thick layers of the dust, even the two pails of water and utensils and sculptures lined on the shelves. The beautiful robes, walking sticks, and other things were no longer in the hut, and she knew Garikai had taken them.

Melinda arrived back to say she couldn't find the keys. She stood outside as though she was afraid to step in.

"Bring me a broom," Zuva commanded.

Melinda hurried off again. When she returned, she placed the broom and dustpan by the door. "I'd love to help you, but I can't. I am afraid of dead animals."

"Don't worry," Zuva said, snatching the broom. "I wouldn't want anyone getting nightmares after cleaning my father's chamber."

Melinda walked away, but soon Mwedzi and the girls joined Zuva, helping to clean the hut of its dead rats, bats, and insects. She was proud of her husband and daughters. How could they be scared of dust? She had trained them well in the bush. How could they be scared of dead animals? They had seen so many.

Later on, after they spent almost an hour cleaning the hut, they went back to sit under the tree on the outdoor furniture. Melinda asked them inside her house, but outside was better. The fresh breeze cooled their hot bodies. Soon, Melinda brought food out for them. Cold homemade lemon juice in a big jar, and warm, crumbling, golden apple pie in a large platter. They served themselves. Melinda didn't stop: she came outside again with bowls stacked on a silver tray, as well as sliced yellow bull–mango fruit next to a white chocolate mocha mousse cake.

Zuva returned to the hut. She ran her hand along the walls that echoed with her parents' voices, remembering every word they said to her when they were training her to become Mambokadzi. One by one, she lifted the clay pots. They were all empty.

A roar announced a car approaching, driving fast along the road. Zuva peeped through the gap of the door and the wall. A blue Range Rover stopped a few meters away from the houses, next to Mwedzi's Peugeot. Zuva pinched her lips. The Peugeot was dented, mud splattered around the wheels. The Range Rover showed no hint of weakness. It beamed under the sunlight.

Her sister hopped out carrying a Gucci purse. Maudie wore a long black wig. Her blue summer dress should have swept the ground but couldn't because of the tall wedges she was wearing. Her little sister hadn't changed after all these years; the jewelry around her neck reminded Zuva of those days when Maudie sneaked into their mother's jewelry box and piled heavy stones on her wrists.

Maudie wasn't alone. Garikai got out of the passenger's seat, supported by a walking stick. He shouted, "Tsano, is that you, Mwedzi?"

"Yes, Tsano, it is me," Mwedzi said.

"Oh, my Lord, you've come back, with my nieces?"

"Yes, Tsano, these are all your nieces."

Garikai and Mwedzi hugged and patted each other on their backs, laughing.

Zuva stepped out of the hut, unsure whether to smile or scowl. Her father's mineral stones were gone, and his chamber was in shambles. Her eyes met Garikai's and then Maudie's. They all stood still, saying nothing to each other. Though he still looked like their father, Garikai had lost his hair and was now bald. His beard had turned gray. Zuva's eyes narrowed, he was holding Togara's brown walking stick—the one her father used to dub her on each shoulder the day they announced she would be next in line to the throne. Who had given it to him?

Everything he had, Garikai took by force, without respect or compassion. Had she not learned years ago that he was the greedy one? Maudie was no better.

"Welcome back, sister," Garikai said.

"Sister," Maudie said in shock, pushing the sunshades back on her wig to see if it was really Zuva.

Zuva didn't respond. She stood there, looking them in the eye. They looked guilty, choking for words, blinking as if the fire had caught their bodies. Zuva wondered what Garikai or Maudie had told Melinda, and what she believed—she must be on their side too.

Three young people climbed out of the Range Rover's back seats—a boy who seemed to be at least ten years old, a teenage girl, and a man in his twenties. Zuva's stomach flipped over. The young man looked like Fredrick. Fredrick, the man she was supposed to marry.

Zuva fell in love with Fredrick at school. It was the 60s, early on in the Second Chimurenga War. Zuva asked her parents if she could leave school to fight in the war, but they stopped her. They wanted to send Garikai instead, but he refused.

When she finished school, Zuva and Fredrick got engaged. She liked saying that Fredrick was her fiancé. Sometimes they met under the baobab tree and whispered love songs in each other's ears, holding hands to share the warmth of their blood.

Five years after they finished high school, Fredrick was planning to come with the lobola. Everything was falling into place. Zuva's parents had announced that she would become the next Mambokadzi, and she was training for it. Her parents were passing on the wisdom for how to deal with problems if they arose (war, drought, pandemic diseases, broken rules), to keep the peace within their region, accepting people as they were and helping one another if in need.

But war between the Rhodesian government and the black majority still ravaged the whole nation. The right thing for Zuva at that moment was to fight for her country first. She decided to ask her parents again. She sat on the zebra mat inside Togara's chamber and asked for their blessings.

"But my daughter, you are about to get married, and what if you die there and never come back?" Togara asked.

"Who's going to rule the land, my daughter?" asked Nyikadzino.

"Father, Mother, if you have faith in me, I'll come back. All I need are your blessings. Fredrick will wait. I need to fight for our land. Bless me, I beg you, my parents?"

A look passed between Togara and Nyikadzino. Zuva sensed their fear. Although she was trained to fight, to hunt, and many more other things, this was different. They expected her to be ready to sit on the throne soon if Togara was ready to move seats. They expected her to marry Fredrick and start a family of her own. Togara and Nyikadzino both reached out to touch Zuva's forehead.

"You, our daughter, Zuva, Princess of Goho, go well and fight for your land. Come back grasping soil in your hand, and we will know it is still ours. Come back and rule it. Bring peace, our daughter." Then they stood and hugged her as never before.

Zuva felt sorry for her parents. But Togara and Nyikadzino loved her, and she was there, strong physically and mentally, determined to do the right thing. They accepted her for who she was.

That evening, after telling Fredrick, she began the journey to the camp of the comrades that was in Manicaland with four of her father's men. They were to protect her under disguise. And they were to fight in the war, too. In the back of her mind, Zuva believed this was a test for Fredrick. She could have taken him too, but his crippled mother had no one to look after her. This was the only way to see if he really loved her and would wait until she returned.

Three years later, Zuva was still at war. She was now twenty–eight years old—without her father's men anymore. With her troop, Zuva spent her days dressed in camouflage combat gear, a bullet strap pulled across her shoulder, weighing her down.

Each season came and disappeared into the thick air. It was summer, and sweat dribbled over her body. She went weeks without bathing. Flies followed her, but she kept chasing them away, wiping her face with the back of her hand covered in scars. A rifle was in her hands, gun tucked in a side pocket, knife tucked in her back pocket, and a pack bumped up and down on her back, filled with essentials for the war. Zuva feared she was never going to see her family again. She also feared Fredrick had moved on.

In the middle of the forest, where Zuva and her father once hunted together, she and other comrades crossed the land now set with bombs, pits filled with dead bodies. She had seen too much. They all ran for cover when bombs fell from the skies like deadly eggs ejected by large birds, the exploding bombs burning and killing. That's how her father's men died.

Bullets flew from her rifle, from helicopters, army trucks, and maxi guns like deadly stings. The noise from explosions blocked her ears for weeks. They traveled at night. When Zuva and the comrades heard dogs barking from afar, they would know a village lay somewhere close by. At night when owls hooted, they headed into the darkness, shooting at the opposition forces who were hiding or running for cover. When she and the comrades were lost in the forest, hallucinating from hunger, they gobbled wild fruit.

In neighboring villages, they searched for the mediums who could speak on behalf of spirits of the dead. Quite often, it was Zuva who talked to them. And when they were thirsty, far away from the river, they drank each other's urine to survive.

The color red was normal. So were broken legs severed from bodies, heads detached from necks, and ravaged skin coated with brown blood. Flies crowded dead bodies and buzzed around open wounds. Children, women with babies on their backs, men still holding weapons in their hands—all of them lay on the ground lifeless. Zuva felt guilty for not being there for them when they were still alive. Sometimes the rotten flesh smelled so bad, she and her comrades bent down to vomit.

If most of the weak and the injured were not killed by disease, then it was by a bullet or an explosion. Zuva had lost weight, but she was convinced she was going to be safe from mosquito bites, bugs, and even snakes because her parents' spirits led her. She held tight to her parents' last prayer. The thought of returning home kept her going. Her strength felt renewed whenever she held her lion's tooth necklace.

In the middle of the summer, her commander told them they were moving to a new region. Their lorry stopped in the middle of nowhere in Matabeleland, away from home and the ground she knew better. Zuva and the comrades were taken to their new camp where they were given real food to eat after such a long time—beef stew, tsunga, and sadza, cooked by local supporters. The sunlight flared through the tree leaves, and the breeze was freshening. The land didn't seem to stink of dead bodies or blood.

Zuva climbed high in a tree to survey the area, while below her comrades sat talking and laughing, enjoying the cooked food. From her tree Zuva saw the bhodifas running in to ambush them. The bhodifas were lawless groups who roamed around the nation during war, with the aim to recruit more people so they could fight and rise above the Rhodesian government and the comrades.

For Zuva, it was too late to warn anyone. If she had not done what her father taught her when they went hunting, she would have been killed too. She stayed still on her branch, hidden by thick leaves, while the bhodifas shot at her comrades. She bit her lips until blood oozed over her chin. They shouted to each other to take cover, firing back, but there were too many of them.

The sound of guns was still popping in Zuva's ears

when the bhodifas gathered the comrades in a pile. They poured alcohol on the bodies and set it alight. Zuva could hear the screams of the comrades who were wounded but not dead; the bhodifas were burning them alive. She kept quiet, tears trickling down her dirty cheeks, while the bhodifas laughed and congratulated each other.

She watched the flames following the tune of the wind and breathed in the smell of humans burning. The bhodifas not only stayed until they made sure the bodies were as black as coal, but set up to sleep on the comrades' camp, ate what was left in the pots, and drank all the water. How could they sleep with burnt bodies around them, with the spirits of the comrades haunting them? Up in the branches, Zuva was exhausted, stuck, still hugging the tree. Her back cramped in pain.

The following morning, the bhodifas walked off into the forest. Zuva didn't want to make a mistake, so she stayed in her tree until the sun had set and the forest was in darkness. She climbed down, stiff and aching, and stared at the black figures glued together and ashy. Some parts of the bodies weren't completely burnt. This close, the smell traveled fast into the snakes inside her stomach, and she vomited.

Zuva wiped her mouth and started to walk, following the direction of smoke she had seen from the tree. Her whole body shook. She gripped her necklace and thought of her parents' faces. The night drifted in, and the cold breeze made her shiver, but she kept moving.

Zuva approached the area where she'd seen the smoke. She heard the same voices she'd heard the day before, so loud, and a woman crying. Zuva clambered up another tree, where she could see the bhodifas, pants down, taking turns to penetrate the woman. There were more than twenty, she could tell with the way they circled her, waiting for a turn. Zuva's body revolted. She pulled out her rifle and began shooting at the bhodifas. They dropped on the ground just like the comrades did the day before. Zuva shot the man who was on top of the woman, and he collapsed on her. The woman screamed.

Some ran to their guns, but Zuva kept shooting, making sure she didn't miss. She couldn't miss. When the men were all down, the woman pulled herself from underneath the bhodifa who was above her. She was covered in blood, shivering, and looking around, hoping to see people. The woman got up and limped toward a young boy who was lying on the ground further away. She held him in her arms, crying. Zuva noticed a couple of other dead bodies that weren't the bhodifas, closer to the huts. She assumed they were the woman's family. Zuva cried too, the tears warm and salty. Just seeing the woman holding her son was enough. She hadn't cried like that in a long time. It felt peaceful, right.

She climbed down and approached the cluster of huts. The woman saw Zuva and ran to her.

"Thank you for saving me," she said, still crying, and Zuva wrapped her arms around the woman.

A tall man in black combat boots stepped out of the hut. He pulled a hand from his cream cargo pants pocket that was tainted in blood. A rifle hung loose on his right shoulder over his torn maroon sweatshirt. He removed a brown bandana that was covering half of his face and adjusted a green kangol hat on his head.

"Very stupid," he said. "Aren't soldiers supposed to check the surrounding before they celebrate victory?"

"Aren't men supposed to protect the women and children of their land?" Zuva demanded. "Not kill or rape them, ha?"

"Who knew a woman could shoot all these men? I take my hat off for you." He threw his kangol hat and rifle on the ground. "Since you're a soldier, let's do what soldiers do, you and I, woman."

Zuva told the woman to run and faced down her enemy. The man lunged at her, and his fist landed on Zuva's left cheekbone. She threw two punches back at him, smacking his face. He stepped back, shaking his head, and spat blood on the ground. He then grimaced, and lunged at her again, but she ducked and punched him in the stomach. He kept coming. He managed to grab Zuva's plaited hair and yanked her backwards, strangling her with his other hand. Zuva, choking, shoved him back and pulled out her knife. She aimed for his stomach, but he jumped out of the way. The bhodifa laughed and grabbed her shoulder and pushed her to the ground. Now he was on top of her, staring at her, licking his upper lip.

"Get off me!" Zuva screamed. She drove the knife up and with all her strength, stabbed him in his stomach.

He growled, touching the wound as blood spilt, forming rivers down the handle. Zuva pulled out her knife, but he wasn't ready to give in. He snatched the knife from her and slit her stomach. It felt like a scratch as she fought the man, for her life.

A sudden wind blew up, dust blinding him. Zuva reached for a branch lying on the ground and swung it at his head. He recoiled from the blow but pulled the log from her and threw it away. He then reached for her necklace and ripped it from Zuva's neck. His hand was on her throat again, strangling her. The lion's tooth lay in the dirt. Zuva felt as though her strength lay there too. She wheezed and struggled; all she could see in her mind was her father's chamber, the zebra mat, the necklace. She was too weak to fight anymore.

When she opened her eyes, they stung with dust, but she could see the bhodifa was raising his knife with his free hand. Zuva summoned up all the strength she had left and punched him in the stab wound. He screeched with pain and dropped the knife. But now he was using both hands to strangle her. She tried kicking him in the groin with her knee, but he wasn't letting go.

When she reached out wanting to snap his neck, the sight of the oozing blood on her stomach, the opened skin, it made her heart pound faster against her rib cage. She feared her womb had been sliced. Suddenly, the pain stung, it was strong like the breaking wheels of a train abrading whatever was in their way. The sparks burning the soft tissue. Unstoppable, the pain still traveled all over her body.

Just as Zuva thought it was the end, she glimpsed the woman she had saved looming over him. She stabbed the bhodifa in the back with a machete and he grunted, tipping over on his side. Zuva struggled to her feet, shaking. The bhodifa was still alive and seemed to be laughing, blood bubbling out of his mouth like lava from a volcano. His eyes were wide open, gazing at the two women, his body twitching.

Zuva didn't shoot him. She wanted him to suffer, just as he had made the woman who lived here endure pain. When she saw him take his last breath and his body fall still, Zuva collected what belonged to her, her necklace. The slit in her stomach stung, and she needed the woman's help to put the necklace on again. It was as though a sister was blessing her with life.

While Zuva dragged the dead family members inside

the hut, the woman crouched in a large oval galvanized tub filled with water. It was Zuva who asked her to do that, wash away the vomit of the evil men.

Later, they walked together in the dark to the highway. Zuva pressed the wound in her stomach; it was still bleeding. The woman limped in front of her. When a vehicle on the highway approached, she ran and waved her hands to stop it. The driver was reluctant to stop but did after he passed her. The woman ran after the truck. He had some people in the open back of his vehicle.

"Woman! You can't stop me at this time of the evening, we are in a war!" he shouted at her.

"Please help me, they killed my family!"

"Where do you want to go then?"

"Salisbury, but you can drop me in any city if you are not going that far."

"Jump in, I can't stop here long."

"I have a comrade who helped me." She looked at him with worry.

"Comrade! Are you kidding me, I don't carry comrades, they get me in trouble," he said, eager to drive away so fast.

"If she hadn't come, I'd be dead now." She pressed her hands together in front of her face, begging.

The moment the driver heard the word she, his face softened. "All right, bring her; I hope I won't get in trouble because of her."

The woman helped Zuva into the back of the Toyota truck, and they squeezed in among other people's bags. Zuva saw the grief in the eyes of the passengers. They looked at her, unsure if she was one of those who killed for no reason or those who wanted to save them and their land. The man drove fast along the highway, and Zuva looked back toward the place they had left. Darkness blinded the death she had seen. It had brought pain to her, but she thanked her ancestors for keeping her alive, even though she didn't know if she would live to see tomorrow.

After traveling so many kilometers, Zuva began to worry when the driver slowed down. She didn't want to stop. She was terrified if they did, death would come down upon them before they arrived where they were going. The woman shared a concerned look with Zuva. She then pulled a zambia from her neighbor and covered Zuva with it. There was a roadblock. The soldiers were holding rifles in their hands, ready to fire. One of them raised his hand, stopping the driver.

Zuva looked through the back window, unsure who the soldiers were. If they were the ones on the opposite side, they would kill her. She grasped her necklace again, looking at the woman and the rest of the people in the truck. They had already succumbed to fear.

"Ho, my man, where are you traveling to in the middle of the night?"

"I am going to Salisbury," he responded with a shaking voice.

"And who are these people with you?" one of the soldiers asked, walking back to see who were in the back. He beamed his torch on people's faces, and then tossed the zambia off Zuva. This was her end, Zuva thought, expelling an awful sigh. Soon, the soldier pulled out a piece of paper. It was a black-and-white photo of a woman. A woman who resembled her.

He then beckoned the other soldiers over. The woman held Zuva's hand. She looked ready to defend her, no matter what the soldiers said. The soldiers all looked from Zuva to the small photo, nodding their heads.

"Soldier, tell us who you are and where you came from?" their leader demanded.

"Comrade Chasunga, from Manicaland. We came to Matabeleland to fight here."

"Where are the rest of the comrades?" the leader asked again.

"Dead. The bhodifas killed and burnt them."

"All right, Comrade Chasunga—your real name?" the soldier demanded.

Zuva had been told not to disclose that information to anyone, but she didn't care anymore. "Zuva Mutongi," she said, leaving out one word. She didn't want it known that she was a princess. She didn't like it when people knelt before her or treated her differently with so much care and loyalty.

"All right, Comrade Chasunga." The leader looked over at the driver, who seemed distressed. "My man, we'll take it from here."

Zuva didn't care if they were going to kill her. She had experienced too much horror already. She was ready to be tortured in a damp room with no light, tied to a broken chair or hung on a chain from the roof, questioned again about who she was and who she was fighting for or, even worse, have a hot iron stamped on her, water poured in her nostrils and beaten to death. Or even made to eat rotten things.

"Please don't kill Comrade Chasunga," the woman pleaded. "She saved me from the bhodifas. You wouldn't know what they did to me."

"No one is killing Comrade Chasunga," the leader responded.

"How do I know?" She started crying, clinging to Zuva.

The driver threw his hand through the opened window.

"Woman," he shouted, "you want me to get in trouble? Get off my truck. I can't take you with me anymore."

"You can go as soon as Comrade Chasunga is off your truck," one of the soldiers said. Some of them had surrounded the truck with rifles pointed at the driver.

Zuva crawled to get off the truck and was led to the soldiers' lorry. The woman followed, so terrified that she grabbed onto Zuva's arm. They all climbed into the back of the green lorry along with other soldiers. In there, no one said anything. When the lorry drove off, the two women fell asleep, until they heard voices speaking outside the lorry in the middle of nowhere. They got up to see the sunlight beaming outside the truck. One soldier of high rank came and called out to Zuva.

"Comrade Chasunga!" He saluted.

Zuva was surprised—they were on her side. The soldiers who took her had kept her in the dark. She hadn't recognized their combat gear.

"I'm Comrade Dhoza, commander of Mashonaland West, and we are going to take you back to Manicaland for now." He frowned. "I'm sorry—I heard your troop were shot and burnt by the bhodifas."

"Yes, Comrade," Zuva said. She was unhappy she was being sent back to Manicaland.

"It seems like you have been injured," he said. "We don't have time, we should be back on the road, but we can see if the comrades can take care of that wound you have there."

"She needs to be taken to the hospital," Zuva said, touching the woman's wrist, forgetting she was speaking to the commander. "Help her get to her family."

Before she parted with the woman, she hugged her so tightly as if they were sisters or had known each other for many years. She had saved the woman, and the woman had saved her too.

That evening, the comrades brought Zuva back to her homeland. No one was expecting to see her alive. Togara had sent a message to the comrades asking if they could find his daughter two years earlier. The word went around the commanders, but it took longer because no one knew if Zuva was still alive, and there were so many comrades scattered all over the country. Still in her bloodied clothes and sore wounds, Zuva walked from the main road up a dusty road, past the armed guards standing around their dwellings, and straight to the room where she slept. She was planning to change her clothes before she saw her parents.

Zuva strolled along the long passage of the big house with its thatched roof. She felt so lucky to be back home, to be able to walk on the floor she used to clean with her sister. Maudie's room was half–dimmed with a slow–burner lamp, and Zuva opened the door in case Maudie was still awake.

She was not only awake: her mouth was pressed against the mouth of a man Zuva loved. The man she had promised to come back and marry. Yet he was on top of her sister, naked, thrusting his body on Maudie.

"Maudie, Fredrick!" she cried.

Something splintered Zuva's heart, fast like a flash of lightning. What she'd feared had happened. The worst thing was that Fredrick had cast her aside for her own sister. Shock absorbed her pain. Zuva couldn't bear to see her own sister and her fiancé like this. The way their hands grasped each other's bodies showed it wasn't the first time they were together in that bed.

Zuva banged the door shut. She paced the hallway,

deciding whether to go back into Maudie's room. Her right hand reached out to her back pocket, where her gun nestled.

At that moment, she remembered what she'd promised Togara: to come back holding soil in her palm. If she shot her sister and her fiancé, how would that be soil to Togara? She turned and headed straight to her parents' bedroom and knocked on the door.

"Mother, Father, I am coming in."

Togara was lying down. Nyikadzino was sitting next to him, her hands laid on his chest. When they saw Zuva, their faces lit up with joy.

"Father," Zuva whispered. Togara looked wizened and gray, and she feared this was his deathbed. Nyikadzino stood up and embraced Zuva with a long hug.

"Oh, my daughter, you are hurt," she said, trying to open the torn bloodied uniform. 'With your father's men dead, we didn't know if…"

"Zuva, oh Zuva my daughter, I've been waiting for you," Togara said, a tear flowing from one eye. "How good it is to see you before I leave." He coughed, struggling to breathe, but managed to raise a hand. Zuva moved to the side of the bed. "My daughter, my ancestors have heard me, I'm so blessed," he said, clasping Zuva's hand. "You carry the scent of bravery on you, did you bring soil with you in your palms?"

"Not yet, Father, but I'll go back to get it," she said, kneeling next to Togara.

"You don't need to. It will come to you," he said, smiling.

Nyikadzino began telling Zuva how her father got ill. After a while, Togara took a deep breath, looking at Zuva's face.

"Set me free, my daughter. I was only waiting for you."

"What do you mean, Father?"

"Say a prayer for me, so that our ancestors will open the gate for me."

Zuva lowered her head, withholding her tears. She looked up to her mother, who nodded, allowing her to say the last prayer. Zuva began to whisper words that were only heard by the three of them.

"To my ancestors who bore each one of us in this room, welcome my father, Togara Mutongi, your son who has followed your steps. He's led Manicaland region with so much strength, love, and kindness to the land, to the people, to the animals." She paused, struggling to go on. "Welcome him and…give him the space that he deserves to lay his soul. Remember those he is leaving behind, guide them with light and peace."

Nyikadzino was sobbing quietly. Zuva asked Togara if she could continue.

"Whatever you say, my daughter. Every word brings peace to me. Comfort has already molded my heart. Now that you are here, be strong tomorrow."

"Father, I am not ready for you to go. But if you know it's time, I say go with peace."

Togara closed his eyes, a brief smile on his lips. Zuva watched her father's breath head down to a dark tunnel.

When Maudie tried to enter the room, Nyikadzino stopped her. What they both waited for was already there, the center of their hearts. Zuva held her father's hands and fell asleep with her head resting on his chest.

When she woke up early in the morning, her father's hands were cold. It was Nyikadzino, her eyes red, who had to pull her away from him.

They left the room together. Maudie stood at the end of

the long passage, staring. Zuva kept her head low, avoiding Maudie's eyes. Nyikadzino pulled her out of the house, and they both headed down to Yeredzo River. Still in her combat uniform, Zuva sat in the middle of the river. Her body was stiff, but she wasn't shivering from cold or pain. Nyikadzino unclothed her daughter and tried to wash it all. The pain, the betrayal, the loss. She fetched water with her cupped hands and poured it onto her daughter's forehead, as though she was baptizing her again.

"I am sorry for everything," Nyikadzino said.

Her mother was apologizing as if she was the one who wronged her. But it wasn't Nyikadzino's fault that Maudie was sleeping with Fredrick, or—as Zuva would learn—that Garikai had bought men of the village with his father's gold so that he could rule that land. When Togara died, her mother knew none of this, anyway. Had her ancestors shown Nyikadzino in her dreams what was going to happen?

The stitches on Zuva's stomach were now exposed for Nyikadzino to see what her daughter had gone through. The deep hollowed dent on her shoulder was where the bullet had carved its path before missing her heart by a few inches. The bullet seemed as though it was an airplane taking off, pointing up to the sky. The countless scars were now nothing compared to what she had seen.

When Nyikadzino finished washing her daughter, Zuva emerged from the water and dressed in the new clothes her mother had brought. She walked barefoot on the sand. Nyikadzino stood still in the middle of the river with tears on her face.

"My first and last have killed me," she said.

After the burial of Togara, Zuva sat for hours next to her father's grave on Goho Mountain, only returning home to look after her mother. Garikai had taken over Zuva's throne without consulting Nyikadzino or his father before he died. Zuva and Nyikadzino had to hear it first after the burial when all the village men sat under the shed having a meeting now run by Garikai.

"We've come to mourn with you, our chief, for the loss of your father," they all said. This was a shock to Zuva.

"Who said Garikai is the new chief?" Nyikadzino asked.

"We don't need to go into that, Mother," Garikai said with a smile on his face. "The men of the village have already spoken. They chose me."

"Your father and I have already blessed Zuva. She is next on the throne."

"She is an unmarried woman who chose to fight in a war and forgot her responsibilities. Besides, the men thought she wasn't coming back."

"Well, she is here now. Wasn't fighting for this land her responsibility? It took so much strength from within her. Your father and I thought you'd go and fight in the war since you are a man, but you stayed. It showed us how weak you are." Nyikadzino was showing her disappointment in front of the men of the village. Zuva watched her brother, wasn't he ashamed? Her mother turned to face the assembled men. "If you want my son to be the chief, do it properly, so that tomorrow you won't have anything eating you from within. Because I tell you, you will regret your decision."

The men were now unsettled, and Garikai needed to calm them. Zuva and her mother left the meeting, and Nyikadzino took to her bed. Zuva knew her mother had chosen to follow her father when she said, "Set yourself free, my daughter. Your father and I will always guide you."

One day when Zuva was attending to her mother, one of their guards knocked at the door. He said a man was looking for Comrade Chasunga.

"Let him in," Nyikadzino said, her voice weak. Zuva thought her mother meant in the living room, but she didn't. "In here, Zuva. I want to see him."

A stranger in her father and mother's bedroom? Zuva was puzzled, but she obeyed her mother. A young man entered the room and stopped by the door, holding his hat in his hand. Nyikadzino smiled at him, gesturing for him to come closer. The young man knelt next to the bed. Zuva was confused about why her mother would want a stranger so close to her when she was sick. He looked familiar but she couldn't remember how she knew him.

"Tell me your name, my son?" Nyikadzino asked.

"Mwedzi Taha," he said. "I've come from Salisbury to thank Comrade Chasunga for saving my life."

"Is it love that led you all the way from another city just to come and thank my daughter?"

Zuva opened her eyes wide. She wasn't enjoying wherever their conversation was going.

"Love is what leads you to do the right thing," Mwedzi said.

"That is right, my son." She patted his right hand, her breath wheezy. "Anyway, I am blessed to have seen my son–in–law before I depart. I bless you to marry my daughter when she is ready. Be patient, she is still mourning."

Zuva gestured for Mwedzi to leave the room. She was angry that he'd shown up at such a moment and that her mother was blessing a stranger to marry her. How could she do that to her?

A few days later, Nyikadzino died in her daughter's arms. Before the burial, Zuva was surprised to see Mwedzi was still there, walking down the dusty road, carrying firewood on his shoulder. He piled it next to the meeting shed where men sat circling the fire pit. She was curious, wanting to know the reason he'd remained.

Nyikadzino was buried. People from the village came to help, and yet Zuva was still avoiding Garikai, Maudie, and Mwedzi. Even though Mwedzi hadn't wronged her, she was angry that he'd come to see her when she was most vulnerable. When she climbed the mountain after Nyikadzino fell asleep, she would cry sitting next to her father's grave. This is where Mwedzi found her one day, when he was carrying firewood down the mountain. He didn't say anything. He placed the firewood onto the flat surface of a rock and walked over to Zuva. Mwedzi pulled out a handkerchief, and she took it hesitantly, shy because he'd seen her crying. Before she could ask him why he had come, Mwedzi picked up the firewood and left.

The day of their final meeting with the whole village, Zuva had packed her bags. She got up that morning and told everyone that she was leaving. The only way she was going to control her feelings was by getting away. She feared the anger inside her would make her pull the trigger, killing people she was related to by blood. Her emotions were already getting the better of her. The night Nyikadzino was buried, Maudie had found her in their parents' bedroom and whispered, "I am sorry, sister. It just happened."

Zuva shoved Maudie against the wall, her hand gripping her sister's throat. When Zuva looked into Maudie's eyes, she saw no remorse. Maudie wasn't sorry. She was in love with Fredrick.

She let go of Maudie and walked out fast. At that moment, she felt the way she did when the bhodifa was on top of her. How her necklace was snatched from her neck, and she felt powerless, defeated. How could she stay here and face that feeling again? Garikai, moving on the throne without asking her or their parents first, Maudie falling in love with her fiancé, and Togara and Nyikadzino passing on. What more pain could she endure?

Her siblings didn't object to Zuva's announcement. Her leaving would give them room to do whatever they wanted. Garikai would rule the village without feeling guilty all the time. Maudie would marry Fredrick and start a family without feeling that she'd betrayed her own sister.

That day Mwedzi stood up and told them he was leaving too. It was an honor for him to have met the family of a woman who had saved him. He'd been coming from Chimanimani when a group of comrades surrounded him. One held a rifle to his head. Then Zuva walked toward them and said to the comrades, "Leave the man alone. Lives should be saved, not destroyed because of pride or anger."

The villagers nodded their heads, agreeing that what Mwedzi said was true. Garikai stood up and thanked Mwedzi for helping throughout the funeral of Nyikadzino. Zuva wondered if Garikai was going to follow the path her parents had taught them as a chief.

Later that day, Zuva hoisted her bags onto her back. She climbed the mountain heading toward the graves of her parents—to say goodbye. Mwedzi was already there at the gravesides, carrying his own bags. When he saw Zuva, he bowed at her and left. She wondered why a stranger had gone to the graves of her parents, whom he barely knew.

Zuva said a few words to her parents for the last time, then walked down to catch the Nyamwenda bus along the Umtali Highway. Mwedzi was on the same bus, sitting further back. Though she didn't know where she was going, Zuva felt better knowing there was a familiar face on the same bus she was on. Even if it was someone who had seen her at her very worst. And though she never hoped they'd end up in the same city, at least she had done something right: this stranger she saved in the war, was still alive.

YEREDZO RIVER

Summer 1993
ZUVA AND NYEREDZI

Everyone in Goho Village knew that the waterfall was Selina's dwelling, but to them, it was also their source of water. Mother Earth's saliva poured from the cliff, forming the bridal veils that were divided by a horned rock about eighteen meters high. Sometimes the water flowed smooth as glass, and other times, depending on the weather, the deafening roar raged on people's faces and bodies if they were standing too close.

People said the horned rock was Selina's crown and that each day she lived was her wedding. Others called it the curtain divider, which allowed people to peer through, eager to see what was behind the water. They hoped that maybe one day they would see Selina herself lying on a bare rock within the cave. She had inherited this specific cave from her mother, Heroshina. It was wide, deep, and curvy. And the rest of the area, where the water bumped onto the boulders and flowed along the meandering valley, was for the villagers and other creatures.

Women from the village of Goho came to fetch water from the river before the sun rose, and before it headed west, beyond the bald heads of their ancestors lying in the earth. At that time of day, the water was still clean, untouched, and undisturbed.

During the daytime, after the women had finished making food for their families, sent the children to school, cleaned their houses, and swept their yards with African traditional brooms, they brought their laundry to the Yeredzo River and washed it while sitting on the rocks. It was their meeting place. They knew the time: the sun never misled them. They knew the perfect spot that didn't have any algae, where the rocks weren't slippery, where their pre–schoolers could play in shallow waters and not drown. They gossiped about other people in the village and their love lives, all their secrets unfolding before the river.

It became their holy place, too, because they repented without realizing it. This was where Mother Nature lifted the burdens that oppressed them and where their sins could be washed away with the water. This river invigorated them. It watched them come of age, sang to calm them down, cooled their bodies raging with hormones, washed away their blood, until they struggled to get up from where they sat.

Once the women were done with laundry, when all the clothes were laid out on the grassy patches and bushy trees to dry, the women and their children were cleansed. Each of them stayed close to their little ones, some carrying their babies on their backs. Though the river was special to them in many ways, safety was not guaranteed. Sometimes the long, slim creatures that slithered on their tummies appeared from nowhere, uninvited. The people of Goho were always cautious when it came to wild animals and sacred places, like Selina's dwelling.

Zuva was cautious as well, even after all this time

away. She brought her daughters to the river, stepping into the shallow water, feeling so much respect for Selina. Her daughters sank their feet in the soft sand alongside her. In her heart, she knew this visit home meant introducing her daughters to the values she had long held and telling them what was not accepted in their village. The lifestyle here was different and for her daughters to understand, Zuva had to tell them what happened to her sister, Maudie.

Maudie had broken so many rules in their village throughout her life and she seemed to have lost respect for their culture. Even though Zuva hadn't seen her for a long time, the rumors were already swimming through her ears. It proved that Maudie hadn't changed at all.

When they were still young, the freedom that ran in Maudie's blood made her lips loose. Once they had been at the river when Maudie shouted, "Heroshina's dwelling reeks."

At that time, Heroshina was already dead, but Selina was offended. Zuva told Maudie she had crossed the line and before her sister had finished bathing at the river, she was visited by a dangerous creature. Zuva had seen it coming, the green snake slithering between the gaps in the rocks, while Maudie stood on a flat rock, shaking her waist sideways, laughing.

Zuva whispered, "Forgive."

Her friends and cousins screamed, trying to warn Maudie, but Zuva stood still, knowing in her heart that Selina would have heard her whisper, begging forgiveness for her sister. But Selina couldn't just forgive without warning Maudie of her wrongdoings. The snake circled her, and Maudie screamed in terror, dropping the towel and a bar of soap she was holding. As she ran away, she slipped and fell hard onto the rocks. Blood spilt from her mouth and by the time the river washed her tongue of her insensitive words, she was left with a chipped tooth.

When Zuva told her daughters the stories of her childhood, Selina was listening, enlivened by Zuva's presence. Zuva made a lot of people feel at peace when she was around them. It wasn't just Togara and Nyikadzino, it was also Selina, and the people of Goho. In the Second Chimurenga War, she calmed injured people who, in the end, were swallowed by death. They didn't moan or scream: they fell asleep in her arms as if Zuva had put them to bed.

Later, as the sun began falling in the sky, Zuva walked out of the water and used the same dusty, narrow path she used years ago to walk home. Its edges had been washed away by rainfall. Her daughters followed. They passed by Goho Primary and High School which Zuva once attended. The long red–brick blocks of classrooms stood in small rows. The school ground was green, surrounded by gum and wild berry trees. She tried to point out her old classroom but too much had changed. The office was further away, now guarded by the black tarred car park. The assembly had a stage in front and the back section was an orchard.

Next to the padlocked wrought iron gate was a noticeboard. Zuva's gaze was drawn to Maudie's name on the board. With Maudie's success in education, she was now running a college in Harare. Though the villagers had honored her for developing the school, she also wanted to change a lot of things in the village. This meant Maudie was a main topic at the river when women were bathing or doing laundry.

People would know Maudie was back by the way she

revved the engine of her blue Range Rover as she raced home along the dusty road. They talked about how her feet were no longer touching the soil. Her Gucci wedge sandals defined her steps, lifting her butt in the air, walking as though she was on a seesaw. She seemed more unearthly, someone who thought they were superior to others.

Zuva had witnessed this first-hand the afternoon they arrived from Harare, when the whole family sat outside for lunch together. Maudie was obsessed with her long, polished nails and she didn't want food stuck in her claws, so she used forks and knives even on the food that needed to be picked with bare hands.

Zuva walked away from the school noticeboard, her sister's behavior gnawing at her thoughts. She talked and laughed with her daughters, but she was wondering how so many things had changed in her absence. How so many families were now visiting throughout the summer holidays to celebrate Christmas with their loved ones and how often they brought chaos.

Zuva's brother Garikai was the chief, so he and the elders held meetings once or twice a week to inform visitors about Selina's dwelling, but the young ones wanted to explore and know what lay beneath the deep curves of water, behind the thick veils. Curiosity kept knocking at the back of their skulls each day they walked past, on their way to and from herding cattle or weeding maize. The more curious they grew, the closer they got to Selina's dwelling, walking by as though it was not a sacred place.

During the Christmas season, it was hard for the elders to control everything that happened in the village. The young ones would be found diving into Selina's pool and none of them seemed to understand how serious this was because the lines had become blurred. They wondered if Selina really existed. Why they had never seen her sunbathing? Why had they only heard about her from other people? Why did the villagers claim she was there when none of them had ever come across her? All this stirred confusion within the village.

People had always relied on the information they were told by their elders, just like Zuva's daughters. This included learning about the signs that warned them of Selina's emotions. The villagers knew what to do if something happened, but the Christmas visitors were ignorant.

When the water was bubbling around the curvy pool, it meant Selina was ready to sleep. It was forbidden to disturb her, even by diving from the edge of the cliff. Some mornings, when there was a fresh breeze, words would appear in the overlapping ripples on the water, and it meant Selina was in love; her body was craving a man but only the desired man would be able to read the letters.

When this happened, women of the village were afraid to lose their husbands to Selina. It was believed that some men were infatuated with her. Her breath whistled in their ears, echoing love songs. Others saw her in their dreams, her body beyond the definition of beauty. It melted their souls and drained all their strength into their groins.

The temptation was undeniable. A man would follow Selina into the cave where it seemed dark from the outside, but once he was in there, everything glittered. Her utensils, her clothes, the passages that took him to other rooms, even her body changed colors. She would ask three times if he really wanted to be hers. If he agreed, she would marry him. Quite often, when this took place, people would see flame lily flowers floating within her territory for a full month. It amazed everyone, how the flowers could remain fresh for that long. This honeymoon phase meant a man was never coming back, dead, or alive. If he chose not to stay with Selina, the man would wake with a fright from the dream and never remember what he saw in the cave.

When the thick bridal veils flowed violently from the cliff, Selina was in a vortex of despair, grieving for her long–lost mother, father, sister, brother, and husbands. Her hormones swirled in and out of the river and the water was dirty for days. Dead leaves and branches would be scattered everywhere, frothy edges and boulders covered in Selina's green slime vomit. The water was unsafe for drinking, washing, or bathing. The chief and the mediums of the village would be called to ask Selina to calm down, and let the other creatures live in peace.

During Togara's time as a chief, it was unusual to see this happening. People behaved very well. Now that his son Garikai had taken over, a darkness had begun to grow. Corruption began the moment he bought the men of the village with his father's gold so he could become the chief.

Years back, when Heroshina existed, there was a prediction that the villagers' disrespect toward Selina's dwelling would create havoc and bring death. But people had forgotten the warning. They thought it would never occur in their lifetime and for a long time, life was peaceful. Though the young ones sometimes trespassed on Selina's dwelling, she forgave them. She was more kind–hearted than her mother. Heroshina was impatient, and any obnoxious behavior was punished ferociously.

But after so many decades, people were beginning to take Selina lightly. Their lifestyle had changed. The village had developed. The round huts with thatched roofs had been demolished to make way for brick houses with corrugated zinc or tiled roofs. Electricity lit their rooms at night, and the people no longer relied on Mother Moon and her children. Each roof in the village had a thin spiked horn to watch the moving pictures. They might think this horn resembled Selina's crown, but the worlds were far apart.

The village looked like a modern suburb. Now people went to the river for pleasure or to get away from the crowded houses. Women still enjoyed their meetings, though. Just because the villagers were moving along with the world didn't mean Yeredzo River had stopped flowing. Selina's dwelling was still there, and she watched the newer generation who came to bathe—the grandchildren of the elders who now used walking sticks to guide them as they walked.

A few days after Zuva and her family arrived, she was still waiting for the spirit mediums to go with the whole family to Togara and Nyikadzino's graves. There was to be a prayer to put her parents at rest and this was the only reason she'd come back.

Zuva had already taken her daughters to see where their grandparents lay. While they were waiting for the visit with the mediums, she encouraged the girls to bond with their cousins—Garikai's two sons, Revie and Taurai, and his daughters, Chenai and Mazvita.

She and Mwedzi were sleeping in her father's chamber. The very night they arrived, before supper, Melinda her sister-in-law came into the hut and knelt before Zuva.

"My sister, Zuva, I'm sorry for everything that has happened. You and I barely know each other, but I come to ask for forgiveness." She touched Zuva's hands. "Open your heart for my children and me. And please, when the right time comes, forgive Garikai and Maudie?"

Neither her brother nor her sister had come to apologize for their wrongdoings, so Zuva was surprised to hear Melinda say this. Clearly, no one had asked her to do that. It was time to make things right. Zuva lifted Melinda up and asked her to sit next to her.

"Melinda, my sister, I have never held anything against you. If anyone should apologize, it is me. I was hard on you when I arrived. I guess emotions were coiling inside me."

"Please come and sleep in the house. We have more rooms."

"The girls can come and sleep in there. Mwedzi and I will sleep in here but thank you for your kindness."

"Anything you need, please let me know I'm here," Melinda said, and Zuva thanked her.

Zuva's daughters were already getting along with their cousins. And whenever they sat outside to chat, Maudie's children, Emmanuel, Lydia, and Munya, joined them as well. While Zuva sat in her father's chamber during the day, she listened to their conversations. She was surprised that Maudie's children often talked about their fancy lifestyle. How they had traveled with their mother and father abroad to Europe and America and bought nice things that lasted longer. How they were planning to go and study there.

Zuva's family was still living in an unfinished house that didn't have electricity, and yet here in a village, they flicked the plugs on and off as if they were in the city. Zuva wondered how Maudie and Fredrick had got so much money.

As the days passed, the temperature rose. It was hot. There were times when the children isolated into groups according to their ages. Some sat under the mobola tree to talk. Others spent most of their times in their bedrooms gossiping about dating. Zuva and Mwedzi often wandered off and ended up on the mountain at Togara and Nyikadzino's graves.

The young ones explored the village even under that heat. Nyeredzi and the other girls followed Munya, who was showing them around. Munya had participated in different sports at Peterhouse Boys' School and promised to teach them to swim. Nyeredzi had seen the school several times when they lived in Marondera. It was a private school, and she dreamed that one day her parents would enroll her at one of those fancy schools.

At the river, Munya first swam out into the deep areas, showing the others how to float, but he grew bored quickly and started to climb up the cliffside.

"You can't go up there," Nyeredzi shouted at Munya. "Mama said so—it is forbidden."

"What do you know?" he shouted back. "You just came here a few days ago."

"I know everything," Mazvita said. "I'll tell Papa you climbed there."

"Boo–hoo!" Munya stuck his tongue out and kept climbing the rocky cliff while his cousins waited down by the curvy pool. At the top he strolled along the edge of the horned rock, then tucked his right hand behind his head as though he was posing for a photoshoot. He counted down from five and jumped, spinning his body twice in the air. When his body met the water, a big splash showered his cousins. His head rose above the water and they applauded. Munya's charms had made them forget the rules. Nyeredzi couldn't believe it.

"That was brilliant," Chenai said, "but don't do it again, unless you want to be Selina's husband."

"Oh, chill. Nothing is going to happen to me. I can swim faster than Selina." Munya wiped water from his face with his dry shirt. "Just you wait—you haven't seen the best of me yet."

"And what's that?" Abigail asked.

"I've got something better, something we can all enjoy."

"I'm serious. You can't do that again," Chenai said with a shaky voice.

Munya dashed off toward a little bush where he was hiding his stuff. He pulled out a bottle of cherry blossom body wash. "It's my mother's. I suppose we can borrow it, just for now."

The cousins watched him twist the cap. His smile promised them it was going to be fun.

Nyeredzi shook her head, looking at her cousins, hoping they would say something, but they didn't. "You know very well smelly things aren't allowed here, right?" she asked Munya.

Zuva had told her girls that soap and anything with a fragrance muddled with Selina, and people were encouraged to bathe far from her territory. Any dainty sip of spoiled water in Selina's mouth would mean severe consequences. There were stories of lives stolen, dead bodies floating down the river like leaves, veins popping out of their skin.

"Yeah–yeah!" Munya scoffed. "Too many rules for one place. If you don't want to have a bubble bath with me, you are free to go. Anyway, you and Abigail have only been here for a few days, so I wouldn't expect much from you."

Abigail and Chenai left, shaking their heads in disbelief, walking away into the valley of trees and grass. In the distance, birds chattered, and children could be heard crying from their houses. Nyeredzi wanted to go too, but she had to make sure Munya would get out of the pool safe and sound. She and Mazvita stood at a distance, both worried.

Munya held the body wash upside down and began pouring it in the pool. Bubbles formed, circulating the pool before flowing down the river. When the bottle was half empty, Munya placed it aside and jumped into the curvy pool. He began to swim slowly in circles and then increased his speed. Nyeredzi and Mazvita stood a meter away, watching him perform all kinds of somersaults as he circled along the edges of the pool. His feet flapped like a dolphin's tail, putting to use all he'd learned at his expensive school.

"Why won't you come in?" he asked them.

"We can't do what you are doing in there," Mazvita said. "You know the rules."

"Well, your loss. Throw me the bottle—I might as well finish the body wash. I need more bubbles in here. They are all flowing down the river."

"It's a river, not a tub," Nyeredzi shouted. "I am not handing you the bottle. Mama will be mad at me."

"I can't believe people of Goho have spent all these years without even trying to do this. This is amazing. Hoo!" Munya reached for the bottle at the edge of the pool and poured the rest of the body wash into the water. He then swam back to the middle of the pool. "And that Selina you always talk about, she doesn't exis—"

In an instant Munya's body was submerged, the force of the water tumbling him. Nyeredzi and Mazvita ran around the pool, calling his name and hoping they could grab Munya and pull him out. Fear rushed through the streams of Nyeredzi's blood, goosebumps rose on her skin, and the hair that was glistening in sweat before all stood at attention. The bubbles floating in the pool made it impossible to see Munya.

When the girls realized that Munya was really swallowed deep into the bowels of the Earth, Nyeredzi sent Mazvita back home to call the elders. She waited by the pool. Perhaps Munya would rise again. It was evident Selina was angry.

Nyeredzi pushed the foam away with her hand so she could see, the water became clear for a second and a ripple parted a bubbling circle that was in the center of the pool. If it was a message, she didn't think it was wise to dip her hand inside the water again. So, she stood there, next to Selina's dwelling, hoping for a miracle, for Munya to show his face again. She hated herself for not listening to her mother and staying away.

Soon, the elders arrived. Nyeredzi stepped away to give them room to see but she was still in shock. She didn't know whether to apologize or do something else that would ease her guilty conscience.

The elders looked horrified, but Nyeredzi was sure they would be able to do something. Emmanuel, Maudie's oldest child, had taken diving lessons. He ran to the edge of the pool and said he could make out a blurry object that looked like a body deep underwater.

"He could be caught with roots or under a rock," Emmanuel said.

"I can get him out," Maudie responded, taking her shoes off so she could dive in.

"No, I'll go." Emmanuel dived in. Everyone else knelt beside the pool, calling out to Munya. Within a few seconds, Emmanuel emerged from underneath the pool and shook his head. "That's not Munya. I can't find him," he said, his voice thick with worry.

He dove down again, and this time he took longer. Everyone was now only waiting for him. Maudie was trembling, Nyeredzi realized, and her uncle Garikai seemed lost. The ferocity he'd shown the past few days wasn't there anymore. Maudie climbed to the edge of the pool so she could dive in, but Garikai stopped her. It wasn't the time to show who could swim or not, this was serious. There was a protocol to follow, and they didn't have much time; the boys had been gone for too long.

"What should we do now?" she screamed at Garikai. "I want my sons back!"

"We have to make an offering," Garikai said, shivering.

Maudie lay by the edge of the pool. "I beg you, Selina, please return my sons," she begged. "I'll give you all I have, please."

The commotion had drawn more of the villagers, and everyone seemed to feel for Maudie. To have a person, a child be taken—that hadn't happened in years. The fear of the unknown, the creature that lived under the water, terrified them to their bone marrow. Garikai stood there frozen, as though he'd forgotten the correct procedures. Finally, one of the village men asked if he could bring the offering to Selina, and Garikai nodded.

Garikai crouched down, clapping his hands, and looked up into the heavens. "To the Kings of this region, I ask from the core of my heart for you to rise from where you lie right now. Your blood has been pulled from the soil you have stepped on. Haah! I am stranded. Come and help me with this battle, the Kings of this world, whose spirits linger in the air." He paused, clapping his hands three times, and let out a long sigh.

Nyeredzi wondered if something would happen. When the offering was brought to the river, the bubbles were still visible, the water was disturbed and murky. Maudie was still lying by the poolside, wailing, begging Mother Earth to hear her.

"Selina, I apologize for saying nasty things about your mother and for not believing that you exist," Maudie cried. "All I want are my sons back and alive. I beg you, Selina!"

Nyeredzi overheard an old woman ask where Zuva and Mwedzi were. No one could tell her, so Nyeredzi whispered in her ear that her parents were working on the mountain, pulling weeds by her grandparents' graves. The woman ran off to fetch them, and Garikai made another speech. This time he offered Selina a woven tray, holding the flame lilies that Heroshina loved, a cup full of diamonds, two blocks of gold, five native fruits, and one bluestone. His hands trembled as he mumbled.

One of the mediums took the tray from him and slid it onto the water. They waited for Selina to swallow the offering. The skies had turned dark gray. A sandstorm spiraled toward them and blinded them. While they were trying to regain their vision, Selina returned the offering. When the dust cleared and everyone could see again, the offering was scattered on the ground—and all over Maudie.

Garikai collapsed. Nyeredzi didn't need one of the elders to explain what it meant. It had been rejected, but she didn't know the full story. That her uncle had snatched this position from Zuva, and just wanted to be a chief surrounded by people who knelt before him and brought him presents while he wore robes accessorized with gold and diamonds. He took his duties too lightly and left everything in the hands of village men whom he paid with his father's gold.

The wind howled amongst the trees and blew soil from the ground, slapping those gathered by the water. It blew dead leaves into the river and as the sky grew more oppressive, the clouds started spitting on them. In a deafening roar, the veils washed away the bubbles of cherry blossom body wash. Everyone was cold and nobody knew what to do except beg for Selina's mercy.

Zuva and Mwedzi arrived with the old woman, Mrs. Kaundi.

"How long have they been under the water?" Zuva asked, looking at Nyeredzi.

"Too long, Mama. I am so sorry," she said, shivering. "I tried to help him, we all tried to stop him, but he didn't listen."

Zuva touched Nyeredzi's shoulder before walking to the pool. Everyone was watching. Some people seemed shocked that Zuva had asked a young child instead of the elders. Even when she stepped close to the pool and dipped her hand in the water, they looked skeptical. How could she come and disrespect her brother by dipping her hand in the water when that was only done by the chief? But how could Garikai have known the procedure when he wasn't trained for it? This position he had snatched from Zuva wasn't easy.

"I demand you to come out, Selina," Zuva said, her voice thick. "For these people's sakes, so that tomorrow no one will disrespect you."

People raised their eyebrows, looking at each other, but a voice echoed from the dark cave, Selina's voice. Zuva knew what would happen would shock everyone, but when she glimpsed at Nyeredzi, she saw terror in her eyes.

"Ever since I was conceived, you all know what I do not like. Why would any of you disrespect me? Those who wrong me shall be punished."

People waited, no one daring to speak, but Selina must have dived into the pool from her cave, because there, in the middle of the water, a svelte creature emerged. Long red motsi swayed like kelp behind her. Perhaps that was why Heroshina liked the flame lilies so much. A large gold pendant hung loose around her brown neck. Everything else was flawless silver: it sparkled on her wrists, fingers, nails, and shimmered from her tail under the water.

Her movement lured everyone closer to the pool. They all gazed in awe. No one in the village had ever seen Selina before. But then, her long arms pushed Munya's body toward the surface and everyone watching gasped in horror. His lifeless body floated in the pool. Selina looked straight at Zuva, and blew air onto the water's surface.

"I have so much respect for you, Mambokadzi," Selina said. "You've always protected me and my dwelling even though you were far away. I hear your prayers all the time. You begged the ancestors of this land to look after the villagers and me. In my heart, you never left."

Everyone around them stood with their mouths opened in shock. What they didn't know had come to light.

"It is my duty to protect every creature and this land that my father and mother left in my hands," Zuva said.

"It's a shame it was your nephews today," Selina told her. "I don't want to make you unhappy but at the same time, I can't let people disrespect me."

"Forgive them."

"This is not the first time I've heard that word from you. It makes me feel bad whenever you ask me to do that, Mambokadzi." Selina lowered her head.

If Selina could bow down to Zuva like that, why did her own siblings disrespect her? Why did the villagers treat her as if she was not enough when she came back from war? They had shamed and betrayed her before their own ancestors.

"Begging is not something one should be ashamed of and—"

"I'm so sorry for everything," Maudie said, looking at Selina, "but please let me have my sons?"

"How dare you interrupt Mambokadzi when she is speaking?" Selina shouted. "Wasn't stealing her husband enough?"

People gasped in shock.

"I have moved on from all that," Zuva said. "You shall not bring it up again."

"I apologize, Mambokadzi," Selina continued as she scowled at Maudie. "Between you and Garikai, you took your father's stones that belong to Mambokadzi and used them for selfish reasons. Give them back to Mambokadzi or I'll destroy all of you."

When Garikai heard this, he threw himself before Zuva. She looked away, but when Mwedzi knelt before Zuva too, and said, "Mambokadzi," the rest of the people there threw themselves on the ground as well. Nyeredzi stood with mouth agape, watching Selina inside the pool. Zuva glanced at Nyeredzi, looking surprised, but Mrs. Kaundi pulled her down.

Selina dipped her red head into the water and when she came out again, her hair was parted in the middle. Zuva opened her mouth. When she was trained by her parents to become the queen, she was told that only one who could communicate with the ancestors would part Selina's hair. So, among these people surrounding her, one of them was her link to the ancestors.

"The peace you bring is the one that dwells in your

blood, the one of generations to come," Selina said. "I felt it from a smaller hand, and it stopped me from doing more harm."

Zuva understood Selina's language. She dipped her hand in the water again and whispered, "Peace!"

Selina bowed her head and closed her eyes. It wasn't only peace Zuva brought to all creatures, it was also a deep understanding her siblings lacked: forgiveness, love, courage, and so many other things. Had all this not made Selina show herself for the first time?

"Your voice brings peace to my soul," Selina said, "and your hand brings warmth to my home. Something I haven't felt in such a long time. I am grateful for that. I will give Emmanuel back, but Munya will stay and shall become the protector of this place."

"Selina," Zuva asked, "how can Munya become the protector of your place when you have killed him?"

"He is not dead. His body is getting ready to transform. I had to let you see him for the last time. For you to say the last words before he entered his new kingdom."

"What about his mother?" Maudie was still lying on the ground, sobbing.

"A punishment must be given if one has broken so many rules." Selina looked down the valley. Emmanuel's body lay on the riverbank. "I will not keep the reminder of a bad deed. It shall make the mother know what she's done will never be erased. I could have killed him, but I saved him because I can't take much from you."

Some people ran down the river toward Emmanuel, but Zuva remained in front of the pool. "Give my brother another chance to make amends with my parents," she said. "My role will remain the same. I will be ruling from where I now live, but Garikai will do the right thing by looking after the village, and its people."

"Whatever you wish, Mambokadzi. We are only creatures that bow to you."

"And you won't take any more lives."

"As I have said," Selina said, bowing her head, "we live under your rules, Mambokadzi."

Maudie crawled toward Zuva, as though she was no longer able to stand. "What about Munya?" she asked. "I want my son back. Please ask her to give Munya back?"

Zuva knelt next to Maudie and looked deep in her eyes. "She could've taken both of them. We can't choose right now, so let's accept things as they are." Maudie wept as Zuva wrapped her arms around her. "I am sorry, my sister," she said. This was the first time in years that Zuva had come close to Maudie or called her sister.

How could she not? If she'd not forgiven her sister and brother, Selina would've struck them, and death would fall upon them. Zuva rose and readied herself. Selina blew air on the water's surface again and it rippled, turning Munya's body to face Zuva who mumbled words that no one else could make out. Everyone looked at Munya, who was now blinking with twinkling brown eyes dappled with golden spots. Shirtless, his lower body had changed, and his bronze tail flapped within the water, glowing. His body now resembled that of Selina's.

Selina's own sparkling body had dissolved into the water, leaving a steady, swirling motion. Maudie stretched out her hand toward her son, who was swimming in circles, going deeper. Zuva stopped her sister because she understood what it meant. Munya would remain here, in Selina's realm, forever.

DÉJÀ VU

Midsummer 1994
ZUVA

Zuva rolled down her window and the breeze hit her straight in the face. She wanted to breathe in the fresh, clean air that was free of industrial gases. It felt euphoric to watch the world pass by. The huge mountains in the distance appeared bluish and shadowy. They passed farms where people bent down weeding amidst the long rows of maize and wheat. The granite rocks circled with lush green trees was a sign that things were going to be okay, that life would keep flourishing.

In 1970, Zuva had left with a black ball sitting in the core of her heart. This time her shoulders were light. She now left knowing Togara's and Nyikadzino's prayer was done, and she was endowed with peace because her parents' souls were at rest. Zuva had promised the villagers that she would be coming back to check on them, but Garikai was going to look after the village.

She had placed the clay pots of minerals one by one on the shelves of her father's chamber. It was peaceful to put them back where they belonged, even though Garikai and Maudie had sold some so they could live a luxurious life. It was also peaceful to see her father's chamber painted in

NDIMA NDIMA

fresh white paint after she and Mwedzi fixed it up.

Zuva had returned to the mountain to say her final words to her parents, but this time Mwedzi stood before Togara and Nyikadzino's graves with their daughters. The last time he stood there with his bags, he was a stranger. Back then, when they were young, Zuva had asked herself why Mwedzi was there, but she learned he had lost all his family in the war.

When Mwedzi was speeding, overtaking the Marcopolo buses and other private cars, Zuva tapped on his left thigh so he would slow down. She pretended to fall asleep while her daughters talked about village life and what had happened to Munya, their cousin. Could she have done more than she did to save her nephew? Could she have asked Selina to take her instead? Deep down, Zuva knew she'd done all she could, but she kept thinking about Maudie, and her sister's long walk back home with two children instead of three.

"My love, we are in Marondera now," Mwedzi said, touching Zuva's shoulder.

Zuva opened her eyes. "Already?" she said, turning to face Mwedzi. They must've been driving for two hours. "I'd like to revisit some of the places we remember."

A couple hundred meters away from the city center, Mwedzi pulled over exactly where the Nyamwenda bus was raided by the Rhodesian soldiers in the Second Chimurenga War. The land on their left was now fenced, and zebras were grazing on the green grass. A few buildings in the distance looked as though they were a lodge or private property. Ruth and Hannah stood by the fence watching the zebras. Abigail and Nyeredzi were busy pulling daisies that grew on the sides of the tarred road.

Here was the exact place where the Rhodesian soldiers

harassed everyone and told them to get off the bus. On the opposite side of the road, another bus was already stopped, some people were pushed on the ground, and those who traveled alone were considered spies. Zuva couldn't help but watch a woman being forced to drink 750 mls of cooking oil.

"Well, it's either you drink the oil, or we take you aside, your choice." The soldier's voice sounded as if his nose was pinched.

Zuva didn't like the language the soldiers used, and whenever they said, "we are taking you aside," it meant torture, but for a woman, it was mostly one thing, so the woman began to drink the oil.

"Who did you buy the cooking oil for?" the soldier asked.

"My family," the woman responded.

"Liar! You're planning to cook for the terrorists, hey?"

Everything was happening fast, and on their side, Zuva was astonished to see Mwedzi stepping in front of her, shielding her from the soldiers, though they hadn't spoken on the bus.

A dark–skinned soldier stepped in front of Mwedzi and asked, "And you two, what is this?"

"My wife," Mwedzi said.

Zuva was taken aback, but she tried not to show it on her face. She stood behind Mwedzi quietly. She could have gone back to war. After all, there was nothing left for her in Goho. If she wanted to take the easy way out, she could've disclosed to the soldiers before her that she was a comrade, and they would have killed her with one bullet—but Togara had asked her not to go back to war, to live longer, and she'd made a promise to her father before he died that she would not.

　　　　　　　　NDIMA NDIMA

One of the passengers shouted, "He's lying, they weren't sitting next to each other."

Mwedzi thought quickly, raising his hands in the air. "Am I not allowed to give my wife time to grieve for the parents she just lost?" he asked, staring at the passenger.

Mwedzi was standing the way he had the day he almost got shot, the day he fought six comrades and urinated on them. When Zuva rescued him from death, she told the comrades to let him go. At that time, Zuva was a comrade too, and she didn't know she was saving the love of her life. She raised her hand and touched Mwedzi's shoulder, calming him down.

"When did you get married?" the soldier asked, smiling.

"Recently, customary," Mwedzi answered. "We will wed when things get better."

"Where are you going? Shouldn't you two be in bed?" The soldiers laughed. Zuva's eyes caught those of a light-skinned soldier blowing smoke from his mouth by the bus, smiling.

"This is our destination, Marandellas," Mwedzi said.

"Well, if this is your destination, you better get going then. I am in a better mood today, so leave." The dark-skinned soldier gestured for them to go.

Zuva and Mwedzi left the rest of the passengers still sitting on the bare ground. She didn't look back. It was as though she had become someone who walked away from everything she believed in. Back in Goho Village, she'd left her father's kingdom in her brother's hands. Her sister's claws were now dug into Zuva's fiancé. She had to bury the urge to keep fighting for her people's freedom in the war somewhere in the back of her brain. Yet here she found herself walking with a stranger whom her mother had blessed to become her husband. At that time, she didn't care about the future nor what would happen to her.

Now her memories were disturbed by Nyeredzi, who tapped on her elbow.

"Mama, why are we stopping here?" Nyeredzi asked.

"We are just taking a rest. Would you like for us to drive through our old street?"

"Yes. I want to see my old friends, Cleo and Tariro."

Mwedzi walked around the car, checking the tires, before they set off again. As they drove, he pointed to all the houses he'd built for people in Dombo Tombo suburb. Opposite Proton Bakers was Marondera Country Club. A few white men pulled their golf cart bags across the rolling green golf course and disappeared behind the trees.

Mwedzi turned left toward Marondera City Center. On the left was a TM Supermarket, and the fruit and vegetable market, which was noisy and crowded. Large glass buildings sandwiched the black tarred roads. Some people bustled in and out of the shops, offices, and banks. Others sat around tables at outdoor restaurants and cafes. Buses and trucks waiting in a queue for petrol and diesel kept roaring while they crept toward the service station.

Zuva raised her hand, directing Mwedzi which road to take. He passed by the service station and then turned down a road that led them to the park. He slowed down by the hardware building, where their oldest daughter, Ruth, was shot in the war. He reached out and placed his palm on Zuva's leg and she put her hand on top of his, her eyes glistening. Everything was still vivid in her mind: the blood droplets on the pavement, on Zuva's dress, Ruth's unstoppable screaming, the marathon with her daughter on her back to the hospital amidst all the gunshots.

When Mwedzi turned onto the street where they used

to live, Zuva gasped for air and the girls looked through the windows at their old neighbors' houses. The wheels of the Peugeot car kept rolling on the tarred road, lined with plastered and painted houses that had large yards, fenced with Durawall or overgrown hedges. The telephone poles and streetlights along the road were like ghosts holding hands. Nothing much had changed since they moved to Harare.

Zuva saw Mr. Davidson watering his flower beds, his light–skinned face and forearms spotted with freckles. He was the one who sold them a house he owned on the same street. Instead of money, she handed him a piece of gold Nyikadzino had given her when she turned twenty–one. At the bank, Mr. Davidson was told that the gold was worth more than he was asking for. He returned some of the money to Zuva, and later she used this to buy extra furniture for their house.

The deeds were given to Zuva, and the deal was done. At that time, she wasn't planning to marry Mwedzi, but somehow, she had included his name in the deed. She didn't even know the reason why. She had told him to stay in the cottage at the back of the main house. Perhaps it was a sense of wanting to have company but not ac-knowledging that she needed it from him. They'd met Mr. Davidson after they were released by the soldiers. They saw him packing cement and buckets of paint in his truck by the hardware shop. Zuva was left in awe when Mwedzi approached Mr. Davidson and said, "I am a builder. I can help you build your house if you want?"

Zuva wondered if Mwedzi was someone who said things without thinking. The way he'd done before, claim-ing that she was his wife. Even if it had saved them, she didn't like the idea of being owned when they barely knew each other.

"Well, I am not a builder," Mr. Davidson said. "But I certainly am looking for someone to build a cottage at the back of my house. Where do you live?"

"We only just arrived," Mwedzi said.

"Are you two married?"

Zuva spoke quickly, "If you know anyone selling a house nearby, we could stay here, and you're guaranteed Mwedzi will build your cottage."

It was a done deal.

They passed Mrs. Kau, the gossiper of the street, walking her dog as usual. The bulldog waddled from side to side with its thick legs and a round stomach, too big for its body, and stopped after every few steps. Zuva recalled the day she was walking with Nyeredzi back from the supermarket, and Mrs. Kau greeted her.

"I see that you've been associating with Mrs. Brayton?" she'd said, pointing at the house next to Zuva's. "I saw you the other day handing her a basket of vegetables from your garden."

"What's wrong with sharing with my neighbor?" Zuva knew where their conversation was heading.

"Have you forgotten not long ago, we were in a war because these people took our land?"

"Didn't we all just celebrate our independence a decade ago?"

"You mean after blood was shed?" She frowned at Zuva. "Aah! On top of that, you are growing vegetables for them?"

Zuva stepped closer to her. "Doesn't your husband work with Mr. Davidson at his farm?"

She clicked her tongue. "Mr. Davidson only gives my husband peanuts."

"Peanuts enough to buy food for your dog, huh?" Zuva asked, looking at the fat bulldog that was now sleeping on someone's green lawn.

"You know you sound like those stupid kings who signed our land away."

"Yes, I suppose so." Zuva smiled, taken aback. As though something in that sentence had some truth in it. As though Mrs. Kau could see through her, see what lived inside her left rib and what flowed in her veins. Wasn't she a Mambokadzi herself?

Mwedzi came to a stop outside their old house. The girls got out and ran to peer through the black wrought–iron gate. They all held onto the bars, gazing at the long rectangular yellow house. Zuva told them to give the new owners privacy, although she stood next to Mwedzi, staring at the house for quite a long time.

Nyeredzi then ran next door, opened the gate, and stepped into Mrs. Brayton's yard. Soon, there were screams of joy. Nyeredzi and Cleo were hugging each other, loud with excitement. Mrs. Brayton came out and welcomed Zuva's family. She made them afternoon tea while all the girls sat outside, talking about what they had been up to. Tariro had joined them as well.

After they had tea, Mwedzi went out to get some supplies for the rest of the trip. Zuva got up from the brown suede sofa and walked over to look at photos displayed on the wall. One was a black–and–white photo of Zuva clasping Mwedzi's hand. She was in a white wedding gown, revealing the necklace she was given by her parents. A diamond crown, which seemed to be sparkling in the photo, sat above the white patch on her head. Underneath her long gown, she had her black combat leather boots she used in the war. She'd refused to wear the white high–

heeled stilettos.

Next to her, Mwedzi was in black except for the white shirt and a bowtie. His tailcoat had silver buttons that appeared white on the photo. The long trousers sat on his ankle boots. They both were half–smiling, but their eyes reflected sorrow buried deep in their skulls. Mrs. Brayton and Zuva's relatives were on either side of Zuva and Mwedzi. Zuva had ended up falling in love with Mwedzi after all.

"I had so much fun that day," Mrs. Brayton said, walking over to stand next to Zuva, "even though we were still in the war."

"I couldn't have done it without my best friend." Zuva touched Mrs. Brayton's hand. Wasn't Mrs. Brayton more than a friend? She was a surgeon who saved Ruth's foot in war, although she couldn't do more about the hollowed scar.

They sat down again and talked for a long time. Zuva wanted to stay longer, but the clock was ticking. They had another long journey ahead of them.

On the way to the highway, while the traffic lights were red, Mwedzi opened the dashboard to pass the girls the food he'd bought. He handed Zuva a warm lamb pie, like the ones he used to buy her when they first started living in Marondera. Zuva chewed on the warm pie, her mind thick with memories.

Once again, she was leaving the city in which she bore all her daughters, the place she fell in love with Mwedzi. Zuva went quiet, drawn back to the time she married him. After one and a half years living with him, he wasn't a stranger anymore, even if half of that time she didn't speak much to him. He stayed in the cottage, and she lived in the main house. But Zuva watched him from afar, questioning why her mother blessed him as his son–in–law. What had she seen in him?

Day by day, she grew closer to Mwedzi. Gradually, the energy she felt whenever Mwedzi stood next to her became too intense. He was selfless and he helped her without being asked to. He even nursed her when she fell ill from an infection that had developed from the scar on her stomach. Every day he came into the main house with a tub half–filled with warm water. He would open the dark green curtains to let the light in and asked Zuva if she'd slept well.

When he used a warm towel to gently wipe around her belly, their eyes would lock, making it difficult for them to think straight. And when his fingers ran across her skin applying the medicine, the tingling couldn't stop.

"I'm much better now," she would say to stop him, to stop herself from the temptation that sat next to her, even if she was still in pain. Though she was in and out of consciousness the second day she fell ill, she still heard him say, "If you could love me, I promise to love you forever."

And when she was better, she sat outside on the veranda to get some fresh air. Mwedzi came to check on her and brought food he made in his cottage. He placed a cup filled with hot tea and a plate with two sandwiches next to Zuva.

"Do you promise to love me forever?" she asked, looking straight in his eyes.

"You heard me?" Mwedzi asked in return.

"Yes. I wasn't dead."

"I came to look for you because I fell in love with you the first time I saw you."

"What do you mean? You didn't know me."

"Do you need to know someone first so you can fall in love with them?"

"I don't know. What do I know? I was engaged to Fredrick, and he cheated on me with my sister, so I don't know anything about love."

"Sometimes it's not about knowing what love is. It's how you feel about someone."

Mwedzi crouched in front of her with his legs wide open. She was sitting with her legs crossed, a padlock that was never opened. He reached out to touch her hand, but Zuva pulled it from him. The temptation was too strong.

"I know you are a woman of action, and you don't like to talk much, but tell me." He paused, looking in her eyes. "Have I won your heart?"

She was silent for a while, struggling to admit her feelings. "You should take my lobola to Garikai and my uncles."

He tilted his head, looking at the ground. When he lifted his face to Zuva, his eyes were glistening with tears. He reached out to touch Zuva again; this time she didn't pull her hand away. "Yes, my love, I've heard you."

At that time, asking Mwedzi to go back to Mutare and sort her lobola wasn't meant to measure the perimeter of his love, but Zuva was a woman who stuck to her values. She wanted everything to be done according to their culture.

The next day, Zuva was astonished to see Mwedzi with a satchel on his back. She was sitting by the veranda enjoying the sun, a yellow shawl around her shoulders. He crouched in front of her, and said he was heading back to Goho Village.

"Do you have enough wealth?" Zuva asked.

"Yes, I do." He looked hard at Zuva's face. "Look after yourself, and make sure you eat."

She pulled her shawl off and handed it to Mwedzi.

"Take this, and make sure you bring it back."

"My ancestors have led me to you, so I will not die anytime soon."

"I know." She paused. "It shall bring you comfort when you feel alone."

"I am not alone anymore," he said, leaning forward to clasp Zuva's hand.

"If you take it, at least I will know you are coming back."

"I am coming back, my love."

Mwedzi put the shawl in his satchel and set off with a smile on his face. Zuva was scared that he might not make it back. With all those bullets still flying, not to mention his temper when he came across soldiers, he might get killed. Sitting in front of that big house alone, she missed him and yearned for his touch. The irresistible touch that wove a strong connection between them. *Mwedzi will come back*, she told herself. As he said, his ancestors had led him to her.

FULFILLED

Winter 1994
ZUVA

Mwedzi had finally finished their main house. It took him four years because his clients didn't always pay him in time, and when this was happening, Zuva offered to assist Mwedzi but he refused. The house they lived in before in Marondera—it was Zuva who used her gold to buy it.

Now, Mwedzi wanted to do it on his own, and when his clients paid him, he used all the money to buy the building materials that were needed to finish off their house.

They both stared at the large L–shaped plastered house. The gray asbestos lay in lines accordingly on the asymmetric roof.

"Why L?" Zuva asked.

"Love!" Mwedzi answered.

"Yours or mine?"

"Mine, my love to you," Mwedzi said with a smile on his face.

Years earlier, when Zuva married Mwedzi, she'd asked him to build her a home she would never leave. A home where she would raise their children and grandchildren. Mwedzi said yes. He had built a lot of houses for other people, why wouldn't he do that for the love of his life?

"I suppose it took you this long to show me your love."

"I know." He took Zuva's hand. "So, what color?"

"White."

"Why white?"

"I guess it represents your pure love," Zuva said and walked onto the green patch of lawn. Soon, she was running her hand along the dusty black windowsills, appreciating the hard work done by her husband. Below the sills was gray splash coarse–textured cement. Zuva touched the wall, and it was as if she was back in Mutare, feeling the rough surface of the mountains. She wondered how Mwedzi could have known what her heart desired. He stood watching every move she made.

"What do you think?" he asked.

"I love it," she said in a soft voice.

Some of the windows were half–opened, revealing the burglar bars welded to the frames. The black–bricked wide pillar of the chimney popping out of the wall stood tall between the two windows of the lounge. Smoke was swirling at the top of the fireplace and it reminded Zuva of the mountains on a foggy morning in Manicaland. She wasn't going to miss Mutare that much. Her yard was now circled with mature fruit trees.

At the back, the bush was still there, beckoning to her with its trees and rocks. She had even dragged one of the fine granite rocks from the bush to place under her peach tree. It was different from the rest she saw. It was cream, spotted with black. The tiny holes collected water when it rained, and sometimes she would watch birds drinking water from them. Most visitors who came to her place sat on it before they were asked to come in. Sometimes she used the rock when she sharpened her hoes by beating them with a hammer.

In spring this was where she sat, in the shade, with pink flowers or raw peaches weighing the thin branches down. The coolness of the rock made her feel as if she were stepping onto the boulders of Yeredzo River where she bathed when she was young. This was the home she and her husband made. No one was going to snatch it away from her.

By the veranda she waited for Mwedzi, looking at the three–roomed cottage they used when they first moved here to Harare. The cottage was sheltered under the broad branches of the water berry tree and surrounded by garden beds of Covo, and a patch of sweet potato she kept for transplanting in spring. A chicken coop stood against one wall. Some of the hens sat on their eggs while others were feeding on the maize seeds.

The veranda was dusty, so she brushed off her canvas shoes on the mat by the French doors. Mwedzi came around the corner and stopped to brush off excess dried cement on one of the veranda pillars.

Inside, three of their daughters were sitting on the sofa, and Ruth was preparing tea for everyone. Zuva stopped in the middle of the large lounge, admiring the cylindrical crisscrossed pine beams on the roof. She had told Mwedzi not to cover them with a ceiling. She loved the scent they released: organic. Her husband had brought the outside in. Love of nature was what led her to spend hours digging in the fields. Now, she could smell the earthiness from the freshly plastered walls.

Behind her the dining room had two glass–front cabinet displays which stood against one wall. They were filled with chinaware and a few decorative wooden utensils, a carved family of elephants on top. A large painting of the Mosi oa Tunya, Victoria Falls, was hung on one wall. At the center of the long, wooden dining table sat a large vase with peace lilies, positioned on a golden mat. Two palm trees stood either side of the window with its zebra–print curtains.

The photos of her ancestors floated against the walls, crafted by her husband's rough hands. They watched the weight of her daughters' bodies on the sagging vintage sofas drawn close to the fireplace, where the flames and smoke fought to escape through the long zigzag flue.

When Ruth finished making her mother a hot drink, she pulled the coffee table with legs of lion paws, a totem of Zuva's, across the cold shiny floors. Zuva's tongue craved the sweet Tanganda tea Ruth was stirring with a silver teaspoon. The silhouettes of the giraffe sculptures stretched over the bookshelf, the TV cabinet, and the zebra–print curtains sweeping the floors. A large, carved clock hung just above the fireplace.

Mwedzi came in for his tea, and Zuva told the girls to pick their bedrooms. Nyeredzi and Abigail ran to the corridor as though there weren't enough bedrooms to go around. Abigail was first to pick the room next to the kitchen and the master bedroom. Nyeredzi chose the room across from the kitchen, right next to the dining room.

"This is mine and mine only," Nyeredzi shouted to her sisters.

"Who cares?" Abigail asked, mockingly. "I've got mine too."

Hannah went back to the old bedroom she had once shared with Abigail and Nyeredzi before the house was finished. There had been so many fights amongst the girls in there but now Zuva hoped there would be no more arguments in future. Ruth chose the old room her parents once used as a bedroom, opposite the bathroom. There was only one room left, the one that used to serve as their kitchen/dining/lounge room.

Zuva looked at Mwedzi. "I suppose that will be the guest room?"

"I suppose so," he said, holding the back of Zuva's waist. "So, what color for the inside walls?"

"Light green. You must look at your house as ever–growing nature or wealth."

"Mmm!" Mwedzi nodded. "Wealthy color it is then."

Zuva sipped tea from her cup: its sweetness was the icing on the cake. She stood next to her husband, embracing each moment as it came. Her wish was finally fulfilled. This time, she wasn't going to leave. She was going to live here no matter what happened in the future. She could feel her roots already spreading underneath the red soil.

VOODOO CHICKEN

Spring 1995
NYEREDZI

Nyeredzi's days of fighting with Abigail were over. For her plan to work, she had to stay on Abigail's good side, especially now that Ruth—her favorite sister—had moved out and into her own home with her husband.

Mealtimes had taught these sisters to be kind to one another. Since they moved to Harare, it was no longer just their own family sitting around the dinner table. Sometimes they had guests who came for different reasons. Nyeredzi didn't always mind having people visit their house. Usually, it made Zuva dig deeper in her wallet and give Nyeredzi five-dollar notes to go and buy ice cream at the mini–shop for dessert or a liter bottle of Coca–Cola. The spare change was always hers to use.

If Zuva didn't have the money, the girls would make tea. But everything changed when Timothy and his wife arrived from the Chipinge countryside, where he'd grown up with Mwedzi. Timothy wasn't family, but Mwedzi allowed him to stay in the cottage for free. Nyeredzi wasn't happy about that. She'd planned to move into the cottage and call it the girls' domain.

For the first two weeks, Timothy stayed with his

pregnant wife, Thoko. She was due in a few weeks, and they had moved to Harare for Timothy to look for a job. Thoko didn't speak much Shona but she felt at home when Mwedzi and Zuva accommodated her by speaking in Ndebele. Thoko soon went to Bulawayo to be with her family for the birth of their baby, but Timothy stayed behind and continued living in the cottage.

Regardless of the weather, Timothy had developed the habit of coming to the main house every evening. He would knock on their French doors, wearing his orange–and–black striped sweatshirt, black trousers, and black sandals.

At first, Nyeredzi didn't mind, but his constant self-invitation to dinner was driving her insane. She didn't want to be his servant or chef whenever his tummy needed filling. She also didn't want to hand him what they were meant to eat for dinner. At times like this, Zuva always said, "Sharing is love," as though Nyeredzi and her sisters didn't do that at all. Nyeredzi had always had to share, ever since she was born; being the youngest child wasn't easy.

When her sisters refused to give some of their new blankets and sheets to Timothy and Thoko, Nyeredzi ended up doing it. How could she not, with Zuva's eyes watching her? Those eyes made her say yes even when she didn't want to. But there would be severe consequences with this extra love she was obliged to give. Timothy never showered and Nyeredzi was pretty sure that when she finally got her blankets back, they would stink. They might even be ripped because he didn't cut his toenails or fingernails. He'd let the dirt build up underneath. Nyeredzi noticed this each time she knelt on the shined floor in the lounge room, holding a jar to pour water onto his grubby hands.

Everyone else had deserted the dining room because of the stench from Timothy. No one wanted to sit next to him. Mwedzi sat with him in the lounge, and sometimes Zuva if she was not too tired. Whatever water Timothy used turned the color of black tea. Nyeredzi had no idea what Timothy touched to make his hands so dirty, except for the old Coca–Cola bottle caps when he played checkers with the other loafers outside the mini shop. He never looked for a job, which was the reason he came to Harare in the first place. But Nyeredzi had heard Timothy saying he didn't need a job: he got everything for free.

Nyeredzi always knew he had arrived at the house because Timothy was a loud talker. Once Zuva heard him talking, her demeanor changed. She would add another plate to the counter, a sign that Abigail and Nyeredzi's night had turned upside down. Darker. Starless. Moonless. A dense, gray cloud hanging over them.

All their effort to make dinner, which often took most of the afternoon, went down the hole and into his throat. They would spend a lot of time trying to catch a hen in the garden. The chickens would run and hide under the coop or jump up on the roof to the rotten branch of the peach tree in front of the veranda. Sometimes they landed on Nyeredzi's shoulder before flapping their wings, attempting to fly away.

If the chickens ran toward the bush, the girls chased them, which always took more time than they expected. The chickens sensed death, but one was always unlucky, no matter how hard it tried to set itself free by using its beak and claws on their skin: either Abigail or Nyeredzi would step hard on the hen's wings with their foot. All it took was a clutch at the head and a slit of the neck with a knife. Blood would run like a river onto the soil, its body pulsating for a few final movements. Hot water in a tub would burn the girls' fingers while they plucked the feathers off and later, Zuva would cut the chicken in pieces, rub on herbs, and butter, and toss it in the oven.

After an hour, the chicken was done; sadza, Covo, and soup were all ready. Zuva would look at Abigail and Nyeredzi and say, "Sorry, girls."

Then she'd scoop up the golden–brown pieces they were meant to have and put them in a dish for Timothy and Mwedzi to serve themselves. Since Nyeredzi was the youngest, Zuva bribed her with a chicken head still attached to the neck.

"Nyeredzi, do you want this? Eat the brain. It will make you smarter."

She would place it on her plate before Nyeredzi even said no, its eyes staring at her. Its beak was either shut or gaping, and there was no meat to eat. It was as if she was being asked to fast that night. Zuva would give Abigail the thin legs. Hannah was lucky: she would get a wing. Drumsticks, thighs, and breasts went to Mwedzi and Timothy. Of course, Mwedzi deserved to eat the big, delicious parts of the chicken, but so did the girls.

It was hard to get Zuva out of the kitchen, especially the days she came back from the field so tired. She would sometimes sit on the bench next to a rutsero filled with vegetables from the field. When this happened, Nyeredzi asked Abigail why their mother couldn't put the meatless, skinny pieces on Timothy's plate? This constant need to please visitors like Timothy had gone on too long. The girls were tired of sucking the juice from chicken bones.

Nyeredzi came up with a plan. Something that would save them from malnutrition caused by Timothy. Abigail's bedroom was right next to the kitchen, but it was a long way to the lounge. The girls had to put an empty container by the dresser in Abigail's bedroom. Whoever Zuva handed the meat dish to had to make a turn into Abigail's bedroom, open the dish quickly, and chuck some pieces into the container before Zuva noticed. The other one was supposed to distract their mother.

The first time they tried out their plan, it was a success. Abigail managed to take out a drumstick attached to a thigh and a breast. After the girls did the dishes, Nyeredzi and Abigail sat on the bed and ate the chicken while Timothy, Mwedzi, and Zuva were chatting in the lounge. While Hannah talked to her boyfriend outside, Abigail and Nyeredzi rinsed the container and put it back in the bedroom.

The next day, Nyeredzi knew Timothy would be back again. Why wouldn't he? The smell of roasted chicken swirled in the air through the opened windows and summoned him from the cottage. She heard him pulling the heavy metal door open, trying to shut it before he dragged his sandals on the concrete pathway to their house. Sometimes he whistled as though he was going somewhere else. Nyeredzi listened to the whistle's tune fading toward the main road, cheering her little soul, but then the loud knock on the glass door startled her.

"You know we really need iron and protein in our bodies," Nyeredzi said to Abigail. "Our mother has forgotten we need to grow up healthy."

"Hear–hear, we aren't going to let Timothy get what we deserve," Abigail said.

Mwedzi was sitting in an armchair across the passage, so he could see what was happening. Zuva handed Abigail the chicken dish.

"Distract Papa," Abigail muttered to Nyeredzi. "He's

looking at me."

Nyeredzi started dancing along the passage, Mwedzi shook his head, and when he looked away, Abigail took a sudden turn into the bedroom. She appeared again with a half–opened dish. When she placed it on the coffee table, Mwedzi frowned. Abigail adjusted it quickly.

In the kitchen, Zuva asked if the girls were playing with dinner in the passage.

"It's Nyeredzi's fault," Abigail said, and Nyeredzi looked away, avoiding her mother's interrogating eyes. Later, when they checked the container, Nyeredzi could only see a small nibble and a drumstick.

"What? Only this?" Nyeredzi complained, raising her hands in the air. She paced the room, and swore she was going to talk to her father about his friend coming every evening to have dinner with them.

"There wasn't much in the dish," Abigail said. "I think Mama saved some for tomorrow. I'll try to get more pieces next time."

The third night, they had beef stew for dinner. No one complained because the cubes were easy to share, but day four, it was chicken again. Nyeredzi walked into the lounge with a small silver bowl and a jar of warm water. Mwedzi had adjusted the lights so they were bright. The three–seater sofa was in front of the chimney and the two armchairs were across the long passageway, facing the French door and its closed curtains.

She placed the jar and bowl underneath the coffee table already set with water glasses, cold water in a glass jug, and round, woven mats. She moved the vase of lilies aside. The TV was switched off, and Timothy was practically shouting, even when Mwedzi spoke quietly.

She knelt before her father and poured water on his

hands, then Timothy's. A strong odor lingered around Timothy. She wanted to pinch her nose, but she couldn't because she was holding a bowl and a jar. Some of the water splashed on the sofa and floor as she tried to hurry the washing of his hands, so she could move away from his smell quickly.

Nyeredzi wondered what Thoko had seen in Timothy. In her eyes, Timothy was lazy, and he must've had a god who wasn't fond of cleanliness. He was different to her hard–working father. She wondered how they even became friends. This man here was snatching a lot from them— uncountable meals, time with their father. They'd stopped eating dinner together like before, and Nyeredzi was becoming more jealous and angrier.

When it was time to eat, Zuva handed Nyeredzi the dish of meat. On her way to the lounge, she turned into Abigail's bedroom and tipped all the chicken into the container. When she placed all the covered dishes on the coffee table, she could see her father and Timothy were excited to eat. She walked back to the kitchen quickly before Mwedzi had a chance to uncover the dishes.

Just as she entered the kitchen, her father called out to her mother.

"My love—what happened to dinner tonight?"

"What do you mean?" Zuva shouted back. "Everything is there, just eat."

"The chicken dish is empty!" he responded.

All the women in the house marched into the lounge. Even Hannah who'd just got out of the shower, her hair still wet, wrapped in a towel. They all stared down at the empty dish. Zuva looked at Nyeredzi, and she stared back into her mother's eyes. Words bubbled in their throats, waiting to come out, but Abigail was the first to speak.

"It's him, Papa," Abigail said, pointing at Timothy.

"Eh!" Timothy leaned back, shocked.

"You can't trust him," Abigail said. "He lies to you. He has voodooed you to provide for him—his friends said so. If you are not careful, he's going to steal all your money."

"Yeah," Nyeredzi agreed. "He's already used his magic to eat all the chicken."

"No, I didn't!" Timothy sounded confused.

"Papa, your friend here also asked my friend out, but he's married," Hannah chimed in.

Zuva raised her hands in the air.

Nyeredzi ran to Mwedzi, knelt before him, and made herself cry. "I'm so scared, Papa," she said.

Mwedzi got up and opened the door with a serious face. He turned to face Timothy. "I can't believe you perform voodooism, and you are using it on me, your friend. You have to leave right now."

Timothy got up from the couch, trying to explain. He said some words in Ndebele that the girls couldn't understand.

"Hai, haikhona," Mwedzi responded. He shook his head, holding the door open. Timothy left, still protesting, and Mwedzi returned to his armchair.

"Nyeredzi, go and take out the chicken you've put in Abigail's bedroom," Zuva said. "And then you can tell me where you saw Timothy performing voodooism."

Soon, Nyeredzi placed the container on the coffee table, scared of being scolded, but Mwedzi just picked up one piece and pushed the rest to his girls. "To be quite honest, I didn't know how to get rid of him. He was eating most of the food everyday, and I was left hungry."

"Why didn't you say so?" Zuva asked. "I would have put out your meal separately."

"What could I have done? I'm the one who brought him here, thinking he would look for a job."

"Some people are strange," Zuva said. "You should remember that."

"Oh, you girls! Whose idea was it to frame Timothy?" Mwedzi asked.

Abigail looked at Nyeredzi and Hannah laughed, each of them holding a piece of chicken. Zuva walked to the kitchen and came back with a dish of chicken she'd left from the other day and handed it to Abigail and Nyeredzi.

"I kept this for you two, but it looks like you've found a way to survive in the world."

Nyeredzi stretched out her hand to pick a drumstick, but couldn't avoid the look in Zuva's eyes, the one that made her feel empty and guilty. Although these golden pieces of chicken told a different story, deep down inside, she knew she shouldn't have doubted her mother.

WOMANHOOD

Late Winter 1996
NYEREDZI

Izzy arrived to work as a maid for Ruth. She'd grown up in Machipanda, Mozambique, but moved to Zimbabwe when she was twelve. In Mutare, she had lived with one of Zuva's relatives, and now Izzy was to stay with the Taha family for a few weeks while Zuva taught her how to look after Ruth's twins, Gabriel and Gabriella, who were about fifteen months old. During this time, Nyeredzi followed the girl around so closely, she practically became Izzy's tail.

This new girl was vivacious. She was the same age as Hannah, six years older than Nyeredzi. Everything about Izzy was different, like the clothes she wore, which hugged her curves, and most of the time she had to cover herself with a zambia because Zuva would complain. The way she brushed her hair back, it was as if it were waves of kelp laying on a round rock.

While the girls wore simple necklaces and diamond studs, Izzy made sure she wore bright and attractive dangling jewelry. The earrings pulled her earlobes down, and whenever she raised her hands, the bangles on her wrist jingled. When it was sunny, her silver nose ring sparkled under the light. Nyeredzi and her sisters were fascinated.

Izzy spoke Portuguese, Shona, and a little bit of English. Her accent made everything sound unique, and her laugh pierced the quiet of their house like a bolt of thunder. Nyeredzi followed her everywhere—around the house, to the fields where Zuva asked them to do work, and to the shops, where men gawked at Izzy's curvy body.

Even Nyeredzi couldn't keep her eyes from following Izzy. In the kitchen, she stopped wiping the water glasses with a tea towel several times just to watch Izzy. Her chest looked as if it was going to burst out of her brassiere. Every size she tried in the clothing shop at Thorville Shopping Center couldn't accommodate her mountains. Nyeredzi watched every move Izzy made, each jiggling step she took from the counter to the sink. It was as if that's where all her power came from, and she seemed to never stop bragging about it.

"Oh, you city girls," Izzy said. "You bathe your bodies a million times a year, but you don't know where your wells are at."

A look passed between Abigail and Hannah, who sat on the bench by the door. Nyeredzi frowned, trying to understand what Izzy was saying. "What wells?" Nyeredzi asked.

"You are still young—that's why you don't know." Izzy laughed and turned to look at Hannah and Abigail. "They know what I'm talking about."

Nyeredzi looked at her body, skinny as a twig, chest starting to pop, a slight curve to her hips. "It takes time for a girl to grow," she said, feeling offended. "I don't need you to make me feel as though I am not enough."

"Relax, I was only kidding! You, my sister, are coming in strong and soon you'll overtake me." Izzy smiled and Nyeredzi's heart lightened.

At some point, Nyeredzi had started hating her body but perhaps she wouldn't always feel that way. She thought she was the only one in the dark about what Izzy was talking about, but when she glanced at Hannah and Abigail, they looked as if they didn't know either.

"Why won't you just tell us?" Hannah asked. "Show us where the well is?"

"Yeah, we might be learning different things since you grew up in a different country," said Abigail.

"This has nothing to do with where I grew up," Izzy responded.

"Honestly, show us," Hannah said, "and we will show you what we know?"

"All right, all right," Izzy said.

When Izzy unwrapped the yellow zambia cloth covering her lower body, all the girls looked away. They didn't want to see her sacred part. The day before, when they went to the taro garden, Izzy was wearing a baggy brown dress with white dots. It was long enough to touch her knees. Her hair was covered with a white bandana. In the middle of the taro plants, Izzy spread her legs out and urine poured out of her. Nyeredzi and her sisters were shocked.

"Really? You couldn't walk away from the garden and choose a spot?" Nyeredzi asked. "Plus, aren't you wetting your underwear?"

"Sorry girls, I apologize for peeing in your mother's garden," Izzy replied. "If my body doesn't feel like wearing underwear, then why should I wear them?"

"Are you telling us you don't have underwear on right now?" Abigail asked, widening her eyes.

Izzy didn't say anything. She just nodded, looking across the bush. "Have any of you been at that bar?"

"No! Men go to the bar," Nyeredzi said.

"Who said only men go to the bar, women are allowed to have fun, too."

The girls didn't respond to that, and now, they were not interested in seeing her sacred part in the kitchen.

"Relax, I am wearing underwear today," she said, laughing.

Underneath her wrapper, she was wearing a silver miniskirt that hugged her thick round waist. She ran her hands over her silky skirt and unbuttoned her top button and pulled her skirt down to her thighs. She was wearing purple lace underwear.

Abigail and Hannah stood with their mouths agape. Nyeredzi stepped closer to see what Izzy was going to do next. Izzy's hands traveled over her underwear and between her legs.

"This is your well, my dear friends, in case you didn't know." She paused, pulling her skirt up again to button it. "This well is meant for one thirsty person who deserves to be hydrated. Oh, you city girls, don't tell me your mother hasn't sat down to teach you the procedures that need to be done before you age."

Izzy straightened her skirt and put her yellow wrapper back on. Nyeredzi couldn't understand why Izzy didn't just tell them what their wells were without taking off her clothes at the same time, but she was also curious as to what kind of things Zuva was supposed to teach them.

"Oh, one more thing, you girls," Izzy said. "I've never heard any of you clapping while you bathe."

"What do you mean, why do we need to clap hands while we bathe?" Hannah asked, through a mouthful of sugarcane.

"That's why I said you city girls bathe a million

times a year with warm water, but you don't know the procedures." Izzy crouched next to the working bench and pretended there was a tub filled with water. She cupped her palms and began to clap, producing a deep sound from her hands.

"You clap before you wash your sacred part," she said, looking at the girls. "You must respect it." Izzy moved her hands outwards and Nyeredzi couldn't figure out what she was doing.

"What is that now?" Nyeredzi asked.

"Oh, this is you, washing your sacred part."

"I am not ever going to crouch down and clap before my sacred part as if it is a god, plus Mama never said anything about this," Nyeredzi said.

Izzy got up from the floor. "Oh, my dear sister, you as you sit there, you are a god." She pointed at each one of the girls in turn. "Didn't your mother give birth to you? Don't tell me you didn't know a woman is a god? After all, it is your waist that does all the work."

Now Nyeredzi was wide awake: she took every word Izzy was saying and stored them inside her skull. She wondered where Izzy had learned all this stuff. Was it in Mozambique? Was it here in Zimbabwe? Was it in the rural area where she lived? Perhaps women there knew a lot more than the city girls, as Izzy kept on repeating. Now it felt as if she was missing out on so much by growing up in Harare. She'd heard her mother say that in the countryside, women bathed together in the river and no one was shy of being seen by another woman. The elders taught the young ones their values. Nyeredzi felt as if her mother was withholding some details she deserved to know.

Zuva walked in, holding the twins' hands.

"It's time for their bath," she said, and Izzy left the

kitchen with the twins. Zuva asked the girls to start preparing dinner. She pulled out a basket underneath the working bench and passed some potatoes to Hannah so she could peel them.

"I'll be back soon," Zuva told them. "Make sure everything is ready before your father is back."

"Can I come with you, Mama?" Nyeredzi asked. Abigail elbowed Hannah, but they were standing behind their mother, so only Nyeredzi could see.

"Yes, you can come with me," Zuva answered. "I'm not going very far."

She walked down the passageway, and Hannah whispered to Nyeredzi, "Don't tell Mama what we were talking about."

"Obviously you'll have to give me half of your lunch money if you don't want me to tell," Nyeredzi whispered back. Zuva gave Hannah money each day before she went to the University of Zimbabwe where she was studying economics. Zuva didn't want her to end up like other girls who dated sugar daddies who would buy them what they wanted.

"I'm not doing that," Hannah hissed.

Nyeredzi knew her sisters were desperate for Izzy to show them stuff they didn't know. Though she too wanted to learn from Izzy, she pretended as if she didn't care.

"Okay, don't say I didn't try to negotiate with you," Nyeredzi said, walking out.

"All right, I'll give you only one day's lunch money."

"Deal!"

Nyeredzi walked with her mother down Sunset Street, toward the orangey–peach sky. The light shone on their faces, making it difficult for them to look into the horizon. Zuva greeted almost everyone she came across. They regarded her with respect, and she treated them the same way. A motorbike roared past them and a dog began barking behind their neighbor's Durawall. When Nyeredzi wasn't talking to her mother, she listened to people chatting from inside their fenced yards or to the music playing on their loudspeakers.

They turned onto another street and Nyeredzi looked at her mother with a questioning face, though she didn't say anything.

"Yes, Nyeredzi, what is it?"

"Nothing," Nyeredzi responded. "Where are we going?"

"To the Tuze family. I need to talk to them about this Sunday's services at the church."

Nyeredzi was still thinking about what Izzy said to them earlier on in the kitchen.

"Mama, why haven't you told us things that girls are supposed to be taught by their mothers before they come of age?"

"Nyeredzi, who's been saying such things to you?"

"No one," Nyeredzi answered quickly.

"Are you sure that this is your thinking?"

"Yes, Mama," she said. "So, there is nothing we should learn before we get married?"

Zuva reached out to touch Nyeredzi's shoulder. "First of all, you are too young to think about marriage. There is nothing I have to teach you before you come of age. Your body will ready you on its own, and when you have questions then, come to me."

Nyeredzi couldn't bring herself to ask any other questions.

Zuva smiled. "Nyeredzi! No woman should change their body to please a man, do you hear me? If your body is ready to develop then let it be in its own time. Never rush or force your body to do anything it's not made to do."

"Okay, Mama." She wanted to ask about clapping in the bath, but she felt shy.

They finally reached their destination: a large yellow house fenced in with Durawall. Broad branches from avocado and mango trees seemed to float at the end of each Durawall corner. Zuva pressed the button by the electric gate but no one responded on the intercom.

It seemed no one was at home, so Zuva and Nyeredzi turned to leave. The evening breeze raised goosebumps on their skin. The streets were busier now: they passed men in suits, holding portfolios in their hands, and women in suits and floral dresses who clicked along in high heels, their purses hanging loose on their shoulders. More cars and bicycles zipped along the road. They were nearly home when Nyeredzi spoke to her mother again.

"Mama, can you not ask Izzy or Hannah and Abigail about what I asked you?" she asked, rubbing her arms. "Otherwise they will never let me in their rooms, which means I'll never know what they are planning or doing, and then you'll never know what your daughters are doing inside your house."

Zuva didn't respond. While Nyeredzi was someone who'd learned to trick people with words, she also knew her mother didn't like to be told what to do. The silence between them meant there were no promises from Zuva.

"Mama, please don't ask them?" she begged.

Zuva still didn't respond. They walked through their yard and past Mwedzi's pickup truck. Nyeredzi slowed her pace. She didn't want to go inside anymore. She was scared of what she'd done, and regret burned inside her.

These kinds of questions usually ended in a family meeting which included a heavy interrogation, word by word pulled out of each child.

Zuva opened the French door and stepped into the house. In that moment, Nyeredzi knew her sisters would never allow her in their bedrooms and Izzy would never let her go places with her ever again. She wouldn't get the promised ten dollars of Hannah's lunch money. Nyeredzi sat on the veranda, watching people coming home from work. Darkness arrived and the sky lit up with stars. When her mother opened the door and called her inside, Nyeredzi walked in, afraid of what would happen next.

Mwedzi was sitting in the armchair next to Zuva, listening to the news.

"Good evening, Papa." She curtsied.

"Good evening, Nyeredzi."

"Mama, I am here," she said in a low voice, and Zuva told her to go help her sisters in the kitchen.

Nyeredzi was worried that after dinner there would be a family meeting, but she tried to act normal. She planned to deny everything if Zuva asked the girls, and to say that Mama had already heard everything before she stepped into the room with the twins. At dinner time she didn't even go in the dining room. Instead she ate her sadza with Covo and fish stew in the kitchen.

No family meeting was called that night, but in the following days, Nyeredzi avoided her mother. Izzy, however, kept teaching the girls new things: how to use lipstick and nail polish, how to dress when going out with a boyfriend. The girls already knew all of this, but the way Izzy explained it made everything seem new to them.

A few days later, Ruth came to collect the twins. Izzy was leaving to go with her. Outside by the veranda, Zuva said goodbye to her grandchildren. Then she looked straight at Izzy. "Izzy, you see yourself as a god, but a god shall never misuse her powers." She paused. "You are going to Ruth's house for one reason, to look after her children while she works at her bakery. Nothing more, do you understand me?"

"I do understand, Auntie," Izzy said.

"Who ever told you that you are supposed to clap hands when bathing?" Zuva asked.

"No one," Izzy answered.

"Then don't feed people with wrong information," Zuva said.

Izzy lowered her head.

Nyeredzi glanced back at Hannah and Abigail, searching their eyes for who had told their mother about the god conversation and clapping while bathing. Abigail was blinking too fast. Nyeredzi realized then that she wasn't the only child who fed her mother information from their conversations.

Once a month, Ruth brought her family to spend a weekend with her parents and sisters, and that's when Nyeredzi would go back to enjoying her days with Izzy. The girl hadn't changed: she was still vivacious, with loads of knowledge to share about womanhood.

One weekend, the older girls were sitting under the peach tree chatting with Maison, Ruth's husband. Maison was a plumber. Sometimes he finished work earlier than Ruth, who only closed her bakery at six every evening. He'd arrived early that day while Zuva was out at her usual late afternoon prayers. Nyeredzi was in her bedroom, but she could see everything happening outside. Maison was standing close to the dining room window, watching Gabriel and Gabriella run around. Izzy sat on the bench next to Abigail and Hannah.

In one quick movement, Izzy opened her legs wide, revealing her pink underwear to Maison. Nyeredzi's brother-in-law licked his upper lip, looking at Izzy, but Hannah and Abigail didn't notice. Nyeredzi sat up on her bed. At first, she didn't take it seriously. Some men looked at women even when they were married, she reasoned. Soon, she heard footsteps along the passageway. She got up to look out the window again, but Izzy and Maison were not there anymore. She could hear them inside the kitchen.

Nyeredzi opened her door slowly to avoid making a creaking sound, and she slipped along the passageway, her steps as silent as a cheetah's. The kitchen door was half-closed, but when she peeped, Maison's hand was rubbing Izzy's chest in a circular motion. What was happening? Nyeredzi hurried back to her room, her mind racing. Had Izzy found a thirsty person to hydrate with her well? No. Nyeredzi shook her head. How could her brother-in-law touch the chest of a woman he was not married to?

When Ruth arrived, Nyeredzi didn't know how to tell her what she'd seen, or if she should say anything at all. She remembered the first time her sister brought Maison home to meet their parents and they were both so in love. Maison used to bring Ruth presents on weekends, and they would all go for picnics at Harare gardens together. Sometimes Ruth asked Nyeredzi to pass by Maison's workplace and ask him to drop in after work.

Nyeredzi lay on her bed, unsure of what to do. She recalled the day she'd gone with Izzy to the mini shop to buy bread. A few young men stood by the counter and one looked rich in his fancy clothes. He placed his car keys on the counter and pulled out a wallet. Inside there were plenty of $50 and $20 notes.

Izzy told Nyeredzi to stand by the door. She walked up to the rich man and said, "Won't you be kind and buy us ladies drinks to cool off our bodies?"

The man shook his head and continued with his shopping. Izzy didn't say anything, but she bent down a few steps away from him. He looked at her curves. Her skirt had risen up a little bit revealing lines of stretch marks on her thighs. His eyes lingered on Izzy's waist. Soon, he pulled out $20 and handed it to Izzy. She nodded, thanking him.

Nyeredzi had felt bewildered; she didn't know whether she should see Izzy as cool or wild. Zuva had warned her about girls who used their bodies to get what they wanted from men and now, Nyeredzi wondered if Izzy had some kind of medicine she used to lure men to her. Perhaps Izzy had voodooed her brother–in–law.

Darkness crawled inside her room and Mother Moon was shining through her window. She heard Ruth's voice echoing from the lounge, talking to their parents and her husband. The other girls were in the kitchen. When she heard footsteps along the passageway and Ruth's old bedroom door open, Nyeredzi got up. She dashed to Ruth's room. "Hi, Sis."

"Nyeredzi, you look sad. Is everything all right?"

Nyeredzi's heart started pounding. She stepped closer to Ruth and blurted, "I think brother–in–law is doing bad things with Izzy." She said it quickly, a habit she had when whatever she was about to say was unpleasant.

"What makes you think so?" Ruth stared at Nyeredzi. "Maison is my husband. He wouldn't do anything to hurt my feelings."

Nyeredzi leaned against the wall, head down. She

couldn't bring herself to repeat what she'd seen. "I'm sorry, sister."

Ruth opened her purse and took out a receipt, which she studied for a while, and Nyeredzi returned to her own bedroom. Ruth didn't believe her, she thought. But soon, she heard her sister calling for Maison to join her in the bedroom. Their conversation started quiet, but Ruth's voice grew louder. Nyeredzi opened her door to try to hear more, and her sister rushed past her.

Ruth charged into another room and emerged, holding Izzy's bag. Maison was there too, trying to calm her down, but Ruth turned to slap him in the face. Nyeredzi was shocked, her sister was not violent. She'd said nothing about Maison licking his lip when he saw Izzy's underwear, or about him touching her chest. The passageway seemed small because everyone crowded in to see what was happening. Ruth marched into the kitchen, and Nyeredzi followed.

Her sister grabbed Izzy's wrist. "You, you need to leave, now!" Ruth shouted.

"Daughter, what's going on?" Zuva asked, still standing in the passageway, her face serious.

Ruth didn't respond. Mwedzi chucked the newspaper he was reading on the coffee table, looking angry. Nyeredzi shook. It seemed as if they already knew what had happened.

Izzy frowned. "What's going on?"

Ruth pushed Izzy into the lounge. "What's going on?" she repeated, glaring at Izzy. "You don't know what's going on? Really?"

She threw Izzy's bag in her face and turned to Zuva.

"Mama, ask your son–in–law what he's been doing with our maid," she said, tears flowing down her cheeks.

"Ruth, you're overreacting now," Maison said.

It was as if he didn't take it seriously, the things he'd done. Nyeredzi knew it wasn't fair to blame it all on Izzy. Anger swirled inside her chest. "You think my sister is overreacting?" Nyeredzi raised her voice at Maison. "If she's overreacting, then why did you lick your lip when Izzy opened her legs outside? Why were you touching Izzy's chest in the kitchen?"

"How could you do that to my daughter?" Mwedzi shouted.

Her father stood up from his armchair and charged toward Maison. His right fist landed on Maison's face, then the left in his stomach. Her brother–in–law staggered backward, colliding with the dining table. Before he could react, both of Mwedzi's hands were on his collar. Their shouts echoed around the room. Ruth collapsed on the floor, sobbing. Nyeredzi realized this was her fault, for talking to Ruth. She knelt next to her sister. "I'm sorry I got angry," Nyeredzi apologized. "I didn't want to say anything."

"Take the kids out of here now," Zuva commanded Hannah and Abigail.

"Make sure you kill him, Papa!" Ruth demanded, still sobbing.

Zuva pulled Mwedzi off Maison and stepped between them. Mwedzi's chest was rising and falling. Maison's mouth was red with blood; the lip he licked earlier was split in half. Izzy was outside now, wailing and apologizing. Nyeredzi suddenly hated the sound of her voice. She wrapped her arms around her sister. She wanted her shoulders to collect all Ruth's tears.

"Ruth, will you give me the keys? I can't stay here," Maison said, wiping blood off his chin.

"What keys?" Ruth spat at him. "There is nothing of yours in that house. Take your whore and leave and never come back!"

"What? My kids are here! I'll come back when everyone has calmed down."

"You should've thought about the kids before you slept with Izzy," Ruth sobbed, pulling out the receipt she'd been studying in her old bedroom. "Here is the receipt of the lingerie you bought her a month ago. I bet you she is wearing it right now."

Maison stepped forward as if to touch Ruth, but Nyeredzi shoved him back. Her mother led Maison outside, and Nyeredzi followed her.

Zuva walked up to Izzy, her face disgusted. "The day you left here, I told you that you were only going to Ruth's house for one reason. Nothing more was asked of you, and you said you understood very well. Did I ask you to sleep with Maison?"

"No, Auntie, you didn't ask me to sleep with Maison," Izzy said, glancing from Zuva to the ground. "I crossed the line. Maison kept coming on to me. I never wanted any of this to happen."

"Why didn't you come to me if he was forcing you to do things you didn't want to do? I thought you were a god, and a god is in control of everything. Now you've broken my daughter's marriage. I don't know what happiness this will give you tomorrow."

Nyeredzi regretted listening to everything Izzy ever said about being a god, about womanhood. Everything sounded like a lie now. Izzy seemed so small.

"And you," Zuva said, pointing at Maison. "I thought you loved my daughter. If my daughter doesn't want anything to do with you tomorrow, do not come back here, do not come to claim the children. If you try to do so, there will be severe consequences. And I will make sure you never win. Do you understand me?"

"Yes," Maison replied, looking down.

"Now leave," Zuva commanded.

Maison and Izzy walked away, and Zuva went back inside the house.

Nyeredzi had never heard her mother threaten anyone before. Zuva's voice was thick with anguish, with a fierceness that no one could ever take away from her. Nyeredzi stood near the veranda, staring into the darkness for a long time. She could hear her father apologizing to her mother inside for losing his temper. Ruth wandered out the back door without her canvas shoes. She was holding Maison's clothes and a bottle of paraffin. She threw the clothes on the ground by the cottage, poured paraffin on them, and scratched a matchbox she was clasping in her palm.

"Sis, I am so sorry for what I did," Nyeredzi said. "It's my fault Maison is gone."

"Nyeredzi," Ruth said, "your brother–in–law was cheating on me all along. It's not your fault he couldn't keep it in his pants. I was in denial." She paused, wiping away tears. "If anyone is to apologize, it's me. I'm sorry I was rude to you earlier; I shouldn't have done that." Her voice quivered.

Nyeredzi stared at her sister's feet. She'd never seen her sister walking outside without any shoes. Even in the dark, the scar on her foot wasn't brownish anymore; both her feet were pale, like peanut butter. Could this be Maison's fault? Was he making her wear shoes and socks all the time?

Something was boiling inside Ruth, she was shaking

and crying. Nyeredzi watched her sister's anger in the flames. Ruth burned Maison's clothes as though she was burning her husband. It felt as if there was no coming back from this. Even though Ruth had said it wasn't her fault, a small part of Nyeredzi couldn't help but blame herself.

LOVE IN THE MAIZE FIELD

Summer 1997
NYEREDZI

A black lawn had already flourished under Nyeredzi's armpits. She was still thin, but her hips were slightly curved. Sometimes she strolled from wall to wall in her bedroom, crossing her legs the way a female cheetah does. And, when she grew tired of this, she would stand in front of the mirror to examine the two mountains on her chest. Each was almost the size of half an orange. These significant changes to her body weren't new; she'd seen it happening to her sisters, but no one told Nyeredzi that her body was going to betray her.

She blamed it on the hot temperature of summer. To make things worse, the maize crops were still green, still circling one side of their house and backyard, and blocking the breeze that came from the bush. To cool her body, she sometimes ended up playing with Gabriel, and Gabriella, inside the squared pit that was almost a meter deep. A big hump of red soil that surrounded the sides of the pit gave her enough shade if she sat down. Zuva had dug the pit next to the banana trees at the edges of their garden so they could throw away rotten fruits and maize stalks after harvesting the crops.

The twins giggled while Nyeredzi buried their feet in red clay. She stopped, shushed the kids so she could listen to the voices she'd heard within the maize. The afternoon was quiet.

First, it was a young woman's voice. "Oh, Nicholas!"

Nyeredzi looked over the hump through the rows of the maize. A young man in his twenties wrapped his arms around the body of a woman as if he owned her. They dragged each other onto a narrow pathway amidst the maize. They stopped and began whispering in each other's ears. When the young woman turned around, Nyeredzi recognized her.

It was Sharon, who lived across the street, a few houses away from the Taha's house. She was only three years older than Nyeredzi, but Sharon was famous on the street. Some of the girls wanted to be like her, including Nyeredzi. She had the guts to walk with her boyfriend while he held her waist from the back. Not even married couples ever did that in the neighborhood. Sometimes when they crossed paths and greeted each other, Nyeredzi wanted her to stop and have a proper conversation, but she was aloof.

Sharon was still wrapped up in Nicholas's hands. Amidst the green maize with thick stems carrying the heavy cobs at an angle, tassels and silks dangling, the couple were touching each other, hands slipping underneath their clothes. Nicholas whispered something in Sharon's ear again, and she gave a sexy laugh. It made Nyeredzi's body vibrate. A new, weird feeling flowed in her bloodstream. She turned to whisper to her nephew and niece, who were now building castles with red soil.

"If you all sleep on the ground next to each other like you're dead, I'll let you play in here all the time." She paused to place a finger before pursed lips to hush the kids. "If you are perfect, I'll buy you ice cream."

Gabriel and Gabriella jumped up and down, so excited by the idea of ice cream, but Nyeredzi placed her finger on her lips again, and they both dropped onto the squared ground to close their eyes.

Nyeredzi stood up to see what Sharon was now doing. As soon as her head popped above the red soil mound again, Sharon and Nicholas were kissing, unbuttoning each other's tops. Nicholas took off his shirt and chucked it onto the sweet potato bed. He ran his hand on Sharon's thigh, pulling her voluminous skirt up. Sharon was breathing loudly as she lay back on the sweet potato bed. It surprised Nyeredzi how quick they undressed each other. Her gaze lingered on the naked top half of Nicholas and then moved to the two mountains on Sharon's chest.

Nicholas pulled his underwear down to his knees. With a startled gasp, Nyeredzi ducked behind the hump of the soil. Her body was shaking. She grasped the edge of the pit, the earth crumbling and falling onto her feet. Squatting was uncomfortable so Nyeredzi stood up again. Sharon moaned softly. She grasped Nicholas's back, following the motion of his body as their bodies moved together. Nyeredzi's mouth fell open. Their language was music to her, their actions a lesson.

After thrusting his body on Sharon uncountable times, Nicholas produced a deep low growl of satisfaction and Sharon sighed. Nyeredzi was in shock, thinking that this was what Adam and Eve did in the Garden of Eden, except this was not Eden. It was the bush that had offered so many adventures to Nyeredzi. Apparently, she wasn't the only one having new experiences.

Before Nyeredzi could duck back down, Sharon glanced over, and their eyes met. Unsaid words lodged themselves in Nyeredzi's throat. She felt frozen in one spot.

"Come on, we've got to go now," Sharon said to Nicholas, pulling on her purple bra.

"Why? I'm exhausted. Give me some time."

"Look, someone saw us," she said, shimmying into her clothes. Nicholas picked up his own clothes and covered his groin. Both of them ran further down the pathway and disappeared into the maize fields.

Nyeredzi turned to check on the children only to discover they had fallen asleep for real.

"Wake up, wake up, ice cream time," she called out to Gabriel and Gabriella, shaking them. Every couple she knew came to her mind, including her parents. She could not stop thinking about what they did when she was sleeping. Or what had happened while the children were lying here on the bare ground.

Gabriel and Gabriella sat up, the sides of their faces dusty with red soil. They clambered out of the pit still half asleep, fueled by the promised of a treat. When Nyeredzi climbed out too, it was as if she was now climbing onto the other side of the world. A world that had left her wet. Nyeredzi was uncertain about the feelings invading her body. They were leading her to an unexpected place.

That night at bedtime, she switched off the light and opened the curtain to let the moonlight brighten her bedroom. The vision of Sharon and Nicholas kept roaming in her mind. It wasn't easy to erase what she'd seen. She ran her hand from her feet to her hip, emulating Nicholas's actions while sitting on her double bed. She adjusted her night gown, and then continued to run her hand up across her belly button, past her diaphragm, and stopped between her chest.

She imagined Craig from her class, touching her whole

body. The crush she had on him was so intense, building inside of her as she was unable to tell anyone how she felt. His smile, the beard beginning to burst on his chin, and the gap between his teeth made her soft heart melt. She visualized him kissing her, whispering sweet words to her.

When she heard Mwedzi's feet dragging in the passageway, Nyeredzi shut her curtains and threw herself inside the blankets.

Every night, Nyeredzi would write letters to Craig, and then burn them in the fire the following day. She was teaching herself to burn the feelings that were now controlling her. Craig was in love with her friend, so she had to let it go.

A week later, Zuva sent Nyeredzi to buy beef meat at Thorville Shopping Center. Inside SPAR Supermarket, while she stood by the cold breeze of the meat refrigerators, someone called out to her. She was astonished when she turned around to see Sharon and her lover roaming in between the aisles. With a broad smile plastered on her face, Sharon was waving at Nyeredzi who waved too, then went back to comparing prices. She picked one carton with a reasonable price and moved on to the bakery department. Ruth barely made pies at her bakery. She was now standing by the oven, admiring the meat pies when Sharon and Nicholas walked up.

"Nyeredzi, hi."

"Hi, Sharon."

"Nicholas, you should buy a pie for my neighbor," she said.

Nyeredzi was astounded. This was the first time she'd had a proper conversation with Sharon. She didn't know what to say.

"Nyeredzi, which one would you like?"

"Oh no, I'm all right, thanks," said Nyeredzi.

"Don't worry, Nicholas is paying. You should grab a bottle of perfume too. Every girl likes to smell nice, don't they?"

Nyeredzi smiled. She knew Sharon was desperate and would do anything to please her. "Since Nicholas is paying, I could pick some more stuff too, if he is okay with it," she said. "You guys are the cutest couple I've ever seen."

"Oh yes, we are," Sharon said, rubbing his forearm.

Nicholas avoided Nyeredzi's eyes. He seemed uncomfortable.

"Great. I'll meet you both at the counter then."

Nyeredzi ran to the counter to grab a basket. While she looked at the different bottles of perfume, she glanced back at Sharon and Nicholas. The image of Sharon's two mountains pointing at Nicholas came back to her mind. Fresh, yet firm, calling out to her naked lover whose curved biceps were slick with beads of sweat. Although Nicholas had not said anything to Nyeredzi earlier, she could still remember how he sounded in the maize field. How his loud breath was like someone mining gold, grinding deeper into the crevices of Mother Earth, making sure he'd collected all he craved for.

She roamed the aisles of SPAR Supermarket, picking everything her sisters never shared with her, like nice body lotions and hair products. She glimpsed Sharon and Nicholas again, and they seemed to be arguing—probably because Sharon was making her boyfriend spend money on a girl he didn't know. Money he didn't have to start with.

Nyeredzi waited for them by the counter with her basket

full of fancy stuff as well as the toiletries. She had three blocks of chocolates, lemon, and vanilla biscuits, two bottles of perfumes, nail polish, one warm chicken pie, one frozen beef pie to eat later, silky pink lingerie, and a bottle of Amarula champagne. Nyeredzi handed Sharon the basket and saw the girl's eyes widen at the sight of all these expensive things.

"I can't pay for this," Nicholas whispered. "This is too much! Why does she want Amarula? Isn't she younger than you?"

"Who cares? Just pay and she will never tell." Sharon turned to Nyeredzi. "Are you going to tell?"

"I'll never tell anyone," Nyeredzi promised.

"You see, she will never tell." Sharon leaned close to Nicholas, whispering in his ear. "And you'll be getting more of what you've missed. I know you miss me." He smiled and pulled out his wallet from the back pocket of his jeans.

Nyeredzi didn't pass by her sister's bakery because she was loaded. She walked home, holding her two plastic SPAR bags, chewing on the warm chicken pie. She thanked the heat that had been relentless the past few days. Otherwise, she wouldn't have seen Sharon and Nicholas making love and she wouldn't have the opportunity to eat the delicious, crunchy crust of the chicken pie.

When she arrived home, she went straight to her bedroom and hid her bags under the bed. She took out the beef Zuva had sent her to buy and carried it to the kitchen, humming in satisfaction—though it did not compare to the satisfaction Nicholas seemed to get on top of Sharon the other day.

That night when everyone else was asleep in their bedrooms, Nyeredzi opened the bags and laid her new things out on her bed. She munched on the chocolate, the free dessert from Sharon and Nicholas. Then Nyeredzi tore the side of her mattress and hid the bottle of Amarula inside. None of her family drank. The sight of it gave her the shivers. She didn't know why she even picked it from the liquor section.

She tried on the lingerie and crossed her legs in front like a cheetah again.. That night she fell asleep wearing them, without thinking once about Craig. Every night for the next few days, Nyeredzi sat on her bed and ate what was left, bit by bit.

And when she was done nourishing her body from within, she moved onto the outside, moisturizing her skin with scented body lotion. Every week she massaged her skull with hair oil and painted her nails with the new polish. She thought she smelled elegant with the perfume she sprayed under her armpits. All of this made her forget about Craig, and about Sharon as well. There were rumors that Sharon and Nicholas had eloped.

Nyeredzi thought she would never see Sharon again, but some weeks later there she was, arguing on their street with her lover. Sharon wasn't only round on her chest, but her stomach was also curved like a half–moon. Her parents had disowned her because she had tarnished their name, and Nicholas was refusing to marry her. Sharon was crying, and Nyeredzi sympathized with her predicament. She wasn't sure if Sharon was crying because she regretted falling in love with Nicholas or giving him the sacred parts of her body.

Nyeredzi watched the couple fight in the street where everyone could hear them. It reminded her of that day in the SPAR Supermarket when they fought about paying for her things. That's when she remembered the bottle she'd hidden in her mattress.

She decided to confront Nicholas with it and perhaps, she would get something out of it. So, she hid the bottle in one of the SPAR bags and walked out to the street. They were so busy arguing, they didn't notice her approaching, and her first statement made Nicholas step back in shock.

"You raped Sharon!" she said.

"What? I didn't do that."

"Yes, you did. I saw you on top of Sharon in the maize field. You can't deny that now. If I tell anyone what I saw, the verdict will be that you raped her, she's underage."

Nicholas looked from Nyeredzi to Sharon, his face angry, clearly desperate to get away from both of them. "I don't know what you are planning here, but I'm going. Don't come to my house."

"Why are you shouting at Sharon?" Nyeredzi demanded. "That day in the field you were all over her, touching her here and there."

"Young woman, what are you playing at? We are in the middle of a deep conversation here—go away." He reached out to push Nyeredzi away, but she moved out of the way before he could touch her.

"You were just about to touch my shoulder. What kind of a gentleman touches a young woman like me without asking for her permission?"

"I didn't touch you," he growled at her.

Sharon was now sobbing loudly, her face in her hands. Nicholas turned to leave, but Nyeredzi grabbed his arm. Astounded, he turned, glaring at Nyeredzi. She was even surprised herself—grabbing a man's hand in the street when their neighbors were watching.

"Give me the money you used to buy this," Nyeredzi said, opening the plastic bag.

Nicholas peered in at the bottle.

"You still have this?" Nicholas asked in shock. "I don't have the money for this. Just leave us alone."

"I can show it to the neighbors who are watching now. They will know you bought this for me. They can already see what you did to Sharon." Nyeredzi pointed at Sharon's bump.

"What the heck?" Nicholas pulled out his wallet and opened it. There were three $20 notes in there: he took two out, but Nyeredzi shook her head. Defeated he handed $60 to Nyeredzi and snatched the bag from her.

Nyeredzi rolled the notes in her hand. "My mother knows your mother. If I tell her exactly what I saw, you'll be in jail. She's a church leader, and she's also a comrade. I know for sure that the police will listen to her."

"Do you think I care about that?" Nicholas looked unconcerned.

Nyeredzi had come to this couple with the intention of using their situation for the wrong reasons, but now she could see how upset Sharon was. Nyeredzi didn't want her to end up like one of the girls on the train tracks. Zuva had told her about that.

"Look, Sharon is carrying your child, and if she goes to the train tracks to take her life, that'll be on you. Deep down you know it."

Nicholas wasn't shouting anymore. He seemed to be calming down. Nyeredzi realized she'd become her mother's daughter—the person who knew the right words to say. And at the same time, she learned not to ever use her mother's status to manipulate people.

"All right," he said. "I suppose Sharon and I need to talk."

Two days later, Sharon came to the Taha family's house, looking for Nyeredzi. She was the only one home. They sat on a large rock outside under the peach tree, talking.

"So, is it true your mother is a comrade?"

"Yes, she fought in Second Chimurenga War."

"No wonder why she killed all those snakes at the bush when we were young. Damn, she is a fierce woman."

Though Nyeredzi smiled, filled with pride, she knew her mother wasn't just a comrade or a church leader. She was more than that.

"Nicholas has agreed for me to stay with him, and he will sort out the lobola later when he saves some money." Tears glistened in Sharon's eyes. "So, I just want to say thank you for what you did the other day. I thought you only wanted to use me for the wrong reasons, but when you mentioned the train tracks, you saved my unborn child and me. I was actually considering…" She sniffed, clearing her nose.

"I'm glad he's going to look after you, and don't ever think anything like that. If you're stranded in future, come to my mother, she will help you. Me too." Nyeredzi placed her palm on Sharon's shoulder. "For the record, I'm sorry for making you and Nicholas buy me that stuff and the money I took from him. I should give it back now." She paced inside without looking at Sharon who shook her head, refusing.

Shortly, she was back with the notes, more than Nicholas gave her. When Sharon checked, it was $180. "Nicholas gave you $60, and I didn't want the money back."

"You need it more than me, buy stuff for your baby now."

Sharon shook her head, confused.

"I do silly things for fun because I'm bored. If I needed money, I would ask my mother," Nyeredzi said without explaining further, what her mother owned in the pots made of soil back in Goho was worth more.

Sharon sighed, clasping the money. "Thanks again for making Nicholas take me back, and this."

After Sharon left, Nyeredzi stayed sitting under the peach tree. Even though she'd witnessed the ramifications of Sharon and Nicholas's young love, her hormones still danced inside her body. She yearned to be touched by a man's hand. Kissed. Perhaps more, but for now, she sat still on the cold rock, waiting for that time to come.

MAYHEM

Autumn 1999
NYEREDZI

"Pass me the biscuits, will you?" Abigail asked.

Nyeredzi passed a packet of chocolate biscuits to Abigail, who was sitting across from her on the couch. As usual, Zuva had gone to the field, Mwedzi was at work, and Hannah had afternoon classes at the university. The girls were watching *Sunset Beach* but there was an advert break.

"These biscuits are so delicious," Abigail said. "I'm going to ask Ruth to bring another packet next week."

Nyeredzi wiped some crumbs off her chin. "I was going to ask her on my birthday next month. If we ask her now she will say no next time."

"But her bakery is always full of delicious stuff."

"If we keep asking her for food, how is she going to make a profit?"

They stopped talking. *Sunset Beach* was back on TV, and talking distracted their concentration from the plot, so silence was crucial.

In the middle of watching, Nyeredzi heard loud voices outside in the street. Elections were approaching, so groups of people had been running through the suburbs to show their support for their parties. They chanted slogans that told which party they belonged to. This year, Braden Gwenje of United Zimbabwe was up against Memory Chigundu of Regenerate Nation—running for the presidential position. Sometimes disagreement brewed between the groups when they came across each other, and fights broke out.

Five years after independence, the Freedom Fighters gave way to the United Zimbabwe who'd been running the government for more than a decade now, but Regenerate Nation, the new party, was ready to take over, and was promising people a better life—reducing unemployment, improving education, dropping prices of food, and giving capital to small businesses.

Nyeredzi switched off the TV and glanced at Abigail, worried. The noise was unusual this time, nothing like an argument they've heard before. People weren't singing. They heard a clattering, as if something was being banged on the ground. Nyeredzi lifted a corner of the lace curtain to peep through the window and saw smashed vehicles. She ran to lock the doors and Abigail followed, closing all the windows. This was what Zuva and Mwedzi told them to do if things ever went wrong.

From what Nyeredzi could see, armed men were entering the neighboring houses by force. She didn't know which group they belonged to or what they wanted. They held machetes, axes, or sjamboks; some of them even had rifles strapped to their shoulders or hanging loose by their waist.

House by house, they brought people out. Their neighbors, Marvellous and her mum, were thrown on the ground along with other people, crying. Anyone who tried to challenge the armed men or run away were whipped. The women's arms were covered in red bruises. Abigail and Nyeredzi knelt by a window, peeking out. They watched Marvellous's mum begging, asking what they had done wrong, but all she received was a slap from a tall, solid man.

"You think you are all smart," the tall man shouted at the people on the ground.

Another armed man with a scar on his face appeared from the back of the group. "Now crawl on the ground," he shouted.

Everyone crawled along the black tarred road. Nyeredzi couldn't figure out why this was happening in their street. Her only guess was that someone had provoked the other group and now a lot of people were enduring the punishment.

"Go and check in the other houses," the tall guy shouted at the others. "See if we have spoiled brats in there in need of a lesson."

Nyeredzi and Abigail looked at each other, trembling. They could hear the men slamming the doors next door, and Hope screaming. The house their father had built was not safe anymore. Nyeredzi crawled on the gray floors of the lounge to the passage to avoid being seen, her sister crawling behind her.

"Where are we going?" Abigail whispered. "We should stay inside and hide."

"Do you think Hope was not hiding inside too?"

"Mama and Papa said we should stay inside no matter what."

"Look, do what you think is good for you. I'm going to the taro field where Mama is. I'll be safe there, and you will be too."

"Why do you say so?"

"Because Mama was a comrade, remember?"

"People don't care about that, you know."

"If you want to stay, that's up to you, I'm leaving," Nyeredzi said, standing up.

"I'm only coming with you because I don't want to be alone in this house."

When they reached the back door, they heard someone break the glass of the French door with an object. Nyeredzi opened the back door quickly without checking who or what was on the other side. When she stepped outside, she realized how dangerous it was. The people they'd seen outside harassing their neighbors through the corner of the window were not alone. There were hundreds of men with weapons in their hands. Some were in the streets, and others had entered the bush, scanning the area, looking for something.

She and Abigail didn't run. Instead, they walked very fast, taking the pathways they always used without looking back. Abigail was in front. Nyeredzi was right behind her, each breath short, trying to calm her nerves as they headed into the bush toward Zuva's taro garden. Until she heard footsteps following them along the narrow pathway, Nyeredzi was hopeful no one would stop them. The sun cast long shadows on the ground, and she could see figures moving behind them, but Nyeredzi didn't want to turn around or warn Abigail to run. She kept silent as they walked, monitoring the shadows of the people behind her.

When a hand gripped her right shoulder, she almost jumped out of her skin. In an instant, they were surrounded by five young men aged over twenty. She remembered the day she was surrounded by five unkempt teenage boys in the city—street kids wanted some money from her, but she didn't have any except for the yogurt they snatched from her hand. Their big greasy, ripped sweatshirts smelled like urine and tar—hung loose on their bodies while their torn pants were belted with electric cords.

Now, these men before her were in casual clothes such that she didn't know which party they belonged to. Nyeredzi's heart pounded in her rib cage, and all the hairs on her arm stood to attention. She tried to swallow but her mouth was dry.

"Where do you think you are going?" one of the men shouted, scraping on the ground with his black boot like a bull.

"We are heading to the bush," Nyeredzi said, trying to keep herself calm.

"Running away from us, ha?" the oldest one screamed, shuffling toward Abigail who was so scared she tumbled into a dense bush.

Nyeredzi helped Abigail up, trying not to cry as the men glared at them. "No, we are not running away from you." Nyeredzi's voice was quivering. "One of you guys said we should go and summon our mother."

"Liar! Do you think we are stupid?" the oldest one shouted, adjusting the rifle strapped on his shoulder.

"There, that's our mother." Nyeredzi pointed toward the taro garden with a trembling hand.

Indeed, they saw Zuva bending down, digging in her garden. He took a few steps closer to Nyeredzi, and the fresh breeze turned sour with the strong stench of alcohol. She'd seen such movies that involved people hurting or shooting each other, and blood flowing like rivers. Now, in real life, at that moment, she couldn't define what she saw raging in the men's red eyes—except the spirits of the people they may have tortured or killed haunting their sight. They were all standing in the dangerous bush, except this time, danger didn't have anything to do with the thugs or snakes.

A gunshot sounded from her street. Nyeredzi recoiled in fright, but the men didn't. A man appeared, summoning them. They looked at Nyeredzi and Abigail, wanting to deal with them first, but clearly didn't want to disobey their leaders.

"If you are lying, young lady, I'm coming for you," the oldest one said. His skin looked as though it was coated in layers of dirt. "There's more of us, you can't run or hide."

The men walked back to the street, where Nyeredzi and Abigail could hear people still screaming and crying. They couldn't waste any more time, and began to run through the bush, pausing behind rocks and or in dense grass to catch their breath. Just as they had almost reached the steep area, they looked back and saw men coming toward them again.

"This is your fault," Abigail shouted.

"You think I'm the one harassing innocent people?"

"No, but you lied to them. Look, they are coming after us—we are dead."

"If you want to die, then stay here." Nyeredzi swung her arms and started to run.

Mayhem was now following them. She heard three-gun shots, but she kept going. There was no turning back. She wondered about the shots in the street. Was one of their neighbors dead, blood flowing onto the black–tarred road? Hope? Marvellous or her mother? Could it have been just to scare people? Nyeredzi ran, not knowing if she and her sister would be shot as well.

Ahead, their mother was now standing, facing them. *She must've heard the gun shots too*, Nyeredzi thought. It was a challenging long run across the steep land. When they reached the taro garden, Abigail threw herself on the ground. Nyeredzi was heaving and panting. Before she could tell her mother what was happening, Zuva saw the armed men coming toward them like a shadow creeping closer, as though death was approaching.

Nyeredzi sat on the red soil, looking up at her mother. Zuva kept on digging calmly as if nothing was happening. Abigail, her face covered, was very upset.

"Mama, why can't we just run to the Agric company and hide there?" Nyeredzi shouted. "Look, they are coming for us, and we are still here!"

"If you run today, do you think they won't come back tomorrow?" Zuva asked. "You have to deal with your problem before another one comes along."

The men were too close. Nyeredzi trembled and she clasped her hands to pray. Should she not say her last prayer? Should she not beg God to forgive all her sins— like the time she blackmailed Sharon in the supermarket, or the time she lied to Zuva that she was going to see her friend Catherine but was really going to her boyfriend's house? Zuva never questioned her but searched for the truth in her daughter's eyes, which always sold her out. What about the day Nyeredzi asked for money to buy schoolbooks but bought perfume instead? Zuva still gave her the money, more than she'd asked for.

Once Nyeredzi lied to Abigail, saying that Zuva had sent her to one of their church member's houses, just because she didn't want to cook dinner that evening. Nyeredzi knew Abigail didn't like going to other people's homes so she would say, "If you want me to make dinner, then you go." She knew Abigail would choose to stay home and cook dinner. She would go and hide in her bedroom until her sister was done.

When Nyeredzi was on the verge of confessing her wrong deeds to her mother and Abigail, the armed men arrived. "Good afternoon, my sons," Zuva said.

None of them responded. Nyeredzi had learned that her mother's voice brought peace to most people, but these were barbarous men, who paced around their garden, kicking shrubs in anger. They spat at her mother's garden as though they were possessed. The young man Nyeredzi had lied to was with them, walking toward her. He was so furious, he jumped over the dense shrubs that circled the taro garden and walked straight to Nyeredzi, poking her forehead with his gun.

"You do realize you are blessing my daughter to become a soldier like you," Zuva said, looking into the young man's eyes. "She'll come to protect this land like you, my sons. If you decide to bless her, then you should do it properly."

His stiffened shoulders relaxed a little bit when he heard Zuva say he was a soldier who protected their land, but he was still glaring at Nyeredzi.

"She's a liar, this daughter of yours," he shouted at Zuva. "I could just kill her now."

"She only lied to come and seek advice. I'm sure you all have done this before, back and forth, to seek advice from your parents."

"You don't know me, old woman!" he shouted.

The rest of the men watched with wide eyes. On the ground that Nyeredzi had once sat to call upon their ancestors, she trembled, fingers digging into the loose soil. The young man waved his gun in the air, eager to pull it on Nyeredzi, but something was stopping him. Was it the same thing that was pulling Nyeredzi's energy from underneath too? It had been long that she'd forgotten how it felt. What she once experienced after the Ndima Ndima dance was back. It was a feeling she didn't want now, people were watching. They would think she was insane if something out of ordinary took place.

Abigail's head was still buried between her legs, crying. Whether she was now saying her last prayers too or not, Nyeredzi couldn't comfort her, strange things were happening to her.

"Where is your leader, my sons?"

"Over there—he is coming," the other one said with a calm voice.

"Call him to me?" Zuva asked.

The young man whistled, and Nyeredzi could tell he was communicating in code. The leader, a tall and robust man, walked toward them, jumping over the shrubs on the edge of Zuva's taro garden. The sunlight flashed on his tight white t-shirt and black pants. He adjusted his gray beret to one side and stood akimbo, revealing a small gun tucked on his belt.

"Who led us here? What are we doing here?" he asked, looking at the three women.

"Mudhoba did," said the one who had summoned him with a whistle.

"The young woman lied to us," Mudhoba said, spitting on the ground. "For all we know, she could be the traitor— a girl is a gun."

The leader shook his head and ignored Mudhoba.

"You have a beautiful garden, Gogo," he said to Zuva, touching the thick green leaves. When his eyes met Zuva's, he took off his beret and his men who wore different types of hats did the same.

"Thank you, my son," Zuva said. "Your beret reminds me of myself when I was young, though mine was a different color."

"How so?" He looked at Zuva, his face puzzled.

"Way back, before the independence."

"Now I understand why you are so calm."

"What's happening today?"

"We are raiding the neighborhood—you know, things we can't discuss with the public."

"When you look at me, do you see public?"

"No, Gogo, you are nothing like the people I see every-day, but I can't get in trouble."

"I understand," Zuva paused, looking him in the eye. "Your lips are parched. Take a bottle of water from my basket and drink. There are some sandwiches too."

He seemed surprised. "Are you trying to kill us? How do we know you haven't put something in your sandwiches before we got here?"

"Why would I kill a son I've always wished for?"

The leader opened the basket. He pulled out the bottle, uncapped it, drank some water, and passed the bottle to his men. In exhaustion, he dropped onto the ground, close to Nyeredzi. The look he gave her with his red eyes fright-ened her. She was ready to leap up and run for her life, but her energy was being pulled from underneath the ground.

She imagined him trying to strangle her or stabbing her with the knife poking out from his back pocket because she had lied to Mudhoba. Instead, he ordered his men to sit while they gobbled down the peanut butter sandwiches. Nyeredzi wondered if their anger was only because they were hungry men, in need of food in their bellies.

Zuva was still standing and smiling, and when they finished eating, she raised her hand.

"You see this land here?"

Nyeredzi was astonished to see the men laying their

weapons down on the ground and raising their heads to listen. Even Abigail had stopped crying in order to hear her mother.

"When we first arrived here, there were poisonous snakes and thugs who hid here to kill people. The drought came and we performed a traditional rain dance here to summon our ancestors, so they would forgive those who had killed on this land." She went silent for a while, letting her words sink in. "They heard us. It rained, and today this is what we are reaping."

She gestured at the garden. Some of the men nodded their heads in agreement, but Mudhoba still looked angry. Nyeredzi could see him trying to get the attention of their leader, but the tall man seemed to be drawn into what Zuva was saying. A sense of hope kicked inside Nyeredzi. Slowly, her mother's voice was making peace.

"My sons, protect your brothers and sisters. Do not harm one another. Protect this land like our ancestors did. Like they protect us day and night. Do not forget…" She paused, as though she was thinking of what words to say. "We are all related through humanity."

Nyeredzi's energy returned in her body in a way she didn't expect—it forced words out of her mouth, "And isn't humanity something we inherited from our ancestors? And what is humanity without humans?"

"Shut up," Mudhoba pointed his gun at her. "Who gave you permission to speak? Are you forgetting that you lied to us—"

"And who said we only learn from our elders?" the leader interrupted him. "You led us to the wrong people."

Mudhoba flared his nose. Had his energy returned the same time as Nyeredzi's did? Right now she didn't want to be here at all. How could the ancestors make her speak words that were meant to be said by her mother?

"Am I not learning too?" Zuva asked. "Aren't we all learning?"

They all stared at Zuva. They had come with dark spirits dragging behind them, but something was shifting within them. They got up and picked up their weapons.

"Thank you, Gogo," the leader said. "You are the mother of this nation."

"Set the people in my street free," Zuva said to him. "I know they say the wrong things, but they are harmless."

"All right, Gogo. We are leaving."

Zuva walked toward a little bucket where she had placed some taros. She picked it and handed it to the leader. "Ask your wife to cook them for you."

"How did you know I'm married, Gogo?"

"How could I not? I looked at you and saw love inside your left rib."

He put on his beret, and his men did the same. Nyeredzi was surprised to see the leader clapping his hands producing a deep sound, thanking her mother. He took the little bucket from Zuva and jumped over the dense shrubs. He glanced back at them before he turned to head toward the streets. Soon, he raised his hand in the air, coding his men to move. None of them were rowdy anymore. Peace was wrapped around them like a baby blanket.

It always amazed Nyeredzi how people changed after Zuva gave a sermon at church, but this time they weren't inside God's house. These men weren't churchgoers at all, but their stiffened shoulders seemed to relax. The way they dragged their tired feet through the soil of the bush brought Nyeredzi back to the vision she had at the Ndima Ndima dance. *She is the mother of the nation, the peacemaker,* the old woman had said. Now, she heard those words again, but this time they came from a new mouth.

"Mama, are you a peacemaker?" Abigail asked.

Zuva didn't respond. She shared a look with Nyeredzi, bent down to pick the wilting weeds she had been piling up. Although Nyeredzi was keen for her mother to answer that question, secretly, she questioned why she experienced things she did after the Ndima Ndima dance again.

SEPARATED

Late Winter 1999
NYEREDZI

Elections were in two weeks. The closer they got, the more the protesters fought. Today there was a riot at the center of the shopping area. Nyeredzi made her way to the shops to help Ruth close up her bakery. When other people had locked their doors and closed all windows, she was fortunate to have been rescued by a middle-aged woman. Now, at her front door, after an hour hiding, the woman handed Nyeredzi a wet blue towel to protect her from the smoke still swirling in the air.

Nyeredzi ran down the quiet, deserted streets, aware of wailing sirens in the distance and the barks of neighborhood dogs. She jumped over the rocks, logs, and metal bars scattered on the road. All had been used as weapons. It was hot, and she stopped to tie up her braids and open the top buttons of her silky blood red blouse. She pulled up the sides of her voluminous asymmetric green skirt and tucked them into her underwear so she could run more easily.

The smoke formed a thick gray blanket over the ground. Nyeredzi could smell tear gas, a scent that grew stronger near the Thorville Shopping Center, where Ruth's bakery shop was located. The gas burnt her eyes, mouth, and skin so she pressed the wet towel around her mouth. Her skirt was falling down, slowing her pace, but she kept going.

Quite often, some people vandalized buildings and loot the supermarkets. And at times like these, it was usually the policemen in their trucks who pushed the civilians further away from the shopping centers by throwing tear-gas. People picked up the canisters and threw them back. Earlier, Nyeredzi and the woman sheltering her had heard gunshots, loud thuds when metals objects were smashed, and people screaming from the shopping center.

Zuva had sent Nyeredzi to help Ruth close the bakery, but it was a dangerous time to be out on the streets. When Nyeredzi reached the main road near the shopping center, she saw large rocks and rusty barrel drums with holes piled on the black tarred road to stop cars and police coming through. She looked around to see if the protesters and police were still around, then crossed the road. In the fruit and vegetable market, baskets were tipped over on their sides. Some sheds were burning, others were broken. Only a few of the sheds still stood upright.

She stepped over squashed tomatoes, oranges, bananas, carrots, and green cabbages, water squelching underneath her canvas shoes. Sugarcanes were scattered everywhere. Plastic bags floated in the air around her and the sound of distant sirens and barking dogs made her shudder.

She took a shortcut down a dark alleyway that reeked of urine and vomit because of the bar there. Whenever Nyeredzi went shopping, she always avoided that pathway, but there was no time today to run around the buildings. She was desperate to see her sister, and luckily today the bar was closed.

At the shopping center, some of the buildings were burned black and still smoking. Blood was smeared on the concrete pavements and walls. Broken glass was everywhere, and the burglar bars around the Spar Supermarket had been ripped out. It seemed people had looted the supermarket.

In the distance, trolleys and baskets full of groceries reminded Nyeredzi of the day she and Zuva saw a bag of groceries in the middle of the maize field. She'd asked Zuva if she could take it, but the answer was no. Zuva said, "All those products were stolen by selfish people. If you want something in life, you have to work hard to get it."

Here the trolleys and baskets were scattered on the green lawn around the water fountain in the middle of the shopping center. Serene water shot up in the air out of the bronze lion's mouth and poured into the fountain's white–tiled pool.

When Nyeredzi reached Ruth's bakery, it was closed. She peered through the front glass, but it was difficult to see because the burglar bars were in her way, and it was smoky inside too. Someone had tried to break in because the bars were coiled to one side, but the bakery's shelves still looked packed.

She knocked on the green double doors, calling out for her sister, and peered through small holes in the door that weren't there before, but Nyeredzi couldn't see anything. There was no response, so she paced from side to side, stepping around the broken glass, calling out for her sister again and again. She was struggling to breathe, the tear-gas still burning her eyes and nose.

Could Ruth have left already? Nyeredzi's instinct told her she was inside. She knew Ruth would never come out if there were gunshots. They terrified her, and Nyeredzi understood why.

At the fountain she washed her burning eyes, then pushed one of the trolleys back to the shop. By climbing onto the trolley, she could see inside the store through the part of the glass that wasn't barred. Through the smoky glass, Nyeredzi could just make out Ruth lying face down on the floor next to the counter. She wasn't moving.

"Ruth!" Nyeredzi called out again, banging on the glass.

What could have happened to her sister? Had she fainted? Why wasn't she answering? Was it the smoke or the teargas?

Nyeredzi jumped down to pick up a rock and threw it up at the glass to break it. Now she had to put two trolleys on top of each other so she could climb up. She took her skirt off to cover the spiky edges of the frame, the wet towel now stuffed in her brassiere. Her body trembled as she clambered on the wobbling trolleys, and then through the jagged opening in the glass.

Inside, she stepped onto the front display shelf: it swayed under her weight. Cakes dropped onto the laminated timber floor, releasing the delicious scent of vanilla, chocolate, and raspberry. Nyeredzi held onto the beam next to the shelf and looked for any sign of intruders. The till still sat on the counter and the landline telephone was still connected to the wall. Underneath the counter was clear glass, revealing shelves packed with silver trays of croissants, ciabatta buns, baguettes, and biscuits with nuts, chocolate chips, and cream, and pies she'd started making because of Nyeredzi. "You are losing more customers," Nyeredzi had said.

As far as she was concerned, nothing tangible was smashed. Behind the counter, on the wall that separated the kitchen and the shop, big bright letters read Nourish Your Body With Sweetness.

After shimmying into her skirt, Nyeredzi climbed down, coughing because of the smoke, and ran over to Ruth.

"Sis, Sis, wake up!" she yelled, crouching next to her. Her fingers ran across Ruth's neck, looking for her pulse; it was faint. Only now, close to Ruth, Nyeredzi saw the blood flooding around her sister.

She managed to roll Ruth's body over. Ruth's pink chiffon dress was dark with blood. Nyeredzi's hands felt wet and warm when she touched the dress. A strong smell of blood cut through the smoky air and penetrated her nostrils. Nyeredzi lifted the dress and carefully ran her hand over her sister's bloodied abdomen. A round piece of metal had pierced Ruth's flesh and Nyeredzi realized the door had bullet holes. The same holes she'd used to peep through earlier on.

Zuva had told her once that a bullet was not that big, but it could do irreversible damage. Had the bullet that pierced Ruth's foot as a baby come back to finish her off?

She used the landline to call an ambulance and then to ring Zuva.

"Mama! Sis has been shot, please hurry." Nyeredzi's voice quivered, and her eyes flooded with tears. She had to be strong. If she broke down, how was Ruth going to pull through?

She ran to open the double doors. Contaminated air flowed in with the sunlight, and Nyeredzi started coughing again. She assumed the ambulance would arrive before Zuva, because her mother had to walk all the way from their house.

No one was around outside to help. Nyeredzi knew people would not leave their houses any time soon after the riot. It was just her and Ruth in the store. The sun pierced through the smoke and the broken window. She sat praying next to Ruth, pressing the wet towel to her abdomen. She wasn't that old, but she'd seen death before, when her mother prayed for the church members who were departing this life.

Ruth's eyes blinked, then she opened her mouth, gasping for air.

"Nyeredzi!" Ruth said, her voice low and rasping. "You are here."

"Yes, I am here. I've called Mama and the ambulance, they are coming."

Slowly Ruth turned her head to the doors, squinting at the sunlight. "Take me outside? I want to lie under the sun."

"I don't want to hurt you, Sis."

"I'm already hurt. Take me outside."

This sun that Ruth craved was the same sun that had once burnt them as they crossed the bush on the way to the grinding mill. The days they spent digging the red clay, bonding them to their ancestors and each other.

"All right, I'll take you outside," Nyeredzi said.

She slid her hands under Ruth's armpits, lifted her to a sitting position. She thought this would be easy, but the dress was too soft and slippery, making it hard to get a grip. Ruth tried to hold onto Nyeredzi, but her hands were too weak. Nyeredzi was not strong enough to pull her sister up. It was a two–man job. She had to lay Ruth back on the floor to regain her strength.

Ruth looked at Nyeredzi, trying to breathe. "Hurry up, I need the sun on my skin now," she said, her voice weak.

"Okay, Sis."

Nyeredzi gasped for air, her eyes sore from smoke.

She made her way to the bakery's warm kitchen. Trays of golden cupcakes lined the work bench. Ruth must have baked her first batch before the riot broke out. In the store-room, Nyeredzi collected boxes and hurried back to the shop with them. She unfolded and flattened them next to Ruth and then rolled her sister, who whined in pain, onto the cardboard. It took a long time to drag the boxes outside, as she was trying to avoid hurting her sister more. Nyeredzi's desire to fulfill her sister's wish gave her strength. She pulled Ruth to the lawn and sat down next to her, pressing on her wound with the towel. Her hands were drenched in blood.

Ruth opened her eyes. "Thank you," she whispered.

"I'm sorry if I hurt you more."

Ruth shook her head. "You are so brave."

"I don't think so, Sis."

"You are," Ruth said. "You told me the truth when I had chosen to look the other way."

She was talking about the time she hired a maid named Izzy from the Mutare countryside, and Nyeredzi told her she saw Ruth's husband touching Izzy's chest. Ruth chucked both Izzy and her husband out.

"I never meant for you to separate from the love of your life," Nyeredzi said. "I'm so sorry."

"Do you not see yourself as the love of my life? There's nothing to be sorry for. You gave me the strength to accept the truth. My husband was sleeping with my maid—can you believe that?" Ruth let out a small laugh. "You even noticed that I hid my foot from people."

Ruth paused to cough.

"You," she said to Nyeredzi, "everyone in the family knows you are brave."

Ruth coughed again, blood flooding her mouth, choking

her. Nyeredzi tilted Ruth's head on the side so she could spit. Her tongue and teeth were tainted red.

"Hiding the past doesn't mean we are weak." Nyeredi paused. "It means we don't want it to control us. If the past is too painful, why should we expose it in our eyes? Why should we let it make us cry?"

"See, I told you, you are the brave one," Ruth said. "Look after Mama, Nyeredzi!"

"What do you mean? This is not the end, the ambulance is coming, Mama is coming, and…and I am here. Can't you see me? Sis, you can't leave me."

Nyeredzi started crying, her whole body quivering. Ruth opened her mouth, struggling to speak. Her voice was so faint. Her sister inhaled but she didn't do what Nyeredzi expected. She didn't exhale.

"No, no, no, no, no, Sis—please!" Nyeredzi pressed her hand against Ruth's chest, counting. She began to perform CPR. Where was the ambulance? It should have been there by now. It should have taken her sister to hospital already. She wasn't going to let Ruth go like this. She used all the strength that was in her body, pressing hard on her sister's chest while checking for a pulse in between.

The pulse she searched for on Ruth's wrist and neck wasn't there. Had she done the CPR wrong? Had she missed some vital information in her First Aid class? Why wasn't Ruth coming back? In a confusion state, she was lost. But when she recalled what the ancestors told her: *Ask and we will give*—she begged for the power to bring her sister back as she resumed with the CPR.

Why wouldn't they hear her plea? They'd made her do things she didn't expect before, right? What was that burning flame in her eyes—the one the woman at the Ndima Ndima dance saw? Even her parents. Was it all for nothing? If Nyeredzi was that important to them, they wouldn't let Ruth go like that. This was her sister.

After a while of performing CPR, and checking if Ruth's pulse was back in between, Nyeredzi was now covered in sweat mixed with blood, her sister's blood. Ruth was the only sister who had treated her well ever since Nyeredzi was young. She laid her head on her sister's chest, hoping she would hear the music of life thumping from within, hoping for a miracle. But there was nothing. How could she have failed her?

Perhaps she wasn't as close to the ancestors as she thought she was. Tears dropped on her face as she heaved, alone.

A shadow washed over both of them on the green lawn. Nyeredzi raised her head to see Zuva, standing there in shock. Ruth's mouth was open, her eyes unblinking.

"Mama, I'm so sorry—I tried," Nyeredzi cried. She got up on her knees and grasped Zuva's arm. Her nails dug into her mother's flesh. "She was talking to me, she asked me to bring her out. Mama, I don't know what happened, but I tried."

Zuva knelt beside Nyeredzi and Ruth.

"The ambulance didn't show up, Mama."

"The roads are blocked, my daughter." Zuva reached out to hold her, tears falling.

Nyeredzi had never seen her mother cry, and this only made her sob louder. She sobbed because she had made her mother cry. She sobbed because she could not save her sister.

"You did a great job, Nyeredzi," Zuva said, pulling Ruth's head onto her lap. She wrapped her arms around both her daughters.

How could her mother say she did a great job? Even

though someone was responsible for Ruth's death, she'd failed her sister too. She couldn't imagine seeing her mother with only three daughters when she'd given birth to four. Weren't parents supposed to die before their children? Was her mother going to use her gun hidden in a safe under the bed to hunt the person who'd shot her first born?

Nyeredzi knew she would never find peace within herself again. Although she sat wrapped in her mother's arms, she wanted to run away from her failure. The joy that had bound them had been severed. Nothing else sang in their ears except for their grieving breath. Nyeredzi watched with swollen eyes when her mother reached out to close Ruth's eyes and mouth. Her beloved sister was gone.

PARALYZED

Late Spring 1999
ZUVA

Zuva wasn't prepared to stand in front of the parishioners to preach on that day, nor any time soon, but she had to do it. She couldn't abandon her duties.

Earlier on, after receiving a call from Mrs. Tuze at home, Zuva stood at the back of her house, staring into the horizon. The dark gray skies seemed so low, as if they were so close to her, weighing down her soul. She'd hoped to conquer her fears by getting some fresh air, but the spit falling from the skies raised goosebumps on her arms.

Although she was grateful for all the things Mr. Tuze did at the church, he had fallen ill at the wrong time. Mr. Tuze was the leader before Zuva and her family moved to Harare, and since she'd taken over, he had been helping in the church with other things. He ran the counseling sessions and organized the charity for orphans. But when Ruth died, Zuva asked him to take over the services while she mourned for her daughter.

Zuva was in her long olive–green dress, sweeping the maroon carpeted floor. She stood behind the pulpit that was in the middle of the altar. It held a microphone, a pen, and a notebook underneath her Bible. Behind her, the choir gleamed in their white robes, singing a slow tune before the service started.

On their left, the musical instruments were set in order, the drums, saxophones, tambourines. A large piano stood closest to them. An arched white wall held Jesus Christ on the cross, angels looking up to him on either side. The long, cream curtains had been drawn to the corners of the building to let the light in through the large windows. The skies were even darker than before.

She glanced at the opened Bible and then looked at the two rows of pews stretching a hundred meters from her. Somehow the church was crowded that Sunday morning. She couldn't miss her family sitting in the front row, an empty space next to her grandchildren, Ruth's spot. Her chest tightened, and her face tensed with the realization that no one was ever going to fill that void. And with the verse she had chosen, the service was going to be even harder than she had assumed. Was it going to help her let go of her daughter's death?

After finishing the song, the choir and the parishioners stopped singing.

Zuva raised her hands, and yelled out, "Praise the Lord."

"Amen!" the parishioners yelled back.

"Let's look at Ephesians 5 verse 31 today." She paused, looking at the people opening their Bibles.

She continued as people bowed their heads to read along with her. "The Lord said...therefore a man shall leave his father and mother and hold fast to his wife, and two shall become one flesh." She looked at the people nodding their heads.

A sudden memory came to her. She was sitting on

the bed with Ruth. It was a day before Ruth's wedding. The fragility of her daughter left Zuva overwhelmed with mixed emotions. Partly, she was excited, but at the same time, she was sad that her daughter was leaving, starting a new life far away with her husband. She had raised Ruth during the difficult times of their life, and war almost took Ruth from her.

In the long run, the war had ended, they had lived life in peace, and she never dreamed of seeing her daughter laying lifeless on a patch of lawn, covered in blood. She thought she was always going to save her daughters, even though she was not the Creator. How could her daughter die like that? Where had she gone wrong? She had failed to protect her own child this time, and this left her paralyzed, spiritually and physically.

A few days had gone by without her eating food, without her speaking to her other daughters. She couldn't communicate with the living. She could see that her husband was there all the time, but she couldn't feel him when he touched her. When he wanted to comfort her in bed, all she could do was turn, sleep on one side, facing the wall, and gaze in the dark the whole night.

"It's amazing how the cycle of life is already planned for us." She looked at the crowd, staring back at her. "When we are born, we grow, we fall in love, we marry, we give birth to our own children like our parents did; our children grow and they fall in the same cycle we have already lived, and life goes on and on like that, right?"

The parishioners nodded their heads, agreeing with Zuva.

She continued, "So, don't we all love it when our children marry someone they love, start a new life, a family?" She looked at her grandchildren. "Don't we love it when we see them happy, and we are there to send them off?"

"Yes!" A few people from the crowd yelled back.

Zuva nodded with a sad face. Something was not right as she spoke out louder. Her message was not getting through to the parishioners. She could see that in them, so she chose another way of saying it.

"Don't we all love holding our grandchildren in our arms, putting them to bed, playing funny games with them, spoiling them with delicious treats when they are hungry?" She paused. "They call them bundles of joy, right?"

Some people smiled, nodding at what Zuva was saying. She gazed outside through the double pivot doors, open wide; it was now raining. If only she could go and stand outside and let the water pour on her, perhaps her grief would be washed away. Why was it so hard for them to understand what she was saying in front of them? This verse she had chosen wasn't about happiness or marriage to her, it was about losing a child to something, and as she stood there, trying to let people see through her, she realized people were waiting for her to continue.

She pointed to the roof with her finger. "But what happens when death comes to take our children before us?" she asked, looking at the parishioners.

Some of them lowered their heads, others turned to look at each other, reminiscing the death of Ruth. And at that moment, that's when it sank in for them.

Zuva was someone who'd seen so much death, in the war, in the family, in the neighborhood, and in the church, but the death of her daughter came when she was not expecting it. How was it right to see her daughter swallowed by death before her? It broke her. Her world was crushed to such an extent that she couldn't deal with it.

Zuva stared deep between the letters of the Bible, and all the words she had planned to say couldn't come out, it was as if her vocal cords were paralyzed.

A big black block sat in her chest, and it was now heavy, heavier than the dark skies outside. She gripped the edges of the pulpit tightly. The timing was tight, it had created a weak point in her. She took a while before she could lift her head. The corner of her eye saw Mwedzi wanting to get up, to come and comfort her, but she gestured for him to stop before he did so. She glimpsed at the choir sitting behind her before a tear dropped onto her cheek. They began to sing.

Zuva wiped off the tear and lowered her head again. Why would she let herself drown in her own sorrow, in front of all those people? Why would she choose these verses so soon after Ruth passed on, when she was at her lowest point? Zuva breathed deeply and stood tall. She gripped the edges of the pulpit again, trying to pull herself together. Otherwise, she'd have ruined the service by her one–time emotional breakdown. She'd never cried in front of her parishioners, but that Sunday morning, she let one tear drop on her cheek. It wasn't her body that had failed her, but her faith, and with the extended period of grief, it was as dark as the darkest night of the soul. There was no light at all.

Soon, Zuva flipped the pages to Revelation 21:4, where she had marked before. She raised her hand to stop the choir.

"Revelation 21 verse 4." She waited for people to open the page. After a little while, she read out loud again, "He will wipe every tear from their eyes. There will be no more death, mourning or crying or pain…" She stopped. She couldn't finish the verse. Her breath was coming in gasps and it could be heard on the microphone. "For those with Bibles today, you can continue reading to yourselves."

Her emotions were sucking her way deeper than she had expected. To distract herself from these feelings, she strolled away from the pulpit to stand in front of the pianist. She held the microphone in her right hand so tight, moving here and there at times.

"My whole point here, people, is that, who are we to stop death? We can plan this and that in life; to bear a child, to raise them with unconditional love, send them off as Ephesians says, but no one knows when death will come." She looked at the parishioners. "No one knows who dies first, sometimes it's a parent, other times, it's a child."

Some people stared at her; others had lowered their heads. And from where she was, she saw some people wiping tears off their faces too. Perhaps Zuva's preaching had managed to get them to feel what she was going through.

"Death is something we all can't avoid, it's part of the cycle, but at the same time, we have to look up to our Lord to wipe away our tears when we mourn for our loved ones."

"Amen!" the parishioners yelled out.

She had lowered her voice. "There are times when death knocks on our doorsteps, we see it crawling onto our loved ones' bodies, sometimes it doesn't take them, but other times, it does, yet some of us are allowed to say goodbye before or after. We are left with loss but let us hold on to the memories we shared with them, let us hold onto what's left here on Earth with us, for ourselves and for the people we love." She raised her hands toward the people and said, "Praise the Lord!"

"Amen!" the parishioners yelled out again.

She led the Lord's prayer, and the rest of the people in the church followed. A couple of young children started crying from the crowd amidst the prayer.

When they were done, she yelled into the microphone, "I can hear some very important people crying already, in desperate need of that unconditional love I talked about. I suppose hunger is making them complain now." She gave out a brief smile. "With that being said, ladies and gentlemen, I guess our service has come to an end; thank you for coming to church today, be blessed."

The pianist began to play a warm song, sending the parishioners home through the wide, double pivot doors at the back. It was still pouring outside—the skies, still dark as before. Something was still swirling inside Zuva. She could see that dark cloud floating above her, haunting her, day and night.

She stood behind the pulpit while she watched people leave. Some people greeted each other on their way out. She may have managed to finish the service, but she knew deep down, it hadn't gone well. Her message may have gotten through to the parishioners, but who was she trying to convince here? Herself? She'd hoped to chase her demons away with this service. Even if they had started to run on their own, it seemed as though she was now a leader who was lost spiritually, who was physically weak.

She held onto the pulpit again, clinging onto the little faith that was left in her. What else could she have done? Decades ago, when she left Goho Village in 1970, she found peace in the Bible when she read it, even embedded her soul within its spine. Perhaps, she would find peace in it again.

AFRICAN FISH EAGLE

Summer 2000
NYEREDZI

Nyeredzi and Zuva used a combi van to travel to Goho Village from Mutare City Center. First, they had traveled for four hours from Harare in an air–conditioned Marcopolo bus, which was spacious with good quality seats. Nyeredzi had chosen a seat by the window to have a view of the plantations, the mountains, and lakes which whizzed past and stirred a sense of adventure deep inside of her.

Three days earlier, Nyeredzi stood in front of her mother in the garden. The broad green leaves of the Covo hung loosely from their stems, scattered inside the rectangular garden beds where Zuva was bent down, spreading mulch. The red soil was damp from the brief showers that were blowing in and out throughout the day. The maize crops circled the backyard and one side of their house. Maize cobs were hanging at an angle from the green stalks and whenever a strong breeze blew, small pieces of the beige tassels dropped to the ground.

"Mama," Nyeredzi said, waiting for Zuva to get up and face her. "Can I apply for a university outside of this country? I know there are plenty of universities here in Zimbabwe, but my heart wants to study somewhere else."

"If you think it's going to make you happy or help you in some way, then do so," Zuva replied, looking down.

"If I choose another country, can you at least help me not to forget?"

"Forget what, Nyeredzi?" she paused. "Do you fear to lose who you are?"

"No, Mama, I am asking if you can bless me with something I can hold onto before I leave."

"Haven't I taught you everything since you were young?" Zuva asked, stretching her hand to gesture at the bush.

"I suppose I am only asking for one thing I do not know," Nyeredzi said slowly.

"I suppose you are."

Zuva bent down to continue gardening and Nyeredzi walked away. She could see her mother was not happy with her decision. They had not been talking as much since the death of her oldest sister, Ruth. When Nyeredzi sat her final exams in November the previous year, not long after her sister died, she passed. She didn't think she would succeed with all the anger that coiled inside her, but when her results came back, she saw the transcript as her passport to go and step on all the corners of the world—the lands that floated in the middle of the ocean as if they were ships, the lands that sat still while covered in layers of snow in winter, and the ones she read about in the Holy Bible.

Although Nyeredzi promised Ruth before she died that she would look after their mother, it had proved to be a challenging task. Neither of them wanted to talk. Her mother spent most of her time in the garden, or she would go and spend hours at church.

Each time Nyeredzi looked at Zuva, she saw herself as a failure in her mother's eyes. Nyeredzi had nightmares about the day she tried to save Ruth after she was shot. The tears on her mother's cheeks when she arrived to see her oldest daughter lying on the grass with eyes and mouth agape, dead; it cut Nyeredzi so deeply, her stomach was twisted in a knot each morning she woke. Nyeredzi thought if she ran far away, maybe this inescapable feeling of failure would disappear one day.

Now, Nyeredzi was in a packed combi van overflowing with people squeezed against one another on worn–out, padded gray seats. She and her mother were in the back row, four rows behind the driver. The woman who sat next to Nyeredzi wore a sleeveless blouse. When the woman had climbed into the vehicle earlier in Dhaka Village, she was all sweaty. Her round, thick arm pushed Nyeredzi toward her mother, and her fluffy wig kept swiping Nyeredzi's face.

Nyeredzi glanced at her mother and gave her a brief smile, which Zuva returned. Nyeredzi had to peel her skin away from this woman's sticky arm and set her hip free from her neighbor's butt. She shifted forward, letting the woman have all the space she needed. The conductor's loud reggae—a CD of Lucky Dube—had the combi van's windows vibrating and Zuva had to shout twice to tell him to stop by the shopping center in Goho.

The driver pulled over on a dusty road, the van rumbling over the edge of the thick grass. Everyone on the left side of the van in front of Zuva and Nyeredzi got up, folding their chairs. Some clambered out while others were too lazy and just bent their bodies to give way to Zuva and Nyeredzi.

Nyeredzi and her mother collected their bags from the trailer, and the conductor handed Zuva coins and notes.

"Here is your change, Gogo."

"Thank you, my son," Zuva said.

He covered the bags piled in the trailer with a broad dusty green tent, and then retied them with a rope before climbing up to stand by the sliding door. He pounded the top of the van twice with his hand, and the driver stepped on the accelerator. The conductor was holding onto a handle inside the van while half his body hung out, the wind blowing his striped shirt away from his stomach. He asked a woman walking on the side of the road, "Do you want to go to the city?"

The woman shook her head no. The conductor bent down to slip inside the van and pulled the sliding door shut, his face disappointed.

The white combi van drove away, dust swirling in the air. Zuva let out a sigh of relief and closed her eyes for a moment. Nyeredzi turned around, studying the land. The last time she came here was a year ago, but Zuva had returned a few times since then. Nyeredzi stared at the general stores and bars. They still looked the same, letters painted in bold colors on the front of the shops.

Further on, painted houses and a few huts were scattered on the steep land. The lush green foliage swayed from side to side. The mountains in the distance looked very dark. Two boys were herding cattle across a grassy field, the bells around the animals' necks clinking. One of the boys spun his body, doing somersaults with a stick in one hand. When he finished, he let out a loud triumphant laugh.

Nyeredzi turned to her mother with a smile on her face. "Can we go now, Mama? I am dying to see Uncle and his family."

"I am taking you somewhere else, Nyeredzi," Zuva told

her. "You can greet your uncle and cousins, but you'll be staying with Mrs. Kaundi, okay?"

"Who is Mrs. Kaundi, Mama?"

"The woman who welcomed me back to Goho the last time we came here. You know her—she came to look for me in the mountains the day Selina came out of her dwelling."

"Yeah, I remember her. Is she related to us?"

"We are all related through humanity, Nyeredzi."

"So, are you coming to stay with her too?" She looked at her mother. "It's going to be hard for me to stay with a family I don't know."

Zuva stared deep into Nyeredzi's eyes. "I thought you wanted something that will help you not to forget?"

Nyeredzi nodded, wondering how living with someone she didn't know was going to help her to not forget. She wasn't keen about her mother's suggestion, but she had to go along with it. They picked up their bags and began walking down the dusty road. Some people who came across them knelt, greeting Zuva. She watched the way her mother spoke to an older woman she knew with such confidence. Zuva asked her if they were getting enough crops from the fields, if there was peace within the village, if people were helping the elders who didn't have families to support them.

Soon, they reached a dwelling fenced with barbed wire. The granadilla plant was growing along the wire and wooden posts. Inside the fence, there was a vast land of maize crops in the backyard where sugar beans coiled themselves up the green stalks. The fruit trees that circled the buildings on the property included guava, naartjie, wild grape, mobola plum, and monkey–bread, while the apple was closer to the borehole. The path of beige sand led them to three round huts roofed with thatch and a four-roomed plastered house roofed with corrugated zinc. Both the house and the huts were painted in light blue.

A woman was kneeling inside a hut, running her hand in a circular motion on the floor. When the woman turned toward the door, her eyes met Zuva's. Mrs. Kaundi stood up and came outside quickly. Nyeredzi could see her hands were covered in thick green paste and she watched as the woman kneeled on the ground. Her neck had ripples of skin and her face was filled with lines, maps sketched by the sun. Nyeredzi was drawn to her soft voice and could tell she was over seventy years old, but the woman still moved so fast.

"Mambokadzi, welcome, welcome," she said, walking toward Zuva and Nyeredzi. She glanced at her hands. "I apologize, I am working on my floor."

"It's all right, Mrs. Kaundi," Zuva said, reaching out to give her a brief hug.

When Nyeredzi stepped closer to hug Mrs. Kaundi, there was a familiar scent lingering on her, but she couldn't recall where she'd smelled it before. Mrs. Kaundi ran to wash her hands in a small plastic gray bucket. Then she opened the door of the house, letting Zuva and Nyeredzi inside.

"Sit wherever you want, Mambokadzi," the woman said. "Did you just arrive from Harare?"

"Yes." Zuva nodded as she sat on a green sofa, next to Nyeredzi. "Do you remember my youngest daughter, Nyeredzi?"

Mrs. Kaundi was busy opening her cupboards door, taking out glasses, water, and Mazoe orange crush. She placed them on the small round coffee table before sitting on the other sofa across Zuva and Nyeredzi.

"Yes, Mambokadzi, I remember her. She is fully grown now. Please Mambokadzi, help yourself to the drink?"

"You didn't have to," Zuva said, looking at Mrs. Kaundi.

"Please drink. The last people who visited me from your family was your husband. Before that it was only your father and mother." Her eyes glazed with tears. "That's when you were away, at war, and now you are here with your daughter. How blessed am I?"

Zuva nodded, looking at Nyeredzi. Nyeredzi knelt next to the table to dilute the Mazoe orange crush. First, she handed one glass to her mother, then one to Mrs. Kaundi.

"Ashe, the glass is for you," Mrs. Kaundi said, pushing it back.

Nyeredzi pushed the glass filled with orange juice back to Mrs. Kaundi and got up to open the cupboard where she took out a tumbler and made herself a drink. Zuva glanced at Nyeredzi and nodded once.

"Is it all right if Nyeredzi stays here with you for a few days?" Zuva asked, looking at Mrs. Kaundi. "She will be helping you with some work."

"Who am I to order the blood of the royal, Mambokadzi?" She paused. "Eeh! This is too much, but if you think she will fit in my small house here, she's more than welcome."

"She's here to fulfill something missing in her and I think you are the right person to help her," Zuva said, finishing off the orange crush. "Thank you for the drink. It quenched my thirsty throat."

Zuva picked up her bag and walked outside with Mrs. Kaundi. Nyeredzi got up to look around. She picked a few bird plums in a wooden bowl by the kitchen unit filled with clay pots, glasses, and dinner plates on the top shelf. A few wooden spoons and woven trays hung on nails in the wall. In the corner was a medium drum made of cow skin.

Nyeredzi chewed on the sweet bird plums while she stared at a black–and–white photo hung on the white wall. The young woman in it looked like Mrs. Kaundi. She was standing next to a man who was wrapping his arm around her. Mrs. Kaundi returned and stood next to Nyeredzi, gazing at the photo.

"That's my husband, Philip."

"It's a beautiful photo, Mrs. Kaundi." Nyeredzi turned to face the old woman. "Can I call you Ambuya? It feels weird calling you Mrs. Kaundi all the time. Plus, I never had someone to call grandma. And I see one in you."

"I've never had anyone calling me Ambuya, but I am honored to be called Ambuya." She smiled. "Come, Ashe, let me show you where to put your bags."

Nyeredzi lifted one bag and before she could stop her, Ambuya lifted the other one off the shiny floor.

"Ambuya, that can stay in here," Nyeredzi said, opening the bag to reveal its groceries—a bag of rice, cooking oil, tea bags, sugar, corned beef, powdered milk. It was Zuva's idea to buy the groceries, except Nyeredzi thought they were taking them to her uncle's place.

"Oh, my Lord, you didn't have to buy all this," Ambuya said. She knelt on the floor and began separating the toiletries and food in separate piles. "I've never had anyone bring me groceries."

Nyeredzi kept quiet, leaning against the doorframe. She thought about the times her mother came back here, if she gave other families all the groceries she bought. Ambuya packed the food into her kitchen unit and returned the toiletries to the bag. While she led Nyeredzi along the passageway, she opened all the doors of the house to reveal furnished guest rooms. Nyeredzi wondered which room Ambuya slept in. The older woman then opened the last door and said this room was for her. Inside was a double bed tucked in the corner.

"Thank you, Ambuya," Nyeredzi said, turning to face the bed. "What about you? Where do you sleep with your husband if these are all guest rooms?"

"Oh, my husband left me more than twenty years ago." She inhaled deeply. "It was difficult when he died because it was always him and me. I guess death affects the ones left behind a lot more, but it's up to you. You can choose to move on with your life, or stay in one spot, grieving."

Nyeredzi stepped closer to Ambuya. She didn't know what to say at first. How could she have known Nyeredzi was suffering from a loss? Mrs. Kaundi placed the bag with its toiletries on the polished floor. "Moving on allows the deceased to be happy wherever they are."

"I am sorry, Ambuya. I didn't know."

"Nothing for you to feel sorry about, I am the one sorry that I couldn't give my Philip any children." She looked away.

Now Nyeredzi knew why there was only a photo of Ambuya and her husband on the wall. She felt sad for her. Was Mrs. Kaundi stuck in the past, grieving for her dead husband? Did she see herself as a failure because she couldn't give her husband children?

"Well, I am here, and your husband can see a child in your house from up in the heavens." Nyeredzi placed her bag on the floor. "Accept me in your heart as your daughter—your beloved child, and I'll always accept you as my grandmother."

Ambuya wiped away tears, leaning forward to hug Nyeredzi.

"Well, a daughter of mine doesn't sleep in a guest house alone. But I think I should call you granddaughter." Nyeredzi smiled. "Come, granddaughter." She lifted Nyeredzi's bag and strolled back into the passageway. "I don't sleep in here, but in the hut outside."

Ambuya led her to a large hut and opened the door wide. The sunlight flared in from the rectangle window on the wall and the door. Inside was a queen mattress on the floor, neatly covered in thick blankets. Hangers carrying brightly colored clothes were hung on nails on the other side of the wall. Her husband's clothes were still in here, still hanging next to Ambuya's clothes.

Robes made of animal skins hung on the other side of the room. Three drums stood next to a large wooden trunk at the head of the mattress, a large rug of brown and white cowhide in the middle of the shined floor. Walking sticks that were tied together in a silver pail by the door appeared to be her husband's too. Who could she have given her husband's clothes to if she didn't have a son? Nyeredzi realized that Ambuya was only living because she was still holding onto the memories she shared with her husband.

"I'm sorry, I broke the bed frame one winter when I couldn't go up the mountain to fetch some firewood, but the mattress is still firm."

Nyeredzi stepped in, smiling.

"This is where I slept with my husband years ago, but now I am going to sleep with my granddaughter. How blessed am I?" Ambuya smiled.

"And how blessed am I to sleep in a hut, with my grandmother? I've never done that," Nyeredzi said, and Ambuya left to heat some water for a bath.

Nyeredzi ran her hand along Ambuya's clothes. She held some of the printed fabric in front of her body. Her fingers dug deep into the fur of leopard skin placed on the rectangle trunk. She could hear Ambuya in another hut, so she walked to the door to peer inside.

Two wooden windows let the light in, and a whole wall was just shelves. Galvanized and plastic tubs were piled on the floor, next to silver pails filled with water. Black and silver pots were hung on the nails. On one side of the shelves sat decorated clay pots. Ambuya got up to pick a wooden spoon from among the utensils, plates, and cups of different colors stacked on the other side of the shelves.

"Come inside, granddaughter," Ambuya said, sitting on the bonde next to the round metal firewood stove.

Nyeredzi walked up to the tall wooden mortar next to the containers, along with its thick pestle. She'd used one before; it wasn't easy. She'd kept hitting the edges of the mortar with the pestle, tipping out the maize that was inside. Ambuya blew on the flames underneath the stove. On top of a pail filled with water heated and a small clay pot next to it was steaming up. Smoke swirled up to the cylindrical dark beams holding the thatched roof.

"Take the bench, my granddaughter."

Nyeredzi picked up the bench that was next to the firewood piled behind the door. "Do you want to sit on it, Ambuya?" she asked.

"It's for you to sit on," Ambuya said, stirring pumpkin leaf relish inside the clay pot.

"I can sit with you, Ambuya. We do have maponde at home."

"Nice." Ambuya poured water into a white bucket. "This is for you. Come and have a bath."

Ambuya picked up the bucket with warm water and walked outside to the bathroom. She moved so fast that Nyeredzi struggled to catch up with her. The destination was two small rectangular rooms: one side was the pit latrine and the other was the bathroom. Nyeredzi walked in holding the bucket, a towel and a bar of soap. In the corner was a tiny hole for drainage. She looked up to see the blue dome above her patched with white clouds. A branch of a monkey–bread tree was floating above the squared room. Nyeredzi undressed and hung her clothes on the nails in the wall.

In the middle of washing her face, Nyeredzi opened her eyes to see a monkey staring back at her. She screamed, scaring the monkey away.

Ambuya came running to the bathroom. "Is everything all right?"

"It's nothing, Ambuya," Nyeredzi shouted. "It was just a monkey."

"Aah, I forgot to tell you they come to feed on the monkey–bread all the time."

Nyeredzi could hear Ambuya's footsteps retreating to the kitchen. She wiped her face quickly to survey the tree and see if there were more monkeys on it. From now on, Nyeredzi was going to bathe with one eye open. Though she hadn't liked the way her Uncle Garikai surrounded their family's property with an electric fence, now she could understand why. Her privacy had been invaded by those little brown eyes staring at her naked body.

By the time she was finished and dressed again, the sun had slipped beyond the mountains. The stars seemed so far from where they sat under the mango tree eating sadza and pumpkin leaves mixed with onions and tomatoes. It was so delicious, Nyeredzi couldn't stop eating. Sadza was hot and smooth, the relish creamy and perfectly seasoned. Was it hunger, or was it that the food cooked in clay pots tasted different?

"If we go to bed early, tomorrow we can wake up early

to go and fetch water at the river."

"But Ambuya, you have a borehole here," Nyeredzi said, pointing across the yard.

"Yes, I do have a borehole, but this is for you, granddaughter. Have you ever gone up the cliff to fetch water from the river?"

"No."

"So, we shall wake up early. When you finish, go and rest." Ambuya washed her hands in a plastic bowl. "That borehole is only there because of your mother. She sent an engineer to install it for me years ago when she returned here with all of you. Your father built this four–roomed house for me. How blessed am I to have people who care for me?"

Perhaps, Nyeredzi thought, Ambuya was teaching her not to forget the people who make a community. If she wanted to be like her mother, she'd have to soldier up.

When Nyeredzi finished eating her dinner, she washed all the dishes and put them on the dara. They didn't dry completely, so Nyeredzi rushed to stack them in a large plastic bowl; she didn't want to be outside by herself. It was as if the mountains blew a sigh in the darkness. Nyeredzi couldn't even make out the green foliage she'd seen that afternoon when they arrived.

Further away at her uncle's place, electricity lit up the dwelling. If she could go and watch the TV shows she watched last time she visited with her family, maybe she would not notice that Ambuya's dwelling had no electricity. She could see that other houses further away had power too. Still, this countryside was nothing like Harare. The vibrant city filled with people who never slept at night, who strolled in the street of the capital beaming with neon lights. The music that kept them moving, and the fancy food that filled their hungry stomachs in the hotels and restaurants.

Nyeredzi walked into the hut where Ambuya was already asleep. She lay next to her and blew out the candle so the whole room was enveloped in darkness. She listened to Ambuya breathing heavily. She wondered how Mrs. Kaundi had been living alone for so long. She barely had visitors and didn't have any relatives of her own. Nyeredzi was terrified for her. What if she got ill one day and there was no one to help her? Perhaps that's why she ended up breaking the bed frame because she didn't have anyone to help her. What if Ambuya died alone and no one would ever know she was dead?

When Nyeredzi woke, it was so early in the morning, the owls were still hooting. Ambuya was shaking her shoulder.

"Granddaughter, wake up, we have to go now," she said.

"Already? Can't we wait until the sun is out?"

"If we go now, I'll show you the sun coming out."

Nyeredzi got up, still half asleep. Soon, she was outside with Ambuya walking in the dark. They both held pails in their hands. Nyeredzi followed Ambuya, who always moved quickly in everything she did. She was trying to keep up, but the land was unfamiliar. Along the narrow pathway, her body brushed against shrubs. It was hard to see where she was stepping as the mountains were foggy and dark. By the time they arrived at Yeredzo River, whose water sang endless music, the sky was brighter. Ambuya chose a spot for them to fetch water. There were other women there too.

"Morning, Mrs. Kaundi," one of the ladies said.

"Morning," Ambuya responded.

"Who is with you today?" the lady asked again.

"I'm her granddaughter," Nyeredzi responded quickly. "I'm Nyeredzi."

"Oh, nice to meet you, Nyeredzi," the lady said. "How come you never visit your grandmother?"

"I live very far away, that's why." She placed her pail on a rock. "Ambuya, please help me?"

The women looked at each other. Ambuya picked the pail and placed it on Nyeredzi's head. She picked hers up too, and soon, they were walking down the cliff. Nyeredzi overheard the women talking. "Did you hear that she called her Ambuya? Maybe she has children we do not know of."

When they reached a cleared section, Mrs. Kaundi stopped. Nyeredzi was wet because she couldn't keep the pail steady.

"Granddaughter, wait," she said, putting her own pail down on flat granite rock, then helped Nyeredzi lower hers. They sat next to each other on a rock looking toward the east. Slowly, the edge of the sky beyond the mountains in the distance began to yellow. The sun was waking from her slumber. Nyeredzi stole a glance at Ambuya who was smiling. The green foliage was coming alive again, and birds were singing in their nests.

"I am sorry for what those women said when we left," Nyeredzi said softly.

"You can't control people's thoughts. The only way to live your life without letting anyone control how you feel is to look aside, granddaughter."

Nyeredzi nodded. She felt as if she was still processing everything Ambuya had said since she arrived yesterday. This woman before her was filled with knowledge and she now understood why her mother had left her at her house. She wasn't thinking about her uncle's luxury life anymore; she was keen to learn from her Ambuya.

"Your mother was born at sunrise. I was there when I went to help your grandmother, and your grandfather walked out to lift her to the sun shining upon our faces and called your mother Zuva." She smiled. "I don't know about your father though. It's a miracle they met, especially with their names."

Mwedzi meant moon, Zuva sun, and Nyeredz star.

"Maybe he was born when the moon was full?" Nyeredzi said.

"Maybe!" Ambuya looked at the sun. "But when the sun and moon meet, they call it a solar eclipse—isn't that right, granddaughter?"

"Yes. Ambuya, did you study science?"

"Granddaughter, the sun, the moon, and the earth were already here before scientists were born." She stared into Nyeredzi's eyes. "Over here, when the moon meets the sun, they create the ring of fire to bear a star."

Nyeredzi had never thought of her name in that way. She had always asked her mother why she was the only one who wasn't given a Biblical name. Her mother comforted her by telling her the star was first created before those women in the Bible. She'd assumed both her parents just liked the name. Now she looked at Ambuya, staring at the eastern side. Half of the sun was visible, bright, and yellow. She wanted to watch it until her eyes were sore, but they picked up their pails and returned home.

At home, Nyeredzi swept the yard with a broom before cleaning the four-roomed house and the huts. When she reached the hut where she'd seen Ambuya with green paste the day before, she knelt and smelled the floor where tiny pieces of grass were popping up.

"That's cow dung," Ambuya said, standing behind Nyeredzi.

"It looks beautiful, but why did you use cow dung on your floor?"

"Cow dung holds the floor intact, and it stops dust from swirling up. It also chases pests away. Traditionally, people have been using it for a long time."

The day before Nyeredzi had struggled to figure out where she'd smelled Ambuya's scent but now she realized what it was. "Will you teach me how to apply it on the floor, Ambuya?"

"Yes, I'd love to—maybe tomorrow. When we finish eating, I want to take you to the mountains." She handed Nyeredzi a round pad used to carrying wood on top of one's head.

"Are we going to fetch firewood, Ambuya?"

"Yes, granddaughter."

Later, they headed off, Ambuya holding an axe. About 300 meters away from their home, the climb started to grow steep.

"This is the way to the graves of the kings and queens," Ambuya said, adjusting the scarf on her head. "No one is allowed there except for the relatives only. This mountain here belongs to King Mutongi and the chiefs under him. So, we can't use that pathway. People are only allowed to fetch firewood from this section onwards." She pointed to an expanse of forest and told Nyeredzi that most kings and queens were buried in caves. "But your grandfather," she said, "chose to be put on that rock so the sun will greet him first before his people."

Nyeredzi nodded, thinking about her mother: where would she choose to be buried? Would she decide to lie inside a cave or let the sun greet her first before her people? It seemed there was a lot she didn't know about her family, about this land before her, and about life itself. Would she have had the chance to learn all this if she hadn't asked her mother to bless her with one thing she didn't know?

To learn much more would mean she would have to stay here forever. If she could stay here with Ambuya, her mother would go back to Harare on her own. Could this be the place she could escape to? Nyeredzi was still deciding what she wanted to do with her life. Was it worth it to study law so she could become a family lawyer? Perhaps she shouldn't leave Ambuya alone and turn away from all that she was offering.

The pathway up the mountain was narrow because the earth had been eaten away by heavy rainfall. Nyeredzi walked carefully, avoiding the tender plants. Out of sight, baboons were huffing. The monkeys kept jumping from one tree to another and birds were chirping. It was painful climbing up the hillside. Her calves were sore, her feet were burning, and sometimes she slipped on the loose gravel. Nyeredzi gasped for air, trying to catch up with Ambuya.

"If we walk slow, granddaughter, we will come back late."

"Okay, Ambuya," Nyeredzi said, though she wanted to take a moment to look behind her. The few glances she took left her with the urge to soak it all in and thank the ancestors who'd blessed her with Mother Earth.

At the top of the mountain, Ambuya began chopping dry wood from the dead trees. At first Nyeredzi was so exhausted, she couldn't even ask Ambuya to give her the axe so she could try this new skill. After she caught her breath, she stretched her hand out toward Ambuya to take the axe. She chopped a few thin logs and stopped.

Ambuya took the axe from her. "Here, this is how you do it," she said.

The edge of the axe met the dead tree at an angle, making it easy for the logs to fall off without using too much energy. Nyeredzi tried it and began to see how it worked.

"There is a false wild medlar tree behind the granite mangosteen over there—go and try them," Ambuya said.

Nyeredzi walked to the tree, heavy with maturing round green fruit. Usually, the granite mangosteen would be orange if they were ripe. She'd only tried them once, and she couldn't wait for their season to come. When the tender, fleshy inside of the fruit sat on her tongue; its acidic juice was a shock, but the sweetness that followed was delicious.

But today though, she would devour a new fruit. She left the tree with false wild medlars in her hands and went to sit on a large granite rock. Her teeth tore the soft brown skinned fruit. The flavor was subtle—a bit sour but was accompanied by a faint sweetness which she sucked from the tiny pods. She didn't stop eating. They were addictive.

Nyeredzi gazed at the eastern mountains in the distance. If she could get up this mountain everyday just to see the panoramic view, it would be enough. Up there, it seemed as though she was closer to the clouds than she was with the village. She could see the mountain they had climbed was about a kilometer in height.

The valley beneath her was a vast land sketched with roads, the horned rock of Selina's dwelling stuck out among the green wild trees scattered everywhere, grass, maize crops, and houses nesting people who bustled in and out. The gray corrugated roofs of houses were a lake fractured in rectangles. A few thatched roofs of huts looked like chocolate cones with rings on top of them.

Nyeredzi continued gobbling on the false wild medlar while Ambuya cut more firewood.

Now the sun was above her, and soon, it would be behind her. Baboons had joined her in devouring the wild fruit. Some climbed the tree; others stretched hands to pluck off the ripe wild fruit. The biggest baboon began huffing and puffing and Nyeredzi stood up, staring back at them. She wanted to walk closer to them.

"Granddaughter, come here," Ambuya said in a low voice. "Don't step too close or they will harm you."

She and Ambuya walked further away from the baboons where they continued to fetch the firewood. Nyeredzi kept thinking about them—how dangerous would they be if she approached them? And even after being warned off by Ambuya, she wasn't scared. Later, when she walked back to check if they were still there, the baboons were already gone.

They started tying the bunches of wood with a soft, peeled skin of a tree. She placed her pad on her head, and Ambuya helped her lift the firewood.

"I'm sorry, Ambuya, why does this make me so sore and it's also heavy?"

"Because it is firewood, granddaughter." She helped to adjust the pile on Nyeredzi's head. "I know you are a city girl, but you have manners that other people lack, and that is why I feel blessed to have you in my house." Ambuya took off her headscarf and coiled it in a circular pad. Nyeredzi gazed at her gray short hair. "Granddaughter, my hair is the hair of a person who has lived a long life."

"I know. Mama has a white patch here," Nyeredzi said, touching the center of her head.

"Now, your mother is different from me. Her patch is a spiritual crown. I am nowhere close to her." She placed her scarf on Nyeredzi's head. "Only peacemakers have a white patch on the core of their heads."

"Was Mama born with the white patch?" Nyeredzi asked.

"Yes."

Nyeredzi went quiet. They both clambered down the steep mountain, not talking until they reached home. Inside the hut, after they bathed and ate dinner, Ambuya sat on the trunk and held one of the drums, tapping on it lightly, singing.

Dai ndiri shiri,	*If I were a bird,*
ndaibhururuka	*I'd fly*
kunamai vangu,	*to my mother,*
kuti ndinovataurira	*to tell her that*
ndane mwana.	*I now have a child.*
Hiya ooh Mambo vangu…	*Hiya ooh my King…*
Mambo mabva nepi	*King where have you come from*
kundikomborera	*to bless me with*
nemwana?	*a child?*
Hoyeee hoyeee…	*Hoyeee hoyeee…*

Nyeredzi got up to dance. She lifted her feet off the floor, moving her arms and hips outwards. Sometimes she bent down, shaking her head in a circular motion. When Ambuya hit the drum harder and sang louder, Nyeredzi noticed some teeth were missing inside Ambuya's mouth at the back. Ambuya sang and sang, and Nyeredzi danced until she threw herself on the mattress.

Ambuya got up and opened her trunk, laughing. Inside were sculptures of small humans and animals, as well as a face mask, which she picked up.

"My husband made this for me."

"You have beautiful things, Ambuya," Nyeredzi said.

"Your mother told me you want to go far away and study?"

"Yes, I was thinking of that."

"What do you mean, granddaughter?"

"It means I am thinking of staying here with you."

"No, granddaughter. You are the hope I never had." She gazed at Nyeredzi in the candlelight. "If I had children of mine, I'd want them to go and study, wherever they wanted to." Ambuya pulled out a piece of cloth and unwrapped three blocks of gold. She looked at the gold, as though she was considering something. "When your grandparents were still alive, they gave me this on my wedding day," she said. "They said two were for my husband and me. And this one, for my child."

Ambuya held the gold up for Nyeredzi to take.

Nyeredzi kept her hands on the mattress. "Ambuya, I can't take that, it's too much."

"Ha! That's what I said when your mother brought you here." She clasped the gold with both her hands. "You are the child I've always wished for. Take this and ask your mother to sell it at the bank. Then you, my granddaughter—an African Fish Eagle shall fly you to the lands we've never been to."

Realization dawned. The memory of the day Nyeredzi met the ancestors came like a flash of lightning. She was told those exact words. And now Ambuya was handing her gold so she could fly overseas.

"Granddaughter, take it," she insisted. "You are a blessing to me, and you were blessed before you were born."

Nyeredzi felt electrified. All the words Ambuya was

saying, the ancestors had already said. Nyeredzi had met a real ancestor, and now she was living with her. So, she nodded and clasped the gold with both her hands.

"Thank you, Ambuya."

There was no turning back on her decision anymore. Though Nyeredzi had initially made it out of anger, she now knew she was meant to fulfill the wishes of the ancestors—starting with the one sitting before her.

CULTURE TO CULTURE

Spring 2002
NYEREDZI

Nyeredzi had fallen in love with the city before she even came to study law at the University of Cape Town. She was now used to the city; the lifestyle was a little bit different here. People embraced their culture through languages and their traditional values. There were more mother tongues to learn, and she was leaning toward Xhosa because the girl whom she shared the room with spoke it.

At first, she had tried Afrikaans, then isiZulu, but when Sibo moved in, Nyeredzi couldn't dismiss the pride Sibo had in her language. To Nyeredzi, this was a lesson she learned, to be proud of who she was, her language, her origins, and whatever made her who she was.

Even with all the good things that were happening to her in South Africa, the good grades she was getting, the friendships she was making with her classmates, quite often she found herself homesick. During her class breaks, she would sit in the garden away from the buildings and stare at the mountains further away.

She had chosen the University of Cape Town because of these mountains that stood behind the buildings. It was a reminder of her origins, of where her mother and father were born, Manicaland. She knew one day she would return, once she had fulfilled her ancestors' wishes, which were hers too.

The view itself brought some calmness to her, but it stirred some emotions internally. It brought back so many memories to her, of her mother, and the last time they spent time together in Mutare. After they returned to Harare, she left within a few weeks.

Even if she had seen it in her mother's eyes that she didn't want her to go, Nyeredzi had to, for herself. She was still suffering from the loss of her sister and now she was bewildered by the guilt of leaving her mother in that state. They may have not talked about it but when Zuva preached in church about death, Nyeredzi had seen her mother's eyes, red and glassy. This was something Nyeredzi knew her mother would never do. And seeing her mother crying on the day Ruth died was already tormenting her. She wanted this guilty conscience to disappear. Perhaps with her being away, it would fade away with time.

On weekends, when Sibo went back home to spend time with her family, Nyeredzi would stroll in the city of Cape Town, reliving the life she'd left in Harare. All those memories she was choosing to block would flow like a river inside her head. Except for the beaches and salty ocean water scent she was now getting used to—there wasn't much difference between Cape Town and Harare City. The tall buildings made of bricks, glass, steel, and timber were sandwiched by wide black tarred roads taking her to different places.

At night, she would wait for the neon lights to show her the way back to the campus after enjoying a beef burger at Wimpy with a bottle of Coca–Cola. This was what she used to do with her family on those evenings when they had all–night prayers at Harare Christian Centre.

This law degree she was studying required her to memorize a lot of what she was reading, so it shouldn't have been hard to remember her childhood. The memories of her and her mother were the ones she tried to block, but they were so vivid. She missed her whole family—her deceased sister, Ruth, but mostly, her mother. Whenever she had problems in life, Nyeredzi always went to Zuva, but now she was alone, far away from home.

Besides, whenever she rang home on the landline, Nyeredzi was finding it hard to talk to her mother, what she was feeling about losing Ruth, because she knew that her mother was also struggling. So, she would bury herself in books of law. It helped a lot with all the knowledge she was gaining because now she knew how she would make herself useful in future.

In her class, she became the favorite student to lecturers, especially Professor Burner. Nyeredzi envied the way she talked and walked in front of all those students, with confidence and so much wisdom in her. And without her acknowledging it, Nyeredzi had also developed these characteristics. Perhaps Professor Burner reminded her of her mother. She'd grown up watching that kind of behavior; and whenever she had classes with Professor Burner, Nyeredzi would get excited; it felt as though she was closer to her mother.

When she was with Sibo, it was all different. Sibo was nothing like Nyeredzi's sisters nor her friends back home. Although she wore casual clothes like every student at the university, she had this energy that Nyeredzi found intriguing. Sibo was more drawn to her culture. Perhaps South Africans embraced their culture more openly than where she came from.

Maybe it was because Nyeredzi was raised as a Christian, and that's why it seemed as though her people weren't so much into their culture. But hadn't it been proved that time when they did the Ndima Ndima dance? The pride that gleamed in her neighbors' eyes. Because of this new spirit she was learning from Sibo, Nyeredzi became fond of her. And bit by bit, they became close.

Sibo had these brown and black leather bracelets, and a necklace that she never took off. They were meant to protect her from evil spirits, Nyeredzi had learned this from her. Even when she took a bath, she would bathe with them on. Nyeredzi would watch Sibo try to dry them with a towel afterwards while she sat on her bed, leaning on her pillows.

Besides a large window letting in the light in between their beds, the tiny wardrobes and desks carrying a lot of books on either side of the wall divided by a door in the middle, it was really easy to distinguish whose things belonged to who. A double bed covered with a white duvet printed with green flowers, timetables nailed to the wall, family pictures collated in one wooden frame, and three large hooks carrying some clothes that couldn't fit in the wardrobe was Nyeredzi's side.

Sibo didn't have much because she always traveled back home on weekends. A deep–rich quilt of mixed colors covered her bed halfway, revealing creased brown sheets tucked underneath the mattress neatly. A large poster of Nelson Mandela, and a photo of a dark–skinned woman wearing traditional clothes were on her side.

"My hero," Sibo pointed at Mandela one day. "And my inspiration," she said, touching the wooden frame hung on the wall.

Nyeredzi stared at the photo. The woman was in a long

red skirt with a black hem. The black sleeveless top was covered in threaded beads of different colors covering the neck and arms. Her head was also covered with a wide black cloth with decorated edges.

Nyeredzi loved how it was tied, leaving the triangle pointing down at the middle of her forehead. The dangling earrings almost touched her shoulders. Her wide lips were covered in blackberry lipstick. Nyeredzi admired the photo but could still remember how their conversation about it was awkward at first. But she had lived with Sibo longer now, and she came to understand who she was.

"Is that your mother?" Nyeredzi had asked. The resemblance of deep dimples on both sides of their faces, the dark, smooth skin on their thin bodies as well as braided curly hair could tell all.

"That's my aunt, she raised me," Sibo had responded and continued, "but she is there because she inspires me, and that was her traditional wedding dress."

"Aah, are your parents still here with us?" Nyeredzi asked with a low voice.

"My mother died giving birth to me, and my father, he is now married to another woman." She paused. "They live in Johannesburg with their three children."

"I'm sorry to hear that, but your aunt is so pretty," Nyeredzi said, unsure of what to say next, so she changed the subject. "What are you aiming to gain from this course?"

"I need to help people in the rural areas fight against developers and mining companies who take their land by force, but mostly, I need to look after my aunt, she did a lot for me."

"Mmm, I guess you and I are alike, in one way or another," Nyeredzi said, smiling.

It had been more than two years now, and Nyeredzi had attended all the classes she had on her timetable. She had passed all the exams she sat. She was still calling home to check on her family, but she'd decided not to go home in the holidays. She would stay and work at B.K Grant Attorneys in Cape Town to gain some skills before she finished her course. The money she earned, Nyeredzi would send home to her parents and Ambuya back in Mutare. Her mother had found Ambuya a maid to live with, that was Nyeredzi's request.

She and Sibo were more like sisters now. They talked a lot and shared their dreams. Nyeredzi sat on the corner of her bed, while Sibo applied hair cream on Nyeredzi's motsi, which were almost touching her shoulders now.

She would listen to Sibo brag about wanting to own her own firm.

"Nyeredzi, I tell you; you'll come and work for me, and I'll be your boss." Sibo laughed.

"As long as you open another branch in Harare, I don't mind working for you."

"Why can't you just stay here with me?" Sibo asked.

"I have unfinished business with someone close to me back home," Nyeredzi said.

Nyeredzi kept quiet for a little while. She'd been having dreams about her mother recently. Sometimes she would see Zuva so far away from her, calling out to her. The images weren't pleasant, and Nyeredzi could sense she was needed back home.

"My sister, we've been practicing for the Heritage Day next Tuesday." Sibo looked at Nyeredzi in a large mirror glued on the wall. "Do you want to come?"

"Yes, of course, I'd love to."

"You are going to love it."

"So, what do most people do on that day?" Nyeredzi asked.

"Some people stay at home with their loved ones and make a braai or they go out to celebrate the day."

"I'd love to come to the celebration."

On Heritage Day, Nyeredzi sat on a black metal chair outside the community hall along with other people further away from the building. A few trees were scattered here and there on the lush, green lawn. The chairs were set out in a circle, leaving an area for the dancers in the middle. The facilitators had tried to squeeze everyone inside the hall, but a lot of people had turned up to celebrate the Heritage Day. So many of them were dressed in their cultural clothing, and Nyeredzi remembered the day she went to the Ndima Ndima dance.

People were talking in different languages; at times she could understand what they were saying. The youngest children who were getting ready to perform were aged from seven and mixed with teenagers, and adults. It made her feel as though she'd missed out learning a lot on her cultural side, though she didn't mind what she was raised to be.

The sun was starting to get warmer now, heading to the core of the blue dome. She could see Sibo with her aunt, gathering in a circle with her dancers. The ladies looked so beautiful in their white skirts with black stripes, a turquoise apron hanging down the front from their waists. The threaded blue and white beaded necklace fell into the middle of their chest and around the back. The white headband accentuated their beautiful, glowing faces under the sun. She also loved everyone's dress code; the vivid colors drew her attention before they even performed.

First the Zulu people entered the dance area and the energy they had when they lifted their legs in the air took everyone's breath away. They sang in their language, but it still left those who could not understand what was said in awe. The Xhosa went second, and other dancers of different cultures waited for their turn.

The boys started off the dance—their bodies shook as if they were being electrified by their ancestral spirits. While the girls sang along with Sibo, clapping their hands along the drums tapped by three young men behind them, they soon picked the striped sticks and joined the boys who were dancing. Their energetic stomps on the ground grazed the lawn as they shook their hips, performing all difference styles.

It raised goosebumps on Nyeredzi's skin, touching her to the core of her heart. The energy these dancers had when they danced was so significant that it left her with tears on her cheeks. And she knew, when she went back home, she would ask her mother to teach her everything that had to do with her culture. As far as she was concerned, this was lacking in her.

CAN I SEE YOU ONE LAST TIME?

Spring 2003
NYEREDZI

Nyeredzi took a taxi from Harare International Airport, then the ZUPCO bus from the city center to the Tahas' family home. It had been three years since she'd seen her mother, father, and sisters. The last time she came back home was the December after she finished her first year of studying law, but after that, she couldn't come back on holidays because of her internship.

The wheels on Nyeredzi's luggage bounced along the black tarred road. She remembered the days Zuva had warned her that if she sat on the tar, she would get boils. It was only when she grew up that she realized this was a way of keeping her safe from the road. This street was the same road where she once chased after her friends Hope and Marvellous. Nyeredzi glanced at their houses to see if they were there, but the doors and windows were closed.

The wheels on her luggage tumbled over a pothole. The land was dry, the soil on the edge of the road pale. It wasn't as red as it was in her memories. It seemed diluted, as if it had been washed several times.

When Nyeredzi reached her old house, she couldn't believe her eyes. So much had changed in their neighborhood. Down the street, about five hundred meters away, was Southgate 2. There were so many new houses with people bustling in and out and lounging under their maturing trees.

While Hannah always talked about her fiancé whom she'd been dating for more than three years and planning to have a wedding soon when Zuva got better, Abigail was the one who always talked on the phone that new suburbs were being developed closer to their house. Southgate 3 was far across the river that cut through the middle of the bush, sandwiched between the water and the train track. Nyeredzi could see the freshly painted houses bright in the distance.

Tall buildings with colorful signage in Southgate 3 sat further away on the left side and Nyeredzi stared for a few minutes before she realized it was a mall. It was surrounded by houses and then more houses. A school was close to the Msasa tree, where the whole community once gathered to perform a traditional rain dance. That was the day Nyeredzi first witnessed the Ndima Ndima dance.

Now the tree had grown taller, its red leaves beaming from afar as though they were calling out to her. She'd missed climbing on those balanced rocks that sat on the red soil as the shrubs and trees danced to the tune of the ancestors' whistles. Nyeredzi imagined her mother in the taro field, bending down to pull weeds.

She'd walked a fair distance and the heat had drained her strength. She'd not told anyone she was coming home. Nyeredzi had been living with a guilty conscience and it felt as if it was eating her from within. Though she sent some of the money she earned from her internship to her family, she'd missed a lot of things, like digging in the field with her mother, and now even Zuva hadn't been doing that in a long time.

The distance between them was destroying their relationship, and she knew it. The last time she spoke to her mother, it was painful. Zuva had not said much and after their conversation, Mwedzi took the phone and asked Nyeredzi to come home.

And she did. To look after her mother on her deathbed.

A few months earlier, Zuva had been diagnosed with ovarian cancer, and Nyeredzi was told the doctors had taken out the stromal tumor. Zuva got better and she was in remission. But now Nyeredzi questioned why her mother was back on the deathbed again. She couldn't stop thinking about the scar Zuva once showed her, the slit made by a bhodifa in the war. *Maybe the doctors had cut the same spot again to take out the tumor,* she thought. Perhaps the bhodifa had cursed her mother, and that's why the cancer had settled in her womb.

The French doors at the front of the house were half-opened and Nyeredzi dragged her bags inside. She heard her father's voice from her parents' bedroom. Her clumsy hands let go of the bags and they landed with a loud thump.

Mwedzi walked out of the bedroom, long salt-and-pepper beard almost touching his chest. He had lost some weight. "Oh, daughter, you've come back," he whispered and ran to hug Nyeredzi.

"Papa!" Their hug lingered for a little while before she raised her head. "Mama?" she asked quietly.

"She's been asking for you for days," he said, tears in his eyes. "She's stopped everyone from the church and relatives from coming to see her."

"Am I too late?" she whispered.

"I am glad you're here," was all Mwedzi said.

Nyeredzi paused outside her parents' bedroom before she pushed the door open. She feared what she was going to see—her mother in a bad condition. Zuva lay in the bed, on her back, facing the pine beams of the roof. A white sheet covered her up to her waist. She walked slowly toward the bed and Zuva turned her head. The white patch on the middle of her head was still there. Nyeredzi saw it as her mother's wisdom, the spiritual crown of her royal blood.

She knelt to hug her mother, and Zuva's face lit up with a brief smile. Her mother's body had thinned, and she was lighter. Nyeredzi didn't want to let go of her. She begged silently for Zuva not to leave her, holding on tight and swallowing the tears threatening to spill over.

"Nyeredzi, you are here. I thought I'd never see you again." Zuva reached out to touch Nyeredzi's face. "How blessed I am that you are here—that you heard me calling you, my daughter, my Samson."

"How can I stay out there, lost in the foreign forest, when all I hear is your voice, calling me in my sleep?" Nyeredzi asked softly.

Zuva ran her fingers along Nyeredzi's motsi tied at the back. "You're the one who has always reached out to death—in animals and people, so are you going to pick me up from this deathbed?" She paused, trying to breathe. "It's either you share the strength in your hair with me, or, you let me go."

Tears ran down Nyeredzi's face. She glanced at the Bible on the bedside and considered picking it up but couldn't. How was Nyeredzi going to share her strength with her mother? She didn't have the power to do so. In the Bible, it was the mother who told Samson that his strength came from his hair. Where was hers? These were motsi she grew because she was homesick. She was trying to reconnect with her ancestors through the roots that hung from her head. But with her and Zuva, death was the lion. How was she going to tear out death's mouth? It was already swallowing her mother bit by bit.

Usually it was her mother who prayed for other people to get better when they were on their deathbed. Nyeredzi didn't know how to say the words, though throughout her childhood she'd heard her mother saying them.

"I shall make you something to eat. It will give you the strength," Nyeredzi said, standing up. "And soon, I shall cover you with my hair, and you'll have all my strength, Mama."

Nyeredzi headed to the kitchen. Mwedzi was sitting in the armchair, hands clasped. Her father looked sad and lost. "Oh, I wanted to give you time with your mother," he said, getting up.

"Thank you, Papa—can you sit with her? I am going to make something for her to eat."

"Please do so. She hasn't been eating."

Everything in the kitchen was the same as before she left for university. This was where Zuva taught her to cook. The days when she finished school, Nyeredzi would arrive home early only to find Zuva cooking sadza on the paraffin stove before they had electricity. At first, the boiling porridge of sadza burnt Nyeredzi's hands. It was Zuva who showed her the trick to avoid that. Her mother took the pot off the stove for a moment while she added mealie meal in the boiling porridge. Zuva never let the pot stay too long off the stove— otherwise the sadza would have lumps in it.

Nyeredzi moved the empty vegetable basket underneath the workbench and layers of dust swirled in the air.

It reminded her of when she was young; she used to play in or chase a whirlwind, just to smell it. Nyeredzi put water in the kettle and switched it on.

Now she was touching the walls, strolling down the passageway, thinking of what to make her mother. She stopped by the bedroom where she used to sleep. The double bed was still in there, placed against the wall and covered with a big sheet. Zuva had done that before she fell ill. She always kept Nyeredzi's things tidy and safe, as though she knew one day her daughter would come back.

The last time Zuva and Nyeredzi talked, her mother had promised her everything was going to be okay. That she was feeling much better and soon they would see each other again once Nyeredzi finished her course. Nyeredzi had believed her, but Zuva only got worse.

She walked back to the kitchen. The cold floor numbed her feet, which were swollen from all those hours sitting in one spot on the Air Zimbabwe plane. In the fridge she found eggs. She decided on scrambled eggs, her mother's favorite, and warmed bread in the oven to soften it. When everything was ready, she found a silver tray to carry to her parents' bedroom. On the tray were three mugs, a teapot with sweet Tanganda tea, two plates of sandwiches, and scrambled eggs seasoned with shallots.

In her parents' room, Nyeredzi placed the tray on the bedside table and opened the zebra–printed curtains a little to let the light in.

"Is that too much?" she asked Zuva, who was frowning.

"No, daughter, I just don't remember what the sun looks like anymore," she said.

"The sun will always come back for us everyday in the morning and stay with us until the moon arrives to take over." Nyeredzi smiled. "So, Mama, you and I will head out together one day. We will sit on the bare rock and bathe in its heat. We will let it burn us until we are so dark that no one will realize people are laying on the granite rock."

"I like that idea." Zuva smiled back and looked at the food. "This smells nice, Nyeredzi."

"Thank you, Mama."

She poured some tea in a cup and handed it to her father. Mwedzi sipped on the hot drink, staring at Nyeredzi as she lifted her mother to a sitting position. Zuva sat still while Nyeredzi fed her scrambled eggs, sipping the sweet Tanganda. But after a few bites, she took Nyeredzi's wrist, gesturing for her to stop. Nyeredzi took a few bites of the sandwiches left by her mother. She sat watching her sweating even though it wasn't that hot. Perhaps that was why she was covered only by the sheet.

The soft skin clinging to Zuva's bones made Nyeredzi realize that she was losing her mother. She could see it in her father's eyes that her mother was going; his silence since she had arrived confirmed it.

Nyeredzi stood up—she needed to get out of the room.

"Daughter, where are you going?" Zuva asked in a low voice.

"I'll be back soon, Mama. Papa is here, he's not going anywhere."

Mwedzi stared at Nyeredzi, his eyes fearful. Nyeredzi knew her mother didn't want her to leave, but she felt as though she was drowning at the thought of losing her. She'd already lost her sister.

Nyeredzi made her way to the backyard, to look out at the bush. She walked on the red soil on bare feet. Tied around her waist was a zambia printed in green, white, red, black, and yellow. She carried a small basket with a clay pot filled with water, scissors, and a small mirror.

Her mother's taro garden lay about two kilometers away across the steep land. Nyeredzi headed toward the Msasa tree, feeling her hips move with each step. Sweat clouded her armpits, her palms sticky, her face glistening as the sun grilled her from above.

Birds glided above, their shadows twirling on the ground. She climbed a steep hill of red clay laced with the green foliage of trees, following the curved path. The children from the school across the river ran in the school ground fenced with Durawall, cheering, and playing games.

Nyeredzi finally reached the Msasa tree, with its red leaves and gray bark. She knelt down in the red dirt before she stepped into the Msasa's shade. She crumbled a small boulder of the clay in her palm and brought the earth close to her nose to inhale it. The last time she asked her ancestors to give her the power to bring her sister back to life, they didn't hear her, so, she had to try again. Perhaps this time they would hear her call. And it was better they healed her mother, their own way.

"This is the same soil my mother's flesh was born from," she said, crawling toward the tree. "To the ancestors who bore my mother lying on the bed with sore bones and flesh, heed me, your grandchild, Nyeredzi." She looked up at the red leaves. "Togara and Nyikadzino, who bore my mother. Makomo and Chengetai, who bore my father. I never met any of you, but I know your spirits linger within us."

She sat facing the tree, her legs crossed. From her basket, she pulled out the scissors and the mirror which she placed in front of her. Nyeredzi clasped each of her locked hair one by one, cutting neatly the sides and back of her head, leaving the top tied into a bun. She piled them on the soil before crawling around the tree, circling the trunk with her motsi.

"My mother asked me to give her my strength. Here it is. I offer this to you my ancestors, so you can all come and save her." Nyeredzi straightened the circle row of her locked hair on the soil. Now her foremothers and fathers were wearing a chuma made by their great grandchild, guarding their spirits. "Allow me to live a long life with my parents. I need them. Your great–grandchildren who were left by Ruth—your oldest granddaughter— need them too. We all need them."

She moved back on her knees to the clay pot and lifted it. "Forgive me. I only come to you when I am in need, maybe it's because I am scared to talk to you. Can I see you one last time in my mother's body? I beg you, allow me to know you through my mother?"

Nyeredzi bowed her head and lifted the clay pot in the air, her chin shaking so much that she struggled to speak.

"I only need one sign from you to know that you've heard me," she said, her voice quivering. "I beg you, my ancestors, I do not have much time—my mother's breath is heading down a dark tunnel. Do you hear me?"

Warm tears flowed down her cheeks. At that moment, a breeze brushed around her. Nyeredzi placed the pot on the ground before her. When she ran her hand to tie her motsi that were coming loose, two red leaves fell on her head. She threw them in the clay pot, and the leaves rose. She gathered her little basket, scissors, mirror, and clay pot, and rushed home. She struggled to breathe, imagining a life without her mother, and though she didn't want to cry, she couldn't help herself.

When she arrived back home, she heard Mwedzi talking in the kitchen with her sisters and Ruth's kids. She didn't stop to say hello, walking straight into her parents' room. Between herself and her sisters, they held the longest conversations over the phone almost every week. Sometimes Hannah called her from work where she was now an accountant at the Standard Chartered Bank. Abigail often called from the kitchen of Crown Plaza Hotel, where she worked as a chef.

Inside the bedroom, Zuva was still sitting up, but her eyes were closed.

"Mama?"

Zuva opened her eyes slowly. "Nyeredzi, what happened to your hair, my daughter?"

"I thought I should share my strength with you," she said. "Please, drink this holy water from the ancestors."

Nyeredzi raised the clay pot to her mother's lips. Zuva looked inside and saw the red leaves. She opened her lips and drank the water. Then Nyeredzi pulled out the leaves and placed them on Zuva's chest, under her top.

"Thank you, daughter," Zuva said, clasping her hand. Nyeredzi climbed onto the bed next to her mother and fell asleep.

She awoke to Mwedzi shaking her. The lights were on, the curtains closed, and Zuva had eaten some dinner already.

"Daughter, can we let your mother rest?" Mwedzi asked, his eyes on Nyeredzi's chopped hair. He was about to say something but Zuva shook her head.

"Let her stay," Zuva said in a faint voice.

Hannah and Abigail came in to greet her and Nyeredzi cuddled Gabriel, and Gabriella, who'd grown so much. Nyeredzi dragged the armchair by the wardrobe next to her mother's bed. She sat there, talking to her sisters before they left to go to their own rooms.

"Papa, I'll let you and Mama rest," Nyeredzi said. "Mama, I'll see you tomorrow morning?"

"Thank you, Nyeredzi," Zuva said with a brief smile.

Nyeredzi went to lie on the three–seater sofa in the lounge. She didn't go into her bedroom; she wanted to be close to her mother.

A week passed. Nyeredzi was bathing and feeding Zuva in her bedroom. She'd hoped her mother would get better, but Zuva remained in the same condition as the day Nyeredzi arrived from South Africa. Had she wronged her ancestors by asking them to save her mother when they were ready to take her? Was it her fault her mother ended up on a deathbed because she didn't stay to look after her when Ruth died?

Had she mocked her ancestors by offering them her hair? No one had ever done that before, but Nyeredzi thought it was the only thing she could do. She didn't know what elders usually placed under the Msasa tree if they were asking something from their ancestors.

Once again, Nyeredzi feared her ancestors would not come to rescue her this time. When Zuva fell asleep in the afternoons, Nyeredzi walked to the back of the house and stood there, watching the bush, looking at the Msasa tree from afar, still silently begging her forefathers and mothers to spare the life of her mother. Why wouldn't they spare her?

Zuva was a woman who was generous with people she knew and with those she'd never met before. Wasn't she the one who sent Mwedzi and the other men into the bush to save a woman they had heard crying one night? Everyone was scared of the thugs, but Zuva asked men in their neighborhood to go and rescue that woman.

Nyeredzi remembered watching her father and the other men hide small axes inside their coats, then march like soldiers into the bush, headed toward the screams in the darkness. That night, Nyeredzi wanted to go with them, but she was scared to ask. When they reached the woman crying for help, they discovered her husband was trying to kill her because she'd had many miscarriages. He was angry she couldn't give him a child.

The brutality of that night stirred something deep in Nyeredzi and she knew she wanted to study law, so she could represent the vulnerable ones. She'd not forgotten about her cousin Jossey, who once came to their house with scars on her body. Nyeredzi wanted to be like her mother and now, as she stood in the backyard staring off into the distance, she remembered how Zuva had looked after Jossey and protected that woman at their church until her family came to collect her.

She wasn't going to let her mother go like that. Perhaps if her great-grandparents could see Zuva outside, they would have mercy on Nyeredzi. The yellow light above them could reconnect with Zuva—she was named after the sun, after all. Nyeredzi ran back into the house and along the passageway to her mother's bedroom. No one else was at home.

"Mama, can I take you outside?" she whispered.

Zuva opened her eyes. "I don't know if I can manage, my daughter."

"I'll help you, Mama."

Zuva nodded. Nyeredzi dressed her mother with a woollen jersey and a long thick skirt to keep her warm. She ran out again to place a chair under the water berry tree before returning to support her mother, Zuva's footsteps dragging in the passageway. When they were both outside under the sun, she helped her mother sit down and covered her with a small blanket. "Are you comfortable this way?" she asked.

Zuva nodded.

Nyeredzi then sat on the ground by her feet.

"The ancestors came in my dream the day you went to the Msasa tree. You shall go and collect your hair later before the sunset." Zuva pulled her hands out of the blanket. "They heard your prayer, and I asked them if I could give you this."

She lifted the brown twine necklace from around her neck. The tooth of a lion, inscribed with the initial ZM, for Zuva Mutongi, sat in the middle of tiny wooden beads engraved with little stars underneath the letters that read Rugare. The back of the tooth had the word Mambokadzi.

"My parents gave it to me when they announced I would be the next Mambokadzi." Zuva looked at Nyeredzi, not telling her what she was asking of her. "Give it to your father, he will add your initials on the tooth soon."

Unaware of what her mother was asking her, too, Nyeredzi caressed the necklace put on her neck by her mother and said, "Mama, I am honored to keep your name on my chest; because I'll know you are always with me."

"And I am blessed to have you as my daughter." Zuva touched her shoulder, waiting for the right time to explain why she gave her the necklace. Perhaps she waited to get better so she could teach her daughter everything she was taught by her parents. "You have nothing to regret, Nyeredzi."

Nyeredzi let out a long sigh, filled with relief at her mother's words. It was as if a heavy weight had been lifted off her chest, her shoulders.

"Tomorrow, when I can walk on my own, we shall go

and lie on that broad granite rock, and let the sun burn us till we are too dark."

"Till we are too dark," Nyeredzi echoed. "That's a good idea, Mama."

Nyeredzi's mind was still heavy with memories of the bush. Now there were no thugs or poisonous snakes hiding in the bush, just suburbs packed with malls, schools, parks, and houses. Children were playing and riding bicycles on the land of red soil that in the past had soaked up people's blood. Nyeredzi remembered the screams of the people attacked by the thugs and wondered if their spirits had evaporated into the air. Were their ghosts still here, floating unseen?

Would they haunt the new people settling into this land? Was anyone ever going to tell these new residents what really happened here, what people saw with their own eyes—the good and the bad—there, in the deadly bush? This place had helped her to learn things about her mother she might have not known if they'd stayed living in Marondera.

Zuva and Nyeredzi sat under the broad branches, studying the bush and the houses stretching out before them. Nyeredzi dug her toes into the red soil. She felt blessed to be sitting next to her mother in the exact same spot they had stood together all those years ago when they first moved to Harare. The ground and their skin were dappled with the sun flaring through the green leaves of the water berry tree.

In the distance, the Msasa tree shimmered red. It danced, swaying to the whistle of the ancestors. A sudden breeze passed between them. Nyeredzi understood the ancestors had allowed her mother to live longer. And she would forever be grateful to hold Zuva's hand in hers, to know they would always be together, in this life, and the next.

GLOSSARY

SHONA LANGUAGE

Ambuya: Grandmother.

Ashe: Princess.

Bonde: A reed mat. (plural: Maponde)

Chuma: Necklace. (plural: Zvuma)

Dara: A flat surface made from timber raised to dry dishes.

Gabhu–gabhu: (No meaning, word created by the author.)

Hwahwa/Masese: Traditional beer made from sorghum and maize.

Maheu: Drink made from leftover sadza or porridge.

Mambokadzi: Queen.

Mbira: An African musical instrument, traditional to the Shona people of Zimbabwe.

Motsi: Locked hair.

Mukombe: A gourd.

Ndima Ndima: (No meaning, word created by the author.)

Rugare: Peace.

Rutsero: A round woven tray used to sieve grains and store vegetables.

Sadza: Zimbabwean staple food—thickened porridge made from flour (maize, sorghum, millet, cassava, corn meal).

Tsano: Brother–in–Law.

Tsunga: A type of Zimbabwean vegetable.

Zambia: A large piece of fabric used by women to wrap their bodies from waist to legs.

KOLOLO LANGUAGE

Mosi a Tunya: The smoke that thunders—Victoria Falls.

NDEBELE LANGUAGE

Gogo: Grandmother.

Haikhona: No.

Lobola: Bridewealth.

Yebo: Yes.

AFRIKAANS LANGUAGE

Braai: A structure on which fire can be made for the outdoor of grilling meat.

Sjambok: A whip made from a cow hide or rhino skin.

ACKNOWLEDGEMENTS

Ndima Ndima is a pure work of fiction. For any incorrect cultural heritage information, and past events of the Southern African countries in this book I apologize to my readers, but I am also grateful to my informants' knowledge, research done on internet, and in books.

I want to acknowledge what's on the Zimbabwean flag, including its colors used throughout this book. Musicians mentioned in some stories. South African and Zimbabwean cities, landscape, and varied cultural heritage.

A special thanks to all those who helped bring this book come to life in so many ways: my master's supervisor Paula Morris, Carolyn Rudzinski, Tom Moody, Anne Kennedy, Azhar Khan, and my MCW cohort 2019/20 for sharing their knowledge with me, for challenging me to grow as a writer, for offering invaluable critical, sensitive, and intelligent feedback. I'm grateful for the time you were and are going to be there for me.

Then there is my formidable friend/agent Nadine Rubin Nathan. Your guidance and encouragement is invaluable. You always go above and beyond and I appreciate you for that. Thank you for believing in me.

A big thank you goes to my publisher, Jessica Powers, and her publishing team at Catalyst Press: SarahBelle Selig Selig, Ashawnta Jackson, Karen Vermeulen, Jill Bell,

Kathy McInnis, Michael Croy, and those not mentioned here for their professionalism and dedication in bringing this book to print. I feel blessed that you saw my writing worth publishing.

My writing community: the University of Auckland MCW Alumni, Manukau Institute of Technology BCA Alumni, and Black Creatives Aotearoa members; you carry so much love in all of you, and it still pours. Thanks to all those people who make things happen behind the scenes, and to the readers who will support my work.

Lastly but firstly, thanks to all my beloved family members, and to the love of my life, my husband Tendai, my children: Miriam, Moses, and Martha, thank you for your endless love, support, and extra care when I am in need of it.

Endless thanks to Mum and Dad, to whom I owe everything.

Above all, I am immensely thankful to the one who created me, enveloped me in a gracious gift that brings words of imagination to life.

NDIMA NDIMA DISCUSSION GUIDE

*Questions for exploring the themes & plot
of Tsitsi Mapepa's* Ndima Ndima

1. Describe the time period and setting of *Ndima Ndima*.

   If *Ndima Ndima* was set in another country or
   continent, or in another era, what might change?

   What would stay the same?

   How important are specific settings and historical
   time periods to a story?

2. The author starts the book with this phrase:
   '*...when a moon meets the sun, they create a ring
   of fire to bear a star.*'

   How is this phrase relevant to the lives of Zuva
   and Nyeredzi?

3. Consider the following statement:
   'We are all related through humanity.'

   Why does Zuva use this phrase?

   How would you receive it if someone said this to you?

   Are there similar concepts to this one in your own
   culture or spiritual practice?

4. Why did Zuva leave Goho Village in 1970?

   Besides the circumstantial reasons surrounding her brother and parents, might Zuva have had other reasons for leaving?

   What choice would you have made, if you were Zuva?

   What were some of the challenges she faced when making this decision?

5. In a setting that is dominated by males, why do you think the writer chose to give Zuva and Nyeredzi such important responsibilities in their community?

   What might the setting of this novel look like if more women in the story held positions of power?

   If Zuva and Nyeredzi were both males, what would change in the story?

6. If more leaders acted and spoke like Zuva, would it change things for the better?

   Why or why not?

7. If we had more female soldiers, do you think it will help reduce the brutality women face in wars?

   If yes or no, why?

8. Some scenes in this book are intended to shock readers.

   What passages did you find the most shocking?

   Explore the impact it makes when the innocence of Nyeredzi is contrasted with the violence in scenes like that.

9. Even at a young age, Nyeredzi wants to become a better person.

   What are some life lessons Nyeredzi learns in this story?

   In what ways does she mature as the story goes on, and in what ways does she remain the same?

10. How does the writer balance her leading characters Zuva and Nyeredzi with side characters' storylines throughout the novel?

    Why are side characters necessary?

    Who was your favorite side character?

11. Throughout the novel, the writer makes many references to Zimbabwean symbols and cultural objects. List a few and their impact on the story.

12. If Zuva was not a chief, a church leader, and a soldier, would people in her community have treated her differently?

    Why?

    How did her leadership roles affect her relationship with Nyeredzi?

    How did your parent or family member's role in your community affect your relationship with them?

13. Discuss Zuva and Nyeredzi's complicated relationship.

    Could things have been different for them?

    How or why/why not?

14. Some people believe that what you see and experience as a child influences what you become when you are older.

    Do you believe this is true?

    Why or why not?

15. Do you think it's important to be able to see something in order to believe it?

    Or can you believe in something without being able to see it or show it to others?

    Discuss examples of this in the book, and in your own life.

16. When something terrible happens to Ruth, Nyeredzi sees herself as a failure.

    How did this event affect Nyeredzi's relationship with her mother?

    If this tragedy had not happened, do you think

    Nyeredzi would still have chosen to leave Zimbabwe?

17. If you are not familiar with the First and Second Chimurenga Wars, do some quick research.

    Discuss why they came to pass, and the major events of each.

18. Explore Nyeredzi's relationship with nature.

    How does it help her connect with her ancestors?

    What else does it help her do?

19. Everyone comes from a different culture. For years,

people have been relying on the information passed on to them by elders to know their ancestry, but now, the use of technology to track ancestral lineage is possible.

Is an ancestry test something you would be interested in doing?

Why or why not?

20. Do you have a relationship with your ancestors?

What does it look like?

21. What traditions from your own culture or other cultures do you include in your life?

Do you think it is okay to include other cultures' traditions in your life?

Why or why not?

22. Why is culture so important?

What does it offer us as individuals?

And as a community?

What are some ways you can pass on your culture to future generations?

23. How can traditions help us cope with bad things that happen?

24. The ending of the story shows Nyeredzi making an offering to the ancestors, a thing she has never done.

Why do you think she chose this pathway when she was raised a Christian?

HISTORICAL NOTES

Zimbabwe is a landlocked country of Southern Africa, home to many ethnicities and cultures. The nation was brought under British colonial rule in the 1890s, and two wars were fought for its independence: the First Chimurenga War in 1896-1897, and the Second Chimurenga War in 1964-1979. These wars are also known as the Second Matabele War and the Rhodesian Bush War. After a successful campaign against British rule, negotiations were held in London between Zimbabwe-Rhodesia's local government, the government of the United Kingdom, and leaders of the Patriotic Front (Robert Mugabe and Joshua Nkomo), in December 1979. The Lancaster House Agreement was signed, ceasing fire and allowing the first multiparty general elections to be held with complete adult suffrage in 1980.

The country officially gained its independence on April 18th 1980 and was then renamed Zimbabwe, derived from the Shona word dzimba dza mabwe, meaning house of stone. Many of its cities were also renamed (e.g. Salisbury became Harare).

Today, Zimbabwe's population is over 16 million. It has 16 official languages: Chewa, Chibarwe, English, Kalanga, Koisan, Nambya, Ndau, Ndebele, Shangani, Shona, Sotho, Tonga, Tswana, Venda, Xhosa, and Sign language. Christianity is the most dominant faith in Zimbabwe, having been introduced by British missionaries in the late 1800s, but many people of Zimbabwe still practice traditional religions or philosophies. A smaller percentage make up other religions such as Judaism, Islam, Buddhism, Sikhism, and Hinduism.

You will find many references to Zimbabwe's culture in this story, like the Mbira, a musical instrument traditional of the Shona people of Zimbabwe. It is used in ceremonial functions like weddings, funerals, and the installation of chiefs, as well as to call on ancestral spirits and seek their advice.

Sadza is one of the most popular staple foods, served with various relishes including meat, soups, and vegetables like covo, tsunga, and pumpkin leaves. Rich in fiber and nutritious, the recipe for Sadza has been passed down through generations and is an extraordinary part of the nation's culture and cuisine.

Roora, or lobola or bridewealth, is a token of appreciation given by a bridegroom to his bride-to-be's family for raising her. Shona, Ndebele, Shangaan, and Venda are patrilineal societies, and after marriage, a women moves into her husband's home. The Tonga people are matrilineal, and the husband moves to the home area of his wife.

The flame lily is the country's national flower, and the stone-carved Great Zimbabwe bird—as seen on the Zimbabwean flag, currency, and sportswear—is considered its national emblem.

The African fish eagle mentioned in this story represents many things to the people of Zimbabwe, but above all, it symbolizes freedom and hope.

Printed in the USA
CPSIA information can be obtained
at www.ICGtesting.com
JSHW022022291023
51056JS00001B/1